A CHAPTER OF HATS

A CHAPTER OF HATS

Selected Stories

MACHADO DE ASSIS

Translated from the Portuguese
and with an introduction by John Gledson

BLOO SBURY

First published in Great Britain 2008

Translation and introduction copyright © John Gledson 2008

Bloomsbury Publishing Plc
36 Soho Square
London WID 3QY

www.bloomsbury.com

Bloomsbury Publishing, London, New York and Berlin

A CIP catalogue record for this book is available from the British Library

ISBN 9 780 7475 9461 1

10 9 8 7 6 5 4 3 2 1

Typeset by Hewer Text UK Ltd, Edinburgh
Printed in Great Britain by Clays Ltd, St Ives plc

The paper this book is printed on is certified by the © 1996 Forest
Stewardship Council A.C. (FSC). It is ancient-forest friendly.
The printer holds FSC chain of custody SGS-COC-2061

FSC
Mixed Sources
Product group from well-managed
forests and other controlled sources
Cert no. SGS-COC-2061
www.fsc.org
© 1996 Forest Stewardship Council

CONTENTS

Translator's Introduction

JOAQUIM MARIA MACHADO DE ASSIS (1839–1908) lived and died in Rio de Janeiro, and hardly ever left the city. In his time, he was regarded as Brazil's greatest writer, and few Brazilians would question that he remains so, even now, a hundred years after his death. Eight of his nine novels have been translated into English, and he has caught the eye of some of the best critics in English – enthusiastic essays by Susan Sontag and Tony Tanner, even an accolade from Woody Allen. He deserves to be known for his stories, too – in fact, he is one of the great pioneers of the genre as we know it today. Two collections have been published in English, in 1963 and 1977 – a new anthology, with new translations, is long overdue.

He is a Brazilian original, with none of the glorious company of the nineteenth-century Russians to accompany him – and no Constance Garnett to translate him and put him on the map – and he has had to make his own belated way in the world outside Brazil, a task made all the more difficult by the fact that his originality is not flamboyant and 'Latin American' – quite the contrary, it is profound and *sui generis*. In his own lifetime, in fact, he tried to make his own way abroad, but when an offer of a German translation of *Epitaph of a Small Winner* came in 1904, his publishers, for whatever reason, refused to sell the rights. No doubt it was partly because he was ahead of his time – is that why a Portuguese newspaper, which serialised *Epitaph* in 1883, dropped it after chapter twenty-six? One Brazilian critic, when it first appeared in 1880, even asked if it was a novel.

If Machado hadn't existed, it would have been very difficult to invent him. He was of mixed race and born relatively poor, in a country where slavery still existed for the first forty-nine years of his life. In later life he suffered from epilepsy, and developed a stammer. He overcame these drawbacks by hard work and determination, and no doubt with a fair degree of hard-headed realism. In 1869 he married the sister of a Portuguese poet and friend, Carolina Xavier de Novais – no one has ever doubted it was a love-match, but it was also a considerable step up the social ladder. He was friendly, perhaps even intimate, with some of the most distinguished Brazilians of his time – the novelist José de Alencar, the abolitionist Joaquim Nabuco – and eventually became the President of the Brazilian Academy of Letters, set up in 1897 on the French model: a pillar of the establishment, in fact.

It was not a dramatic existence, at least not on the outside. His marriage remained childless, and he lived quietly on the outskirts of Rio, fulfilling his duties in the Ministry of Agriculture with such competence and dedication that he is now held up as a kind of patron saint of civil servants. Writing his biography is no easy task – he kept his feelings and opinions to himself, and went out of the way to kick over the traces. He could have adopted for his own motto the one that

Prosper Mérimée, one of his heroes, and a model when it came to writing stories, had on his ring, in Greek: 'Remember to mistrust'.

Hardly surprising, then, that a great deal is hidden beneath the surface in all his works, stories included. The most famous of the novels – *Epitaph of a Small Winner* (1880), *Philosopher or Dog?* (1891) and *Dom Casmurro* (1900) – reveal how far he was prepared to go to play games with his readers; and, incidentally, show what an arsenal of special effects, and subtle shades, he had at his command when he wanted to hoodwink them. In the first, we have a narrator who is dead, and writes 'from the other side'; in the second, one who is prepared to turn on his readers and tell them that the plot-line they've been following is a red herring; in the third . . . but that would be giving away too much. He knew English, read Sterne, Charles Lamb, Carlyle . . . he seems to have had an eye for the unusual, and to have sought it out. He even read Gogol, though the attraction has its logic – if, in 1860, one had had to name two large, slave-owning empires, Russia and Brazil would have been the obvious choices.[1]

The stories translated here were written between 1878 and 1906, and first published, almost all of them, in magazines and newspapers of the time. I have disregarded his production before 1878, because in tone and subject matter it can strike modern readers as naïve and limited, as if there was a voice trying to find itself, and not quite succeeding – often it seems directed at the marriageable girls of the *carioca* elite, and to share their concerns.

We know Machado wanted to transcend these boundaries and write, potentially, for the world. When he achieved his aim, it was with a single bound – or two, first in a story, second in a novel. In a famous essay of 1873, 'The Instinct for Nationality', he had written that: 'What should be demanded of the writer above all is a certain intimate feeling which makes him a man of his time and country, *even when he treats subjects remote in time and space.*' (My italics.) Five years later, time and space suddenly all but disappear, and we are in Noah's ark, 'floating on the waters of the abyss'. 'In the Ark' is a sardonic little counter-parable, a kind of rewriting of the Garden of Eden myth, but without the paraphernalia of primeval innocence, original sin, serpents and female guile – male aggression, however, does make an appearance. Rio de Janeiro is far away – though Turkey and Russia, bitter enemies throughout the nineteenth century, make a brief appearance at the end. It seems that it was all or nothing – Brás Cubas, the narrator of *Epitaph*, in the book's first chapter compares his work to the Pentateuch, laying claim, this time in the context of the novel, to the same limitless terrain.

It was a daring leap in subject-matter, and it needed a style to go with it. What better than the Bible? – because it is a foundational book, of course, but also because when its style is adopted, every single word becomes ironic, and has to be read in inverted commas. Perhaps Machado envied the importance of the Bible in Protestant cultures – in any case, parody and irony became his lifeblood. Here is his own definition of irony, from a story written a short time later: 'that slight curl of the lips, full of mysteries, invented by some decadent Greek, contracted by Lucian of Samosata, transmitted to Swift and Voltaire, the proper manner of sceptics and the world-weary'. Without it, he would have been unable to write – with it, he created an individual style in which every detail, every word weighs.

'The Mirror' (1882) is a demonstration of this new-found power and ambition. Jacobina, abandoned and alone on his aunt's farm, without even the slaves to boost his sense of himself, nearly disintegrates. We are back in Brazil – not Rio, significantly, but a somewhat abstract countryside: 'Just some cocks and hens, a pair of mules philosophising about life, flicking off the flies, and three oxen.' There are two ways, at least, of looking at this story – it can be read as being about the fragility of human identity, about how we depend on the simplest of props (a pointless if colourful uniform, in this case) to keep it alive. It can also, less obviously but just as certainly, be read as a story about national identity. The mirror itself is supposed to have come to Brazil in 1808, when, under pressure from Napoleon and with the help of the British, the Portuguese king and his court fled to Rio, thus turning a colonial backwater into an imperial capital overnight, and, so to speak, allowing the country to see itself in the 'mirror' of European culture – if a rather moth-eaten one, in keeping with the mirror itself, baroque and tarnished. There is no need to choose between these readings – this story is Brazil's version of Gogol's 'Overcoat' or Dostoevsky's 'Underground Man', which both dramatise a situation that is peculiarly Russian *and* universal – and also turns on identity.

Swift and Voltaire might be seen as the twin muses for Machado's first book of stories, published in 1882. *Papéis avulsos* (*Loose Leaves*) is a collection of sceptical, fantastic tales about human failings and the human condition: the longest, 'The Alienist' (also translated rather anachronistically as 'The

Psychiatrist'), is also the most wide-ranging, including a parody of the political process, from *ancien régime* to revolution and restoration. I have excluded it partly because it is available in more than one translation, but also because its length would have meant leaving out too many others.

'An Alexandrian Tale' is still in the spirit of the stories of *Papéis avulsos*, with their universal themes, though it carries an extra, if somewhat gruesome, kick. It is an excellent example of Machado's satire on science, especially when science presumes to involve itself with the mind as well as the body. The 1870s saw the entry in bulk of new scientific and philosophical ideas into Brazil. Their influence was overwhelming – the words '*Ordem e Progresso*' on the Brazilian flag, dating from 1889, are a positivist motto, and one of the most interesting, if least visited, monuments in Rio is one of the world's three remaining positivist churches. 'Remember to mistrust' – Machado remained sceptical, but when he advised contemporary youth, in 1879, to read their Darwin and their Spencer, we can be sure he had done the same. Perhaps his epilepsy and mixed blood had their effect too, for some social Darwinist theories had rather too much to say on these matters and their connection to 'degeneracy'. The later stories touch Darwin but veer off at an ironic tangent, in Conrado's pompous, pretentious and condescending speech in 'A Chapter of Hats', an insouciant comment by the narrator of 'Those Cousins from Sapucaia!' about the way Nature creates species by accident, or in the title – 'Evolution', no less – of an acute and funny little story about the psychology of plagiarism.

In 1883 came a somewhat surprising turn – Machado returned to Rio in his fiction, and almost all his stories from now on are set there. This has caused a largely unnoticed rift between his readers and his critics. While the latter have predominantly focused on *Papéis avulsos* and its attractively universal themes – useful, too, it might be said, to 'sell' him as a great author – Brazilian readers have continued to favour the later stories, which remain very popular – for good reasons, I think.

Perhaps something was in the air; these were years when the short story was becoming the creature we know today. The early 1880s is also the period when Maupassant began to write – '*La Maison Tellier*' is from 1881, and Chekhov's early comic sketches are from these years, too. Talk of influence can be confusing – Machado had enough to be going on with with Diderot, Mérimée, Poe, Gogol and others we know he had read, and his career has its own internal coherence. Though it is unlikely he did *not* read Maupassant (and impossible he would have read Chekhov), it matters little. He in fact disliked programmatic realism – hated Zola, but loved Stendhal and Flaubert – but that doesn't stop him being a great realist in his own manner, which is not (except perhaps in the sharpness and concentrated drama of a story like 'The Cane') Maupassantian.

One thing is beyond doubt – Machado had discovered a wealth of new subjects and a new style to go with them, and the story must have seemed the ideal medium to exercise his new-found confidence; the next two or three years (1883–6) saw a sudden burst of creativity in the form. In *Epitaph*, he had expanded the range of subjects, moral, social, political and sexual, that he could reach, and had also discovered a myriad ways in which irony, and narrative distance, allowed him to reach them without seeming to. It seems he was enjoying his new-found power.

Take the first two of this 'second burst' of stories collected here, both from 1883. 'A Singular Occurrence' is a dialogue between two men, about a woman they see coming out of a church in the centre of Rio. As one tells the story he knows about her former life as a prostitute and lover of a friend of his, we have to keep our eyes not just on Marocas but on the men themselves, who blithely, if no doubt accurately given the society they live in, categorise her: 'She wasn't a seamstress, she didn't own property, she didn't run a school for girls; you'll get there, by process of elimination.' Is the story they tell, or the way they understand it, in part a reflection of their own limitations? In other stories – 'Those Cousins from Sapucaia!' for instance, or 'The Cynosure of All Eyes', and, later, in 'Midnight Mass' – men tell stories about women, and we can feel the tension between what they say and how we can understand the stories they tell. This is one form of the distancing which is so essential to Machado's style and method – it comes in many shapes, however. It is this, this ironic relationship with characters, and frequently, too, with readers, that so often gives them an extra 'lift'.

Usually the narrator is not a character; but there are other ways of creating distance, as in the first sentence of 'A Chapter of Hats', one of his most brilliant stories: 'Muse, sing of the vexation of Mariana, the wife of the lawyer Conrado Seabra, that morning in April 1879. What can be the cause of so much commotion? It's a mere hat, lightweight, not lacking in elegance, and flat.' The contrast between the muse and the hat is plain enough, and it allows room for a good deal of fun at the expense of the characters – Mariana's friend Sophia, who 'flirted with anyone, left, right and centre, out of a natural need, a habit from before she was married', or the aspiring politician with his tight coat who 'opened up his box of topics, and pulled out the opera'. The original readers of *A Estação* (*The Season*), the elegant ladies' magazine in which 'A Chapter of Hats' was first published, with its models of hats, dresses and their innumerable accessories, must have recognised their own world, but seen it anew. This upper-class social world has its own geography, and two of its fixed points are worth mentioning, since they appear in more than one story – the Rua do Ouvidor, the elegant central thoroughfare of Rio, still in essence a colonial city (it often reminds me of the Nevsky Prospekt in the fiction of Gogol or Dostoevsky, and has some of that symbolic importance), and Petrópolis, the town in the mountains where the imperial court went to escape the heat of the summer, and the yellow fever associated with it.

This is social comedy at its sharpest, but there again, and often between the lines, there's more to it than that. The story also presents to us a marriage, happy perhaps in its way, but based on (voluntary) submission. How does Mariana survive sheer boredom, with her three novels, endlessly reread, no children, no housework, even (slaves or servants would take care of that), and her pretentious, 'authoritarian and stubborn' lawyer husband? We mustn't consider Machado naïve enough to think her contentment is in any way 'natural', or that she is in any simple sense stupid. Adultery remains on the horizon here – in fact, though never mentioned except obliquely, perhaps it is the point where the perspectives of the story ultimately converge: 'She'd heard a lot of stories from her about male and female hats, things rather more serious than just a marital tiff.' Distance, understanding, sympathy – these stories contain all three, and part of the difficulty, and the excitement, of translating Machado is to be sure to get the balance right. When he wants adultery in the foreground, as in 'The Fortune-Teller', or as an 'interesting and violent' prologue to a possible 'novel' in 'Dona Paula', he can put it there. It's a matter of perspective, and every story has its own.

One of the possibilities presented by the short-story form which Machado grasped with both hands is its suitability for dramatising the existences of what Frank O'Connor in *The Lonely Voice* calls 'submerged population groups'. In his major novels, particularly *Epitaph* and *Dom Casmurro*, the narrator is a male member of the upper classes, and while a great deal of the point of both is to subvert their own narrators, it must have been a relief at times not to have to adopt their highly characterised voices. Here in the stories, he can focus more easily on women (as we have already seen), on the poor and on children. On slaves, even – slavery itself was not abolished until 1888 in Brazil, and we should not be too surprised, or critical, if slaves seem more or less incidental to the stories, even if they are given the ironic punchline to 'Dona Paula': 'Ol' missy's off to bed real late tonight!' Perhaps some things are more important than reheating old love affairs.

In two late stories, however, both published after abolition, and set well back in the past, Machado reveals something of slavery's horror – almost as if he were taking revenge on the past for its enforced silence. Even now, however, he concentrates less on the unfortunate slaves than on their immediate oppressors – Sinhá Rita in 'The Cane' and Candido Neves in 'Father against Mother' – themselves the products (Machado would never use the word 'victim', I think) of a slave society, in which they find their place. In the end, the slave has no moral choices to make, and cannot embody a story's tension – or to give him or her that dignity might itself make slavery seem less terrible than it actually is. In 'Father against Mother', in particular, one of the last stories he published, we can feel Machado's anger almost spilling over into overt condemnation of his central character – his barely controlled sarcasm makes this story what it is, just as much as the cosy machismo of 'A Singular Occurrence' or the delicate sympathy tinged with distance of 'Dona Paula' create their own parameters of what can be said and what hinted at.

Machado's sympathy and capacity for charm can be given free rein when the poor, or not-quite-so-poor, are less pressured, as in the opening of 'The Diplomat', with its evocation of a St John's Night party – this June celebration (midwinter, in the southern hemisphere) had some of the atmosphere of Christmas about it, and we can feel the author's affection for the world, with its minor characters – Dona Felismina, João Viegas, Joaninha, Queiroz and so on – as well as his sympathy for the central character, Rangel, whose obsession with rank and status harms no one but himself. The black slave in the story's first sentence – that is what she would almost certainly be, in 1853, though she is only called 'black' ('*preta*') – is an incidental, though we can be sure Machado didn't think so, and put her there quite intentionally. 'Admiral's Night' gives us a glimpse into the world of a lower class yet, the poor who lived in shacks on the edge of

Rio, the forerunners of the modern *favelas*, and sailors, a notoriously maltreated, almost enslaved group; both these stories probably have an element of autobiographical affection in them, though it is almost entirely submerged. As Deolindo makes his way to see Genoveva, he passes the hill where Machado was born, near the 'Cemetery of the English', reserved for a small but important minority. Great Britain wielded huge economic power in nineteenth-century Brazil – cultural hegemony was largely reserved for the French.

It is this narrow band of society, the free whites, mulattos and blacks, that felt most immediately the destructive effects of slavery, as we have seen in the two stories on the topic. Machado enjoys watching the moral choices such people make under pressure, and knows that nothing is ever simple – in this world, divisions between social and individual, tragic and comic can be felt, but they are not the final terms of the stories. In 'A Schoolboy's Story', we see how adult pressures, corruption and betrayal, already impinge on a child's world – unperceived by the narrator, too, we see how the impoverished schoolmaster, furious at the public events he's reading about in the papers, takes his frustration out on the young. At least, that is how I see it – the narrator thinks the political passions sometimes prevent him wielding the cane, but the story, I think, allows us to see differently. This 'transmitted violence', as we could call it, is a situation Machado returns to more than once; in a more comic vein, it forms the ambience of the wonderful 'A Pair of Arms' – Ignacio and Dona Severina are both victims of the authoritarian Borges, but his bark is a good deal worse than his bite, and he, too, has to struggle to make ends meet in an unfriendly world, and – not unnaturally? – takes it out on those around him.

Such situations as these gave Machado a psychological acuity which, again, can remind one of his Russian contemporaries, whom, with the exception of Gogol, he quite possibly never read. Sometimes, in fact, it takes over the whole story, as in 'The Hidden Cause', an exploration of sadism which the BBC was reluctant to broadcast in 1991, so shocking is its central passage, where Machado seems suddenly to enter another realm, as if he himself found a perverse enjoyment in its description of torture. A different case is that of 'Pylades and Orestes', a late story from 1903, an account, it seems to me, of a homosexual in a world where homosexuality 'doesn't exist'. It seems Machado knew all about that too. In a short novel, *The Old House*, published in instalments in the same ladies' magazine as 'A Chapter of Hats', he mentions, just in passing, the rape of a twenty-four-year-old bishop by Cesare Borgia, the son of a pope, as recounted by a sixteenth-century Florentine historian.

Nowhere, perhaps, does Machado's subtlety and reach go further than in 'A Famous Man', the only story he published in abolition year, 1888 – Henry James, we hope, might have appreciated its dramatisation of creative frustration, and its quiet, sympathetic humour.[2] We can recognise this figure, the popular composer who would dearly love to write 'great' classical music – Arthur Sullivan, who wrote the score for one comic opera after another with marvellous facility, came to grief in the insufferable *Golden Legend* and *Ivanhoe*. But everything is given a subtle Brazilian colour – it seems to tip from tragedy to comedy and back again in the space of a single paragraph or sentence. We are again in the realm of the *carioca* free poor; we are also in the world of popular music, which of course has a huge importance in Brazil, and has since its beginnings been associated with the black population. Machado almost never refers to race or skin colour in his fiction, nor should that surprise us, given his own entirely probable sensitivity on the subject. So what about Pestana's 'long curly black hair, cautious eyes, and shaven chin', and his doubtful origins, the probable son of the priest who left him his worldly goods – 'something my story is [naturally . . .] not concerned with'? The polkas he composes with such ease and brilliance were not in fact, or not exactly, polkas, but an acclimatised version of the dance that had arrived in Brazil in the 1840s; these polkas had an extra swing to them which had African roots, and which explains the sudden animation in the room when they are struck up. Their titles may be as pointless as Pestana's publisher says, but they too have a swing, and a degree of sexual innuendo, which is part and parcel of the expressiveness of the music itself.

On the classical side, however, not only do we have poor Pestana's repeated falls into plagiarism – his frustration leads to a kind of perverse cruelty disguised as love. He marries the tubercular Maria, one suspects, so that she will inspire him to greater heights, perhaps to his own 'Ave, Maria' – a subtly deployed comma, that. Machado himself, it should be said, was a fervent lover of classical music, and certainly did not believe, any more than Pestana, that popular music is where it's all at, much as he felt its power and charm, and had some inkling of the 'old and intricate things' in which it has its roots (his words, from a newspaper column written in 1887). Is this a self-portrait, as roundabout as you like, but still a self-portrait, of a man from a provincial backwater, immensely intelligent and cultured, unable to find true expression, 'delirious, tormented, an eternal shuttlecock between his ambition and his vocation' or between two cultural worlds? I don't think so; and Machado hints at this at the very end, when Pestana discovers humour ('the only joke he'd ever cracked in his life') on his deathbed. Since 'In the Ark' and *Epitaph*, humour in all its guises had been Machado's salvation and his trusted weapon. He knew all about his own world, and plenty about others beyond it he never saw, and he was no shuttlecock.

In the Ark: Three
Unpublished Chapters of Genesis

Chapter A

1. Then Noah said to his sons Shem, Ham and Japheth: 'We will leave the ark, according to the will of the Lord, we, and our wives, and all the animals. The ark will come to rest on top of a mountain; there we will disembark.

2. 'Because the Lord hath kept his promise, when he said unto me: I have resolved to blot out all living flesh; evil rules the earth, and I wish to make all men perish. Make a wooden ark; enter into it yourself, your wife, and your sons.

3. 'And your sons' wives, and a pair of all the animals.

4. 'Now, therefore, the Lord's promise has been fulfilled, and all men have perished, and the fountains of the heavens have closed; we will disembark on the earth again, to live in peace and harmony.'

5. Thus said Noah, and Noah's sons were very happy to hear their father's words; and Noah left them alone, retiring to one of the rooms in the ark.

6. Then Japheth lifted up his voice and said: 'Our life will be full of delight. The fig tree will give us its fruit, the sheep its wool, the cow its milk, the sun its light and the night its awning.

7. 'For we will be the only people on earth, and all the earth will be ours, and no one will disturb the peace of a family preserved from the punishment which afflicted all men.

8. 'For ever and ever.' Then Shem, when he heard his brother speak, said: 'I have an idea.' To which Japheth and Ham answered: 'Let us hear your idea, Shem.'

9. And Shem spoke from his heart, saying: 'My father has his family; each one of us has his family; we could live in separate tents. Each one of us will do what seems good: whether that be to plant, hunt, or carve wood, or spin flax.'

10. And Japheth replied: 'I think Shem's idea is good; we can live in separate tents. The ark will come to rest on the top of a mountain; my father and Ham will disembark on the side of the rising sun; Shem and I on the side of the setting sun. Shem will occupy two hundred cubits of land, and I another two hundred.'

11. But when Shem spoke, saying: 'I think two hundred cubits is too little,' Japheth retorted: 'Then let it be five hundred cubits each. Between my land and your land will be a river to divide us, so that our property will be clearly differentiated. I will stay on the left bank and you on the right bank;

12. 'And my land will be called the land of Japheth, and yours will be called the land of Shem; and we will go to each

other's tents, and share the bread of happiness and harmony.'

13. And when Shem had approved the division, he asked Japheth: 'But the river? who will the water of the river, its current, belong to?

14. 'For we possess the banks, and have established nothing concerning the current.' And Japheth replied, that each could fish from either side; but his brother disagreed, and proposed that they should divide the river in two, putting a post in the middle. Japheth, however, said that the current would carry the post away.

15. And Japheth having replied thus, his brother answered: 'Since the post is not good in your eyes, I'll have the river, and its two banks; and so that there shall be no conflict, you can build a wall, ten or twelve cubits away from your old bank.

16. 'And if you lose something by this, the difference is not great, and it is right, after all, so that harmony between us shall never be disturbed, according to the Lord's will.'

17. Japheth however replied: 'Get knotted! What right have you to take the bank, which is mine, and rob a piece of my land? Are you better than me,

18. 'Or more handsome or more beloved of my father? What right have you so monstrously to violate another's property?

19. 'Now I say unto you that the river will stay on my side, and if you dare to enter my land, I will slay you as Cain slew his brother.'

20. Hearing this, Ham was very afraid, and began to calm his two brothers,

21. Who had eyes the size of figs and the colour of hot coals, and looked at each other full of anger and contempt.

22. The ark, however, floated on the waters of the abyss.

Chapter B

1. Now Japheth, afflicted by anger, began to foam at the mouth, and Ham spoke soothing words to him,

2. Saying: 'Let us find a way of reconciling everything; I will call your wife and Shem's wife.'

3. Each of them, however, refused, saying that it was a question of rights, and persuasion was of no avail.

4. And Shem proposed to Japheth that he should make up for the ten lost cubits, measuring out an equal quantity at the other side of his land. But Japheth answered:

5. 'Why not send me once and for all to the ends of the earth? Now you're no longer contented with five hundred cubits; you want five hundred and ten, and I shall be left with four hundred and ninety.

6. 'Have you no moral feelings? Don't you know what justice is? Can't you see this is barefaced robbery? Don't you know I'll defend what's mine, even at the risk of my own life?

7. 'And that, if blood must flow, blood will flow, now, this minute,

8. 'To punish your pride and wash away your iniquity?'

9. Then Shem advanced on Japheth; but Ham put himself between them, putting a hand on the breast of each one;

10. While the wolf and the lamb, who during the days of the deluge had lived in the sweetest of harmony, hearing the noise of voices, came to watch the fight between the two brothers, and began to keep a close eye on each other.

11. And Ham said: 'Look, I have a marvellous idea, which will settle everything,

12. 'And which is inspired by the love I have for my brothers. I will sacrifice the land which is due to me, next to that of my father, and will take the river and its two banks, and you will give me some twenty cubits each.'

13. And Shem and Japheth laughed with contempt and sarcasm, saying: 'Go and stuff dates! Keep your idea for the days of your old age.' And they pulled Ham's nose and ears; and Japheth, putting two fingers in his mouth, imitated the hiss of the serpent, taunting him.

14. Then Ham, ashamed and irritated, stretched out his hands, saying: 'Leave it be!' and went to see his father and the wives of the two brothers.

15. Japheth however said to Shem: 'Now that we are alone, let's decide this serious matter, whether it be with tongue or fists. Either you give me both banks, or I'll break one of your ribs.'

16. Saying this, Japheth threatened Shem with clenched fists, while Shem, arching his body, said in an angry voice: 'I'll give you nothing, you thief!'

17. To which Japheth replied angrily: 'It's you that's the thief!'

18. This said, they advanced on one another and grappled. Japheth had a forceful, skilful arm; Shem was strong in resistance. Then Japheth, holding his brother by the waist, squeezed him tightly, crying: 'Whose river is it?'

19. And Shem replied: 'It's mine!' Japheth made a move to fling him to the ground, but Shem, who was strong, shook his body and threw his brother some distance off; Japheth, however, foaming with rage, gripped his brother again, and the two fought hand to hand,

20. Sweating and snorting like bulls.

21. In the struggle, they fell and rolled over, punching one another; blood flowed out of their nostrils, their lips, their cheeks; first Japheth had the upper hand,

22. Then Shem; for anger spurred them on equally, and they fought with their hands, their feet, their teeth and nails; and the ark trembled as if the fountains of heaven had opened up again.

23. Then the cries and shouts reached the ears of Noah, at the same time as his son Ham, who came to him crying: 'My father, my father, if Cain will be avenged seven times, and Lamech seventy times seven, what will happen to Shem and Japheth?'

24. And when Noah asked him to explain what he had said, Ham told him of the brothers' disagreement, and the

anger that spurred them, and said: 'Run to quieten them.'
Noah said: 'Let us go.'

25. The ark, however, floated on the waters of the abyss.

Chapter C

1. And lo, Noah came to the place where his two sons were fighting,

2. And found them still grappling with one another, and Shem under the knee of Japheth, who with his clenched fist was punching his brother's face, which was purple and bloodied.

3. Then, Shem, lifting his hands, managed to grip his brother by the throat, and Japheth began to shout: 'Let me go, let me go!'

4. Hearing the shouts, Shem and Japheth's wives also came to the place where the struggle was, and seeing them thus, began to sob and say: 'What is to become of us? A curse has befallen us and our husbands.'

5. Noah, however, said to them: 'Be still, O wives of my sons, and I will see what the matter is, and order whatever is just.' And going towards the two combatants,

6. He cried: 'Stop the fight. I, Noah, your father, command and order it.' And the two brothers, hearing their father, came to a sudden halt, and were silent and

stopped in their tracks; neither of them got up from the ground.

7. Noah went on: 'Rise up, O men unworthy of salvation and deserving of the punishment which befell all other men.'

8. Shem and Japheth got up. Both had wounds on their cheeks, their necks and hands, and their clothes were spattered with blood, for they had fought with nails and teeth, spurred on by mortal hatred.

9. The floor too was awash with blood, and each man's sandals, and his hair,

10. As if their sin had marked them with the seal of iniquity.

11. Their two wives, however, came up to them, weeping and caressing them, and the pain in their hearts could be seen. Shem and Japheth paid no attention to anything, and their eyes were fixed on the ground, fearful of looking their father in the eye.

12. And their father said: 'Well then, I want to know what the cause of the fight is.'

13. These words kindled hatred in the heart of each. Japheth, however, was the first to speak and said:

14. 'Shem invaded my land, the land I had chosen to pitch my tent, when the waters have disappeared and the ark will descend, according to the Lord's promise;

15. 'And since no one can usurp my inheritance, I said to my brother: 'Are you not happy with five hundred cubits, that you want ten more?'

16. Noah, hearing his son, had his eyes on Shem; and when Japheth had finished, he asked his brother: 'What answer have you?'

17. And Shem said: 'Japheth lies, for I only took the ten cubits of land after he refused to divide the river in two parts; and when I proposed that I should take both banks, I also consented that he should measure ten more cubits at the back of his lands,

18. To make up for what he was losing; but the iniquity of Cain spoke in him, and he wounded my head, face and hands.'

19. And Japheth interrupted him, saying: 'And did you not wound me too, perchance? Am I not bloodied like you? Look at my face and neck; look at my cheeks, which you have ripped with your nails like the tiger's.'

20. As Noah began to speak, he saw that his two sons seemed to defy each other with their eyes. Then he said: 'Hear me!' But the two sons, blind with rage, grappled with each other again, shouting: 'Whose is the river?' — 'The river's mine.'

21. And only with great difficulty could Noah, Ham and the wives of Shem and Japheth hold back the two combatants, whose blood began to flow in great abundance.

22. Noah, however, raising his voice, shouted: 'Cursed be he who does not obey me. He will be cursed, not seven times, nor seventy times seven, but seven hundred times seventy.

23. 'Now, therefore, I say unto you that, before the ark descends to earth, I want no agreements about the place where you will pitch your tents.'

24. Then he became pensive.

25. And lifting his eyes up to heaven, for the porthole in the deck was open, he shouted with a sad voice:

26. 'They do not yet possess the earth and already they are fighting over frontiers. What will happen when it's the turn of Turkey and Russia?'

27. And none of Noah's sons could understand these words of their father.

28. The ark, however, still floated on the waters of the abyss.

The Mirror: A Sketch for
a New Theory of the Human Soul

ONE NIGHT, FOUR OR FIVE gentlemen were debating several questions of a transcendental nature; though various views were expressed, the discussion was not a heated one. The house was on Santa Teresa hill, near the centre of Rio de Janeiro, and the room was small, lit by candles whose glow melted mysteriously into the moonlight outside. Between the city, with its excitement and agitation, and the sky, where the stars twinkled through the limpid, calm atmosphere, were our four or five enquirers into metaphysical matters, amicably resolving the most arduous problems of the universe.

Why four or five? To be accurate, there were four people talking; but, in addition to them, there was a fifth personage in the room, silent, thinking, half asleep, whose contribution to the debate was limited to a grunt of approval here or there. This man was the same age as his companions, between forty and fifty; he was from the provinces, rich, intelligent, not uneducated, and, it seems, astute and of a caustic turn of mind. He never argued; and he defended his lack of participation with a paradox, saying that arguing was the polite form of the aggressive instinct, present in man and inherited from animals;

and he added that the seraphim and cherubim never ques-
tioned anything, and they were eternal, spiritual perfection.
When, on this night, he gave the same answer again, one of
those present contested what he said, and challenged him to
prove it if he was able. Jacobina – that was his name – reflected
for a moment, and answered:

'When I think about it, perhaps you're right.'

And there, in the middle of the night, this withdrawn
individual held forth, not for two or three minutes, but thirty
or forty. The conversation, in its meanderings, came to rest on
the nature of the soul, a subject which radically divided the
four friends. Each one had his own view; not merely was there
no agreement, discussion itself seemed impossible, partly from
the multiplicity of questions branching from the main trunk,
and a little, maybe, from the inconsistency of the views
themselves. One of the contenders asked Jacobina to give
an opinion – or at least provide some conjecture.

'No conjectures or opinions,' he replied, 'either can give
rise to dissension, and, as you know, I never argue. But, if
you'll hear me in silence, I can tell you of something that
happened to me, which provides the clearest possible demonstration of what we're talking about. In the first place,
there's not one soul, but two . . .'

'Two?'

'Two souls, no less. Every human being carries two souls
with him: one that looks from inside out, the other from
outside in . . . You can be as astonished as you want; open
your mouths, shrug your shoulders, whatever; I'll brook no
answer. If you answer back, in fact, I'll finish my cigar and be
off home to bed. The external soul can be a spirit, a fluid, a

man, many men, an object or an operation. There are cases, for example, in which a simple shirt button is a person's external soul; or a polka, whist, a book, a machine, a pair of boots, a cavatina, a drum, etc. Obviously, the role of this second soul, like that of the first, is to transmit life; the two of them together make a man, who is, in metaphysical terms, an orange. Anyone who loses one of the halves naturally loses half of his existence; and there are not infrequent cases in which losing the external soul means losing an entire existence. Look at Shylock. His ducats were the Jew's external soul; to lose them meant death. "Thou stick'st a dagger in me," he says to Tubal, "I shall never see my gold again." Think about these words – the loss of his ducats, his external soul, was death to him. However, you must know that the external soul is not always the same . . .'

'Isn't it?'

'By no means; it changes its nature and state. I'm not alluding to certain all-absorbent souls, like love for one's country – Camões went so far as to say he died with his [1] – or power, which was the external soul of Caesar and Cromwell. These are forceful, exclusive souls; but there are others, however forceful, which are also of a changeable nature. There are gentlemen, for example, whose external soul, in their early years, was a rattle or a wooden horse, and later, it's being president of a charitable institution or something of the sort. For my part, I know a lady – and very charming she is – who changes her external soul five or six times a year. During the season, it's the opera; when the season's over, the external soul is exchanged for another: a concert, or a ball at the Cassino, the Rua do Ouvidor, Petrópolis . . .'

'Sorry; who is this lady?'

'This lady is related to the devil, and she has the same name – her name is Legion . . . And there are many other cases like this. I myself have experienced some of these changes. I won't recount them; it would take too long. I'll limit myself to the episode I mentioned. It happened when I was twenty-five . . .'

The four companions, such was their anxiety to hear the promised story, forgot their controversy. Blessed Curiosity! Not only are you civilisation's nursemaid, you are also the apple of concord, a divine fruit, which tastes completely different from the other one, the one in the myth. The room, which a few moments ago had been full of the noise of physics and metaphysics, is now a dead calm sea; all eyes are on Jacobina, who pares the end of his cigar, as he collects his memories. This is how he began his narrative:

'I was twenty-five, I was poor, and I had just been made a sub-lieutenant in the National Guard.[2] You can't imagine what an event it was at home. My mother was so proud! So happy! She kept calling me her sub-lieutenant. Uncles, cousins – everybody was simply, sincerely happy. In the town, we might note, some were resentful – there was wailing and gnashing of teeth, as in the Scriptures. The reason was that there had been many candidates for the post, and they were the losers. I suppose a part of the disappointment was completely gratuitous, a simple consequence of the distinction I'd received. I remember some lads, friends of mine, who looked at me sideways, for a time. On the other hand, I had many people who were happy about the appointment; and the proof is that all the uniform was given me by friends . . . Next thing, one of my aunts, Dona Marcolina, Captain Pessanha's widow, who lived many leagues from the town, in a lonely, out-of-the-way place, wanted to see me, and asked me to go and stay with her, and bring the uniform. I went, with a servant, who went back to town some days later, because as soon as Aunt Marcolina had me at her farm she wrote to my mother saying she wouldn't let me go for a month at least. And how she hugged me! She too called me her sub-lieutenant. She told me I was a handsome, strapping young man. She was a bit of a wag, and even confessed she was envious of any girl that married me. She swore no one in the entire province could compete with me. And it was sub-lieutenant over and over; sub-lieutenant here, sub-lieutenant there, at every minute of the day. I asked her to call me Joãozinho as before; and she shook her head, exclaiming that no, I was 'Mr Sub-Lieutenant'. A brother-in-law of hers, the late Pessanha's brother, who was living there, refused to call me anything else. It was 'Mr Sub-Lieutenant', and not as a joke, but quite seriously, in front of the slaves, who naturally followed their lead. I had the best position at table, and was the first to be served. You can't imagine. If I tell you that Aunt Marcolina's enthusiasm went so far as to have a large mirror put in my room, a rich, magnificent piece, out of keeping with the rest of the house, whose furniture was modest and simple . . . It was a mirror given her by her godmother, who in her turn had inherited it from her mother, who'd bought it from one of the noblewomen who came with the court of King João VI, in 1808.[3] I don't know how much truth there was in this; that was the traditional story. The mirror, of course, was very old; but you could still see its gilding, partly eaten by time, some dolphins in the top corners of the frame, mother-of-pearl trimmings, and other caprices of the artist. Old, but good quality . . .'

'Was it big?'

'Yes. And, as I say, it was a sign of great kindness, for the mirror was displayed in the drawing room; it was the best thing in the house. But nothing would dissuade her; no one missed it, she answered, and it was only for a few weeks – and in any case, 'Mr Sub-Lieutenant' deserved much more. What's also true is that all these things, the kindnesses and endearments, the deference, operated a transformation in me, which the natural feelings of youth assisted and brought to completion. I expect you can imagine what?'

'No.'

'The sub-lieutenant eliminated the man. For some days the two natures were in balance: but it wasn't long before the original one gave way to the other; only a minimal part of humanity was left to me. At this point, my external soul, which before had been the sun, the air, the countryside, the look in a girl's eyes, changed its nature, and became the curtseys and the kowtowing in the house, everything that spoke to me of my commission, and nothing of the man. The only part of the citizen I had left was what had to do with my rank; the rest evaporated into the air, and into the past. You find it hard to believe?'

'I find it hard even to understand,' replied one of the listeners.

'You'll understand. My actions will explain the feelings better; the actions are everything. The best definition of love is nothing to kissing the girl you love; and, if I remember rightly, an ancient philosopher demonstrated movement by walking. Let's get to the action, then. We'll see how, at the same time as the consciousness of the man was being obliterated, the sub-lieutenant's was becoming vivid and intense. Human sufferings, human joys, if that was all they were, hardly got a nod of apathetic compassion or a condescending smile from me. After three weeks I was another person, completely changed. I was, exclusively, the sub-lieutenant. Well, one day Aunt Marcolina got some bad news: one of her daughters, married to a farmer and living five leagues away, was ill, at death's door. Goodbye, nephew! Goodbye, sub-lieutenant! She was a doting mother, and soon readied herself for the journey, asked her brother-in-law to go with her, and me if I would take care of the farm. If she'd not been so worried, she'd have done the opposite; she'd have left the brother-in-law, and taken me with her. Whatever the truth of that, I was left alone, with the few slaves in the household. I confess to you that I immediately felt a great sense of oppression, as if the four walls of a prison had suddenly been erected around me. It was the external soul growing smaller; now it was limited to a few uncouth individuals. The sub-lieutenant was still dominant in me, although less intensely so, as my awareness of it weakened. The slaves put a note of humility into their courtesies, which in some way took the place of my relatives' affection and the warmth and intimacy of the household which had now been interrupted. I even noticed, that night, that they redoubled their respect, their cheerfulness, their protestations. It was Massa Sub-Lieutenant at every moment. Massa Sub-Lieutenant's a handsome lad; Massa Sub-Lieutenant'll soon be a colonel; Massa Sub-

Lieutenant'll marry a pretty girl, a general's daughter; a symphony of praises and prophecies, which left me in a state of ecstasy. Oh, what traitors! Hardly could I suspect the scoundrels' secret intention.'

'To kill you?'

'I wish it had been.'

'Worse than that?'

'Hear me out. The next morning I found I was alone. The rogues, whether lured by others or on their own initiative, had resolved to abscond during the night; no sooner said than done. I found myself alone, with no one else, between four walls, facing the deserted terrace and the abandoned fields. Not a breath of human life. I ran round the entire house, the slave quarters, and there was nothing, nobody, not even a slave-boy left. Just some cocks and hens, a pair of mules philosophising about life, flicking off the flies, and three oxen. The slaves had even taken the dogs. Not a human being to be seen. You think this was better than having died? It was worse. Not from fear; I swear to you I wasn't afraid; I was a little cocksure, so I wasn't at all upset, for the first few hours. I was worried because of the loss caused to Aunt Marcolina; I was also in somewhat of a quandary, not knowing if I ought to go to her and give her the bad news, or stay and look after the house. I decided to stay, so as not to leave the house unprotected, and because, if my cousin really was seriously ill, I would only increase her mother's worries, without bringing any remedy; lastly, I expected Uncle Pessanha's brother to come back that day or the next, for they'd been gone for a day and a half. But the morning went by with no sign of him; and in the afternoon I began to feel I'd lost all sensation in my nerves, and could no longer feel my muscles move. Uncle Pessanha's brother didn't come back that day, or the next, nor that whole week. My solitude took on gigantic proportions. Never had the days been so long, never had the sun burned the earth so obstinately, so exhaustingly. The hours chimed from century to century on the old clock in the drawing room, whose pendulum – tick-tock, tick-tock – wounded my internal soul, like a continuous mocking gesture from eternity. When, many years later, I read an American poem, by Longfellow I think, and came across this famous refrain: 'For ever – never! Never – for ever!'[4] I confess to you that a shiver ran down my spine: I remembered those terrible days. That was exactly what Aunt Marcolina's clock said: 'Never, for ever! – For ever, never!' They weren't pendulum beats; they were a dialogue with the abyss, a whisper from nothingness. And then at night! It wasn't that the night was quieter. The silence was just the same as during the day. But the night was the darkness, it was a wider, or a narrower solitude. Tick-tock, tick-tock. No one in the rooms, on the veranda, in the corridors, on the terrace, no one anywhere . . . You're laughing?'

'It does seem you were a bit afraid.'

'Oh, it would have been all right if I could have been afraid! I'd have been alive. But the chief thing about the situation is that I couldn't even be afraid, that is, afraid in the normal sense. I had an inexplicable sensation. I was like a walking corpse, a sleep-walker, a mechanical doll. Sleeping was different. Sleep gave me relief, not for the commonplace reason of being the close relative of death, but because of something else. I think I can explain the phenomenon this way: sleep, by eliminating the necessity for an external soul, left the internal soul to its devices. In dreams, I put my uniform on, proudly, in the presence of my family and friends, who praised my military bearing, called me sub-lieutenant; a friend from home came and promised me promotion to lieutenant, another to captain or major – all this brought me to life. But when I awoke, in daylight, all this disappeared with the sleep, this awareness of my new, unique self – for the internal soul had lost its exclusive sway, and became dependent on the other, which refused to return . . . It wouldn't return, come what may. I went outside, pacing from one side to another, to see if I could discover some sign of anyone coming back. *Soeur Anne, soeur Anne, ne vois-tu rien venir?*[5] Nothing, not a thing, just as in the French story – only the dust on the road and the grass on the hills. I went back to the house, desperate, in a nervous state, and stretched out on the drawing-room sofa. Tick-tock, tick-tock. I got up, walked to and fro, drummed on the window panes, whistled. On one occasion I had the notion to write something, a political article, a novel or an ode; I couldn't finally decide on anything; I sat down and jotted some odd words and sentences, to insert as appropriate. But my style, like Aunt Marcolina, refused to budge. *Soeur Anne, soeur Anne* . . . nothing. At most, I watched the ink blacken and the paper shine whiter.'

'But didn't you eat?'

'Not much: fruit, manioc flour, preserves, some roots toasted at the fire, but I'd have happily put up with everything if it hadn't been for the terrible moral situation I was in. I recited verses, speeches, passages in Latin, poems by Gonzaga,[6] some of Camões's lyrics, sonnets – an anthology in thirty volumes. At times I did gymnastic exercises; at others I gave myself pinches on my legs; but the only effect was a physical sensation of pain or fatigue, nothing more. Everything was silent, a vast, enormous, infinite silence, underlined only by the eternal tick-tock of the pendulum. Tick-tock, tick-tock.'

'You're right; it was enough to send anyone mad.'

'There's worse to come. First I should tell you that, since I'd been alone, I'd not looked in the mirror one single time. I hadn't deliberately abstained from doing so, there was no reason for that; it was an unconscious impulse, a fear of finding that I was one person and two at the same time, in the solitary house. If that's the right explanation, nothing proves human contradiction better, for after a week, I decided on a whim to look in the mirror, precisely with the aim of seeing myself duplicated. I took one look, and fell back. The glass itself seemed to have conspired with the rest of the universe; it didn't show a clearly outlined silhouette, but something vague, hazy, diffuse, the shadow of a shade. The reality of the laws of physics doesn't allow me to deny that the mirror reproduced me exactly, with the correct outlines and features; it must have done. But that wasn't the sensation I had. Then I was afraid; I attributed the phenomenon to my state of nervous over-excitement; I was afraid of staying there longer, and going mad. "I'm getting out of here," I said to myself. And I lifted my arm in a gesture at once ill-humoured and decisive, looking at the glass; there was the gesture, but dissolved, faded, mutilated . . . I got on with dressing myself, mumbling to myself, coughing though I had no cough, shaking my clothes noisily, getting unnecessarily irritated with the buttons, just to say something. From time to time,

I took a furtive look at the mirror; the image had the same confused profile, the same blurred outlines . . . I went on dressing myself. Suddenly, by some inexplicable inspiration, a spontaneous impulse, I decided . . . If you can guess the idea I had . . .'

'Tell us.'

'I was looking at the glass, with the insistence of a desperate man, looking at my own floating, unfinished features, a cloud of loose, shapeless lines, when I had an idea . . . No, you'll never guess.'

'Go on, tell us, tell us.'

'I had the idea of putting the sub-lieutenant's uniform on. I did just that, and dressed from top to toe; and, since I was in front of the mirror, I lifted my eyes, and . . . I'll say no more; the glass then reproduced my whole figure; there wasn't a feature missing, no outline was out of place; it was I myself, the sub-lieutenant, who had finally found his external soul. This soul, which had gone missing with the owner of the farm and dispersed and fled with the slaves, there it was, reconstituted in the mirror. Imagine a man who, little by little, emerges from a state of lethargy, opens his eyes without seeing, then begins to see, distinguishes people from objects, but still can't recognise each one individually; then finally he's aware that this is Tom, that's Dick, that's Harry; here's a chair, there's a sofa. Everything returns to what it was before he went to sleep. That's how it was with me. I looked at the mirror, went from one side to another, took a step back, gesticulated, smiled, and the glass expressed everything. I was an automaton no longer; I was an animated being. From that day on, I was another person. Each day, at a given hour, I dressed as a sub-lieutenant, and sat down in front of the mirror reading, looking, meditating; at the end of two or three hours, I undressed again. With this system I was able to get through six more days of solitude, without noticing them . . .'

When the others came back to their senses, the storyteller had gone down the stairs.

An Alexandrian Tale

Chapter I: At Sea

'What, my dear Stroibus! No, impossible. Nobody will ever, ever believe that a rat's blood, if given to a man to drink, will turn him into a burglar.'

'In the first place, Pythias, you omit one condition: the rat must die beneath the scalpel for the blood to preserve its vital essence. This condition is essential. In the second place, since you choose the example of the rat, you may as well know that I have already carried out an experiment, and have managed to produce a thief . . .'

'A real thief?'

'He took my cloak; thirty days later, but he gave me the greatest happiness in the world: the proof of my ideas. What did I lose? A little bit of coarse cloth; and what has the universe gained? Enduring truth. Yes, my dear Pythias, this is the eternal truth. The constitutive elements of the thief are in the blood of a rat, of the patient man in the ox, of daring in the eagle . . .'

'And those of the wise man in the owl,' Pythias interrupted with a smile.

'No: the owl is only an emblem; but the spider, if we could transfer it inside a man, would give that man the rudiments of geometry and musical appreciation. With a flock of storks, swallows or cranes, I'll make a home-loving man into a wanderer. The essence of conjugal fidelity is in the blood of the dove, of vanity in peacocks . . . In sum, the gods put the essence of all human capacities and feelings into the beasts of the earth, water and air. The animals are the letters of the alphabet; man is the syntax. This is my latest philosophy; this is what I am about to unveil at the court of the great Ptolemy.'

Pythias shook his head and stared at the sea. The ship was bound for Alexandria with its precious cargo of two philosophers, who were carrying the fruits of their enlightened philosophy to that cradle of learning. They were friends, both widowers and in their fifties. They especially cultivated metaphysics, but they were also acquainted with physics, chemistry, medicine and music; one of them, Stroibus, had become an excellent anatomist, having read Herophilus's treatises on the subject many times. Cyprus was their native land; but, so true is it that no one is a prophet in his own country, that Cyprus did not give the two philosophers the respect they merited. On the contrary, it despised them; some young men went so far as to laugh at them in the street. This, however, was not their motive for leaving their homeland. One day, Pythias, on his return from a journey, proposed to his friend that they should go to Alexandria, where the arts and sciences were held in great esteem. Stroibus agreed, and they embarked. Only now, once they were at sea, did the inventor of the new doctrine expound it to his friend, along with all his recent speculations and experiments.

'That's that then,' said Pythias, lifting his head; 'I neither confirm nor deny anything. I'll study these teachings, and if I find they are true, I will willingly develop and help to spread them.'

'Long live Helios, god of the sun,' Stroibus exclaimed. 'I can say you are my disciple.'

Chapter II: An Experiment

The Alexandrian youths didn't treat the two sages with the same mockery as the Cypriots. The country was as grave as an ibis standing on only one leg, as thoughtful as the sphinx, as circumspect as the mummies and as hard as the pyramids; it had neither the time nor the inclination to laugh. The city and the court, which had for many years heard tell of our two friends, gave them a regal reception, showed they were familiar with their writings; they discussed their ideas, and sent them many presents – papyri, crocodiles, zebras, cloths dyed a rich purple. They, however, refused it all with simplicity, saying that philosophy, for the philosopher, was its own reward, and that superfluity corrupts. Such a noble reply filled the wise men, the city's leaders, and even the lower classes with admiration. Moreover, said the wisest of all, what else could be expected of two such sublime men, who in their magnificent treatises . . .

'We've got something better than those treatises,' Stroibus interrupted. 'I have a doctrine which, in a short time, will rule the universe; my plan is nothing less than the reordering of men and nations, through a redistribution of talents and virtues.'

'Isn't that the gods' affair?' someone objected.

'I have penetrated the secret of the gods,' Stroibus replied. 'Man is the syntax of nature, and I have discovered the laws of divine grammar . . .'

'Explain yourself.'

'Later; allow me first to carry out my experiment. When my doctrine is complete, I will reveal it as the greatest gift men could ever receive from one of their kind.'

Imagine the public expectation and the curiosity of other philosophers, doubtful though they were that this recent truth could pension off the ones they themselves held. Nevertheless, they all waited. The two guests were pointed out in the street, even by children. A son thought he might change his father's avarice, a father his son's prodigality, a lady a gentleman's coldness, a gentleman a lady's follies – for Egypt, from the times of the Pharoahs to that of the Ptolemies, had been the land of Potiphar, of Potiphar's wife, of Joseph's coat of many colours, and all the rest of it. Stroibus became the great hope of the city and the world.

Pythias, having studied the doctrine, went to see Stroibus, and said to him: 'Metaphysically, your doctrine is nonsense; but I am prepared to allow one experiment, as long as it is decisive. There is only one way, my dear Stroibus, that this can be done. You and I, because we have cultivated reason and because of our upright natures, are as opposed to the vice of theft as it is possible to be. Well then, if you manage to instil this vice in us, no more will be necessary; if you achieve nothing (and that's what will happen, for the whole thing's absurd), you will abandon this doctrine, and return to our former meditations.'

Stroibus accepted the proposal.

'My sacrifice is the harder,' he said, 'in that I am certain of the outcome; but what may truth not demand of us? Truth is immortal; man is a brief moment . . .'

The Egyptian rats, had they known of this agreement, would have imitated the ancient Hebrews, and chosen to flee into the desert rather than accept the new philosophy. We can only believe that would have been a disastrous occurrence. Science, like war, has unanswerable necessities; and since the ignorance and weakness of rats, coupled with the mental and physical superiority of the two philosophers, constituted so many favourable circumstances in the experiment about to begin, there was no missing such an excellent opportunity to find out if the essence of each human passion and virtue really was distributed through the various species of animals, and if it were possible to transmit it.

Stroibus put the rats in cages; then, one by one, he submitted them to the knife. First, he tied a strip of cloth to the patient's snout – then the feet; finally, he tied the animal's legs and neck to the operating table. This done, he made the first cut in the chest, slowly, and as slowly dug the knife in until he touched the heart, for he was of the opinion that instantaneous death corrupted the blood and removed its essence. A skilled anatomist, he operated with an assuredness worthy of his scientific aims. Another, less dextrous, would have interrupted the task many times, for the contortions of pain and the death throes made it difficult to wield the knife;

but that was precisely Stroibus's superiority: his firmness and accuracy were masterly.

At his side, Pythias collected the blood and assisted in the task, either containing the convulsive movements of the patient, or watching the progress of the death throes in its eyes. The observations made by both men were noted down on papyrus leaves; and science benefited from this in two ways. Sometimes, because their view of matters differed, they were obliged to dissect a greater number of rats than was necessary; but they lost nothing by this, for the blood of the surplus ones was kept and swallowed later. A single example will demonstrate the conscientious manner in which they proceeded. Pythias had observed that the retina of the dying rat changed colour to a light blue, while Stroibus's observation indicated cinnamon as the final hue at the point of death. They were on their last operation of the day; but the point was worth testing, and, tired as they were, they carried out nineteen experiments without a conclusive answer; Pythias insisted on the light blue, and Stroibus on cinnamon. The twentieth rat nearly brought agreement, but Stroibus, with great wisdom, pointed out that he was in a different position. He corrected it and they dissected another twenty-five. Of these, the first still left them in doubt; but the other twenty-four proved to them that the final colour was neither cinnamon nor blue, but a violet colour, somewhat on the pale side.

Exaggerated descriptions of this experimentation had re-percussions on the sentimental portion of the city's population, and excited verbose commentary from some sophists; but the severe Stroibus (gently, so as not to worsen a typical tendency of the human soul) replied that truth was worth all the rats in the universe, and not only rats, but peacocks, goats, dogs, nightingales, etc.; in the rats' case, science was not the only beneficiary – the city gained too, as the scourge of such a harmful animal was reduced; moreover, if the same considerations could not be applied to other animals, such as doves or dogs, for instance, which would be dissected in good time, the rights of truth were no less inalienable. Nature should not only serve the dinner table, he concluded in aphoristic vein, but the table of science too.

And they went on extracting the blood and drinking it. They didn't drink it pure, but diluted in a tisane of jasmine, acacia juice and balsam, which removed all its original taste. They took it in tiny daily doses; they had to wait a long time, therefore, for the desired effect. Pythias, impatient and incredulous, made fun of his friend.

'Well then? Nothing?'

'Wait,' said the other, 'wait. You don't instil a vice the way you sew a pair of sandals.'

Chapter III: Victory

Finally, Stroibus conquered! The experiment proved the doctrine. And Pythias was the first one to give signs that the effects were real, when he attributed to himself three ideas he'd heard from Stroibus; the latter, for his part, stole four comparisons and a theory of the operation of the winds from him. What could be more scientific than these beginnings? Other people's ideas, precisely because they can't be bought at the street corner, have an air of having been shared; it's very natural to begin with them before going on to borrowed books, chickens, forged money, provinces and so on. The very word plagiarism is an indication that people understand how easy it is to confuse this germ of thievery with thievery properly so called.

It's hard to admit; but the truth is that they threw their metaphysical baggage into the Nile, and in a short while had become full-blown pilferers. They would lay their plans on the previous day, and off they went after cloaks, bronzes, amphorae of wine, merchandise at the docks, and good solid drachmas. As they stole noiselessly, no one caught on; but even if they had suspected, how would they have made anyone else believe it? Already then, Ptolemy had collected many costly volumes and rarities in his library; and, because they had to be put in order, he designated five grammarians and five philosophers, among whom were our two friends. They both worked with singular zeal, being the first to arrive and the last to leave, and staying on many nights, by lamplight, deciphering, compiling and classifying. Ptolemy, elated, had the highest of destinies in mind for them.

Some time later, serious gaps began to be noted: a copy of Homer, three rolls of Persian and two of Samaritan manuscripts, a superb collection of Alexander's original letters, copies of Athenian laws, the second and third books of Plato's *Republic*, etc., etc. The authorities set up a close watch; but the rat's cunning, transferred to a superior organism, was naturally greater, and the two illustrious thieves made a mockery of the spies and guards. They went as far as to establish the philosophical principle that they wouldn't leave empty-handed; they always carried something, a fable at the very least. Finally, since there was a ship leaving for Cyprus, they asked leave of Ptolemy, promising to return, sewed the books inside hippopotamus skins, put false labels on them and attempted to flee. But the envy of other philosophers was unceasing; the magistrates' suspicions were aroused, and the robbery was discovered. Stroibus and Pythias were arrested as adventurers who had used the names of those two illustrious men as a disguise; Ptolemy delivered them to the courts with orders to hand them over immediately to the executioner. At this point, Herophilus, the father of anatomy, intervened.[1]

Chapter IV: Plus Ultra!

'My Lord,' he said to Ptolemy, 'up to now I have limited myself to dissecting corpses. But the body gives me the structure, it does not give me life; it gives me the organs, not their functions. I need the functions and I need life.'

'What are you saying to me?' Ptolemy answered. 'Do you want to disembowel Stroibus's rats?'

'No, sir; I don't want to disembowel rats.'

'Dogs? Geese? Hares?'

'None of those; I ask for some living men.'

'Living? That's impossible . . .'

'I shall demonstrate that not only is it possible, but legitimate and necessary. The prisons of Egypt are full of criminals, and criminals occupy an extremely low rung of the human ladder. They are no longer citizens, and indeed cannot call themselves men, for they have relinquished man's two distinguishing characteristics, reason and virtue, by infringing law and morality. Besides, since they have to expiate their crimes by death, is it not just that they should give some service to truth and science? Truth is immortal; it is worth not only all the rats, but all the delinquents in the universe.'

Ptolemy found this reasoning correct, and ordered that criminals should be handed over to Herophilus and his disciples. The great anatomist thanked him for such an exceptional favour, and began to dissect the prisoners. Great was the astonishment of the people; but apart from a few verbal appeals, there were no protests against the measure. Herophilus repeated what he had said to Ptolemy, adding that the subjection of the prisoners to anatomical experiment was even an indirect way of encouraging morality, since the terror of the knife would prevent many crimes from being committed.

None of the criminals, when they left the prison, suspected the scientific destiny awaiting them. They came out one by one; sometimes two by two, or three by three. Many of them, stretched out and tied to the operating table, still suspected nothing; they thought it was a new kind of summary execution. Only when the anatomists defined the object of the day's study did the wretches become aware of what was happening. Those who remembered seeing the experiments on the rats suffered doubly, for their imaginations added the spectacle of the past to their present pain.

To reconcile the interests of science with the impulse to compassion, the prisoners were not dissected in sight of each other, but successively. When they came in twos or threes, they were not put in a place where they could hear the patient's cries, though often the cries were smothered by means of certain appliances; but if they were smothered, they were not eliminated, and indeed in certain cases, the objective of the experiment itself demanded that the emission of the voice should be full and free. Sometimes the operations were simultaneous; but then they were carried out far apart from one another.

Nearly fifty prisoners had been dissected when it came to the turn of Stroibus and Pythias. When they were fetched, they supposed it was for their judicial execution, and commended themselves to the gods. On the way they stole some figs, and explained the occurrence, attributing it to the pangs of hunger; further on, however, they purloined a flute – for this latter action they no longer had a satisfactory explanation. However, the thief's cunning is infinite, and Stroibus, to justify the action, tried to extract some notes from the instrument, filling with compassion the people who saw them pass, who were not ignorant of the fate that awaited them. The news of these latest two crimes was narrated by Herophilus, and shook all his disciples.

'Truly,' said the master, 'it is an extraordinary case, a most beautiful case. Before we get to the main business, let's examine this other point . . .'

The point was to discover if the nerve for thieving was to be found in the palm of the hand, or the tips of the fingers – this problem had been suggested by one of the students.

Stroibus was the first to be subjected to the operation. He
realised everything as soon as he came into the room; and, as
human nature has a streak of baseness, begged them humbly
to spare a philosopher's life. But Herophilus, with an acute
dialectical power, said more or less this: 'Either you are an
impostor or the real Stroibus; in the first case, you have here
one way of redeeming the crime of deluding an enlightened
prince, by subjecting yourself to the scalpel; in the second
case, you will not be unaware that the obligation of a
philosopher is to serve philosophy, and that the body is
nothing compared to the understanding.'

This said, they began with the experiment on the hands,
which produced marvellous results, collected in books,
which were lost with the fall of the Ptolemies. Pythias's
hands were also torn open and minutely examined. The
wretched pair howled, wept, pleaded; but Herophilus
calmly told them that it was the philosopher's duty to serve
philosophy, and that for the aims of science they were
worth even more than rats, since it was better to argue from
one man to another, and not from a rat to a man. And he
went on tearing them membrane by membrane for eight
days. On the third day they took their eyes, to disprove in
practice a theory about the internal shape of the organ. I
won't go into the extraction of both of their stomachs,
because the problems involved were relatively secondary,
and in any case had been studied and resolved in five or six
individuals dissected before them.

The Alexandrians said that the rats celebrated this painful,
distressing event with dancing and parties, and invited some
dogs, doves, peacocks and other animals threatened with the

same destiny; and that none of them accepted the invitation, on the advice of a dog, who said, in melancholy tones: 'The time will come when the same thing will happen to us.' To which a rat replied: 'Till then, let's keep laughing!'

A Singular Occurrence

'SOME REALLY STRANGE THINGS happen. Do you see that lady over there, going into the Holy Cross Church? She's just stopped in the porch to give a beggar some money.'

'The one in black?'

'That's right: she's just going in. She's gone.'

'Say no more. I can see the lady brings back memories, and recent ones, judging by her figure; she's a fine-looking young woman.'

'She must be forty-six.'

'Oh! Well-preserved, then. Come on, stop staring at the ground and tell me everything. She's a widow, of course?'

'No.'

'All right, her husband's still alive. Old, I suppose?'

'She's not married.'

'A spinster?'

'Sort of. She must be called Dona Maria something-or-other. In 1860 she was commonly known as Marocas. She wasn't a seamstress, she didn't own property, she didn't run a school for girls; you'll get there, by process of elimination. She lived in the Rua do Sacramento. In those days too she was slim, and certainly lovelier than she is today; she had quiet manners, and never swore. In the street, modest as she was, with her faded dress buttoned up to the neck, she still had a lot of admirers.'

'You, for instance.'

'No, but a friend of mine, Andrade, twenty-six, part-lawyer, part-politician, born in Alagoas and married in Bahia – he came from there in 1859. His wife was pretty, affectionate, gentle and resigned; when I got to know them their little daughter was two.'

'But in spite of that, Marocas . . .?'

'That's right, she swept him off his feet. Look, if you're not in a hurry, I'll tell you something interesting.'

'Go ahead.'

'The first time he met her was at the door of Paula Brito's shop in the Rossio. There he was, and he saw a pretty woman in the distance, and waited, his interest already aroused, because he had a real passion for the ladies. Marocas was coming in his direction, stopping and looking, as if searching for something. In front of the shop she stopped for a moment; then, timidly and with shame, she held out a piece of paper to Andrade, and asked him where the number written on it was. Andrade told her it was on the other side of the square, and pointed out more or less where it would be. She curtseyed very prettily; he didn't know what to make of the question.'

'Nor do I.'

'Nothing could be simpler: Marocas couldn't read. He didn't even suspect it. He watched her crossing the Rossio, which in those days had no garden in the middle, or the statue it has now, and go to the place she was looking for; even then, she stopped at other houses to ask. That night he went to the

Ginásio theatre to see *The Lady of the Camellias*. Marocas was there, and during the last act she wept like a child. No need to say more; at the end of a fortnight they were madly in love. Marocas got rid of all her other lovers, and it can't have been easy – some of them were really well off. She lived on her own; everything revolved round Andrade, and she wanted no other attachment, no other way of earning a living.'

'Just like the Lady of the Camellias.'

'Right. Andrade taught her to read. I've turned into a schoolmaster, he said to me one day, and that was when he told me the story of their meeting in the Rossio. Marocas was a fast learner. It's understandable: the shame of ignorance, the desire to read the novels he told her about, and finally her pleasure in obeying his desire, of being agreeable to him . . . He hid nothing from me; he told me everything with such a grateful, happy look in his eyes, you can't imagine. I was a confidant to both of them. Sometimes the three of us dined together, and . . . I don't see why I should deny it – sometimes the four of us. Don't imagine we were disreputable – these were happy, but respectable suppers. Marocas liked her language buttoned up, like her dresses. Little by little, we became close friends; she asked me about Andrade, his wife, his daughter, his habits, if he really loved her, or was it just a caprice, if he'd had others, if he might forget her – she showered me with questions; she had a fear of losing him which showed the strength and the sincerity of her affection . . . One day, for St John's Night, Andrade went out of town with his family, to Gávea, where they were invited to a dinner and a dance; two days away. I went with them. Marocas, as she said goodbye, reminded us of a comedy she'd seen some weeks before at the Ginásio – *Dining with Mother*[1]– and told me that, since she had no family to spend St John's with, she'd do what Sophie Arnoult in the play does, have dinner with a portrait; but it wouldn't be her mother's, because she had no mother, but Andrade's. What she'd said would have got her a kiss; and Andrade actually leaned towards her, but seeing I was there, she delicately pushed him away with her hand.'

'I like that gesture.'

'He liked it just as much. He held her face in both hands, and gave her a fatherly kiss on the forehead. We went off to Gávea. On the way, he told me about the wonders of Marocas, about their latest whims, told me about his project to buy her a house in some suburb as soon as he could get the money; he was full of praise for her modesty – she didn't want anything from him beyond what was strictly necessary. There's more, I said, and told him something I'd found out, that is, that about three weeks before, Marocas had pawned some jewels to pay a seamstress's bill. This upset him a great deal; I can't swear, but I think there were tears in his eyes. Anyway, after thinking for a while, he told me he would definitely get her a house and release her from the threat of poverty. In Gávea, we spoke about Marocas some more, until the party ended and we came back. Andrade left his family at home and went to the office to deal with some urgent business. A little after noon, one Leandro, a former agent of another lawyer, came, as was his custom, to beg a couple of *mil-reis*. He was a lazy, vulgar fellow, who lived by leeching off his ex-boss's friends. Andrade gave him three *mil-reis*, and seeing he was exceptionally cheery, asked him why he had a twinkle in his eye. Leandro winked and licked his lips: and Andrade, who had an appetite for spicy stories, asked him if it was some love affair. He chewed it over a moment, and confessed it was.'

'Look, she's coming out; that's the one, isn't it?'

'Yes, that's her. Let's get away from the corner.'

'Yes, she must have been really pretty. She looks like a duchess.'

'She didn't look in our direction. She always looks straight ahead. She'll go up the Rua do Ouvidor . . .'

'Yes, sir. I can understand Andrade.'

'Let's go on with the story. Leandro confessed he'd had a real piece of luck the previous day – unique, in fact, something he'd never expected. He didn't even deserve it, because he knew he was a good-for-nothing. But even poor people were God's children. Anyway, the day before in the Rossio, around ten at night, he'd come across a lady simply dressed, really good-looking, closely wrapped in a large shawl. The lady went after him, walking quicker; as she brushed past him she looked right in his eyes, and went on slowly, as if waiting for him. The fellow imagined she'd got the wrong person; he confessed to Andrade that, in spite of the simple dress, he saw straight away she wasn't for the likes of him. He went on; the woman stopped, and looked at him again, but so insistently that he got a bit daring; she did the rest . . . Oh! What an angel! What a house, what a lovely room! Really chic. And she wasn't after money . . . "Look here," he added, "how about yourself, it'd be a good deal for you too." Andrade shook his head; he'd not sniffed out his rival. But Leandro insisted; it was in the Rua do Sacramento, number such-and-such . . .'

'Good God! You don't say!'

'You can imagine what a state Andrade got into. He himself
didn't know what he was saying or doing for the first few
minutes, or what he felt or thought. Finally he pulled himself
together enough to ask if what he was saying was true; but
Leandro reminded him he'd no need to invent it; however,
seeing that Andrade was upset, he asked him to keep it secret,
telling him that he, for his part, was always discreet. It seems
he was about to go; Andrade held him back and made a
proposition: would he like to earn twenty *mil-reis*? – "Fine!" –
"I'll give you twenty *mil-reis* if you'll go to the girl's house
with me and tell me in her presence that it's really her." '

'Oh!'

'I'm not defending Andrade; it wasn't a nice thing to do;
but in situations like that passion blinds the best of us. Andrade
was a worthy, generous, sincere man, but it was such a terrible
blow, and he loved her so much that he didn't flinch from that
kind of revenge.'

'Did the man accept?'

'He hesitated a bit – out of fear more than dignity, I reckon.
But twenty *mil-reis* . . . He laid down one condition: he
wasn't to be involved in any trouble . . . Marocas was in the
room when Andrade entered. She came to the door to
embrace him; but Andrade, with a gesture, warned her there
was someone with him. Then, looking hard at her, he made
Leandro come in; Marocas went pale – "Is this the lady?" he
asked. "Yes, sir," mumbled Leandro faintly, for there are
actions even viler than the man who commits them. Andrade
opened his wallet with a dramatic gesture, took out the note
and gave it to him; and with the same affected air, ordered him

to go. Leandro left. The following scene was short, but dramatic. I didn't hear all the details, because it was Andrade who told me everything, and naturally he was so stunned that he forgot things. She admitted to nothing, but she was completely beside herself, and when, after saying some very harsh things, he rushed for the door, she flung herself at his feet, grabbed him by the hands, weeping, desperate, threatening to kill herself. She lay there at the threshold as he rushed downstairs in a daze, and left.'

'A vulgar person, in fact, picked up in the street; maybe she made a habit of it?'

'No.'

'No?'

'Listen to the rest of the story. It must have been eight at night when Andrade came to my house, and waited for me. He'd already come to look for me three times. I was flabbergasted; but how could I doubt him, when he'd taken the proof itself to the scene of the crime? I'll not tell you all he said, his plans for revenge, the names he called her: all this in keeping with the style and repertoire of these moments of crisis. I advised him to leave her, and live for his daughter and his wife – so good and gentle . . . He agreed, but then flew into a rage again. Then anger turned to doubt; he even imagined that Marocas, to test him, had invented the whole thing and sent Leandro to come and tell him the story; the proof being that when he had shown no curiosity about the lady, Leandro had insisted on telling him the street and the number. Holding on for dear life to this unlikely theory, he tried to flee from reality, but reality came after him – Marocas's pallor, Leandro's genuine happiness, everything

told him the thing had happened. I even think he was sorry
he'd gone so far. For my part, I was thinking the business over,
but I couldn't come up with an explanation. So modest! So
shy in her manner!'

'There's a phrase from the theatre that might explain this
adventure, from Augier I think it is: "nostalgia for the
gutter".'[2]

'I don't think so. Listen to the rest. At ten Marocas's maid, a
freed slave, very close to her mistress, appeared. She was
searching desperately for Andrade, because Marocas had cried
a lot, locked herself in her room, then gone out without food,
and she'd not come back. I stopped Andrade, whose first
impulse was to go out straight away. The servant begged us to
go and find her mistress. "Isn't she in the habit of going out?"
asked Andrade, sarcastically. But she said no, she wasn't.
"Hear that?" he shouted. Hope had filled the poor fellow's
heart again. "What about yesterday?" I said. The maid replied
that yesterday she had gone out; but I asked no more
questions. I felt sorry for Andrade, who was getting more
and more frantic – his sense of honour was giving way to fear
for her safety. We left to look for Marocas; we went to all the
houses where she might have been, and finally to the police.
The chief or one of the constables, I can't remember, was a
friend of Andrade's, and he related the parts of the story he
decently could – in any case, all his friends knew about the
affair. They went into everything: there'd been no accidents
during the night; no one had been seen falling off the ferries to
Niterói; the gun shops had sold no guns; the chemists no
poisons. The police used all their resources, but to no effect. I
can't tell you what Andrade went through for hours and

hours; the whole day went by in useless searching. It wasn't just the pain of losing her; it was remorse, and the doubts in his conscience, to say the least, at the thought of some disaster having happened, which could only argue for her innocence. He asked me all the time if it hadn't been natural to do what he'd done, and if I'd been as angry as that, wouldn't I have done the same thing? Then he went back to saying it was all true, proving to me insistently that it was, just as the previous day he'd tried to argue that it was false – he was trying to adjust reality to his feelings of the moment.'

'But they did find Marocas in the end?'

'We were eating something in a hotel; it was nearly eight at night, when we got news of a clue: a coachman who'd taken a lady to the Botanical Gardens, where she'd gone into a lodging-house and stayed. We didn't even finish dinner, and went in the same coachman's carriage to the gardens. The owner confirmed the story, adding that the lady had stayed in her room since she'd come the previous day, without eating anything; she'd just asked for a cup of coffee; she seemed profoundly depressed. We went to the room; the inn owner knocked on the door; she replied in a weak voice, and opened up. Andrade didn't give me time to say anything; he pushed past me, and they fell into each other's arms. Marocas was weeping copiously, and fainted.'

'Was everything explained?'

'Not a bit of it. Neither of them ever referred to the topic; they'd escaped from a shipwreck, and didn't want to hear about the storm that nearly sent them to the bottom. The reconciliation was quickly done. Months later, Andrade bought her a little house in Catumbi; Marocas had a little boy by him, who died when he was two. When he went to the North, on a Government mission, their affection for each other was the same as ever, though it had lost some of its earlier intensity. Still, she wanted to go with him: it was I that made her stay behind. Andrade intended to return in a short time, but as I've said, he died up there in the provinces. Marocas was very upset by his death, put on mourning, and thought of herself as a widow; I know that for the first three years, she always had a Mass said on his birthday. I lost sight of her ten years ago. Well, what do you think of it all?'

'Well, really, there are some singular occurrences; that's if you've not played on my youthful naïveté and made up a story . . .'

'I've invented nothing; it's the unvarnished truth.'

'Then it is curious. In the middle of such a burning, sincere passion . . . I'm still of the same opinion. I think it was nostalgia for the gutter.'

'No, Marocas had never descended to the likes of Leandro.'

'Then why did she do it that night?'

'He was a man she thought was separated by an abyss from anyone they knew, that's why she dared do it. But accident, God and the devil rolled into one . . . Well, who knows?'

A Chapter of Hats

GÉRONTE *Dans quel chapitre, s'il vous plaît?*
SGANARELLE *Dans le chapitre des chapeaux.*

(Molière)

Muse, sing of the vexation of Mariana, the wife of the lawyer Conrado Seabra, that morning in April 1879. What can be the cause of so much commotion? It's a mere hat, lightweight, not lacking in elegance, and flat. Conrado, a solicitor, with an office on the Rua da Quitanda, used to wear it to town every day, and to all his court appearances; he only wore something different to receptions, the opera, funerals and formal visits. For everything else it was a permanent feature, and had been for five or six years, the length of his marriage. Well, on this particular April morning, when breakfast was over, Conrado was just rolling a cigarette, and Mariana announced with a smile that she was going to ask him something.

'What is it, my angel?'
'Would you sacrifice something for my sake?'
'Ten, twenty things . . .'
'Well, stop going to town with that hat on.'
'Why? Is it ugly?'

'I'm not saying it's ugly; but it's for wearing round and about, here in the neighbourhood, in the evening or at night, but in town, for a lawyer, I don't think . . .'

'Darling, how silly!'

'All right, but would you do me this tiny favour?'

Conrado struck a match, lit his cigarette, and made an amused gesture, so as to change the subject; but his wife insisted. Her insistence, at first muted and pleading, soon became sharp and demanding. Conrado was taken aback. He knew his wife; usually, she was a passive, sweet creature, pliable and made to measure – she could have worn a royal diadem or a nun's habit with the same divine indifference. The proof of this is that, having had an active social life in the two years before she was married, no sooner did she marry than she settled into quiet habits. She went out from time to time, most often because her husband himself insisted; but she was only really comfortable at home. The furniture, curtains and orna- ments took the place of children; she loved them like a mother, and so perfect was her harmony with her surroundings, that she savoured her knick-knacks in their usual place, the curtains pulled back in the usual fashion, and so on and so forth. One of the three windows that gave on to the street, for example, was always half open; always it was the same one. Even her husband's study didn't escape his wife's demands for monotony; she kept the books in exactly the same disorder, and even went so far as to recreate it. Her mental habits followed this same uniform pattern. Mariana had very few ideas, and had read the same books over and over: *A moreninha*, by Macedo,[1] seven times; *Ivanhoe* and *The Pirate*, by Walter Scott, ten times; *Le mot de l'énigme*, by Madame Craven,[2] eleven times.

This said, how are we to explain the business of the hat? The previous evening, while her husband was at a meeting at the Law Institute, Mariana's father had come to their house. He was a good old man, thin, deliberate, an ex-civil servant, eaten up by nostalgia for the time when functionaries went to their offices in frock-coats. A frock-coat was what he still wore to funerals, and not for the motives my reader might suspect, the solemnity of death or the gravity of the final farewell, but for this, less philosophical, reason – it was an old custom. It was the only explanation he gave, whether for frock-coats at funerals, for eating his main meal at two in the afternoon, or for twenty other old-fashioned ways. He was so attached to his habits that on his daughter's wedding anniversary he went to their house at six in the evening with his meal eaten and digested, watched them eat, and at the end accepted a little dessert, a glass of wine and coffee. Such was Conrado's father-in-law; how can we expect him to approve of his son-in-law's flat hat? He put up with it in silence, out of respect for the qualities of the individual; nothing more. However, that day it happened that he saw it in the street out of the corner of his eye, chatting with other top hats on professional men, and it had never seemed so crass. That evening, finding his daughter alone, he opened his heart to her; he dubbed the low hat the height of abomination, and entreated her to have it permanently banished.

Conrado knew nothing of these details, which were the origin of her demand. Knowing how docile his wife was, he didn't understand her resistance; and because he was authoritarian and stubborn, her insistence ended by irritating him profoundly. Even so he contained himself; he preferred to make fun of the matter; he spoke to her with such irony and disdain that the poor lady felt humiliated. Mariana twice tried to get up; he made her stay, the first time gripping her lightly by the wrist, the second subjugating her with a look. And he said, smiling:

'Look, love, I have a philosophical reason for not doing what you're asking of me. I've never told you this; but now I'll confide everything to you.'

Mariana bit her lip, and said no more; she picked up a knife, and began to tap it very slowly on the table, to do something; but her husband wouldn't allow her even this – delicately, he took the knife away, and went on:

'The choice of a hat is not an indifferent act, as you might suppose; it is governed by a metaphysical principle. Don't imagine that a person buying a hat is committing a free, voluntary act; the truth is that he is obeying an obscure determinism. The illusion of freedom is rooted in the purchaser, and kept alive by hatters who, when they see a customer try on thirty or forty hats, imagine he is freely looking for an elegant combination. The metaphysical principle is the following – the hat completes the man, it is a complement decreed *ab eterno*; no one can change it without self-mutilation. This is a profound matter, one that has never yet occurred to anyone. Wise men have studied everything from stars to worms, or, to give you the bibliographical references, from Laplace onwards . . . You've never read Laplace? From Laplace and his *Mécanique céleste* to Darwin and his curious book about worms,[3] yet they've never thought to stop and look at a hat, and study it from every angle. No one has noticed that there is metaphysics in hats. I might write a memoir about it. It's a quarter to ten; I've no time to say any more; but think about it yourself, and you'll see . . . Who knows? Perhaps the hat isn't the complement of man, but man of the hat . . .'

Mariana finally got control of herself, and left the table. She'd understood nothing of his grating vocabulary, nor his peculiar theory; but she felt the sarcasm, and, inside herself, she wept for shame. Her husband went up to dress; he came down a few minutes later, and stood in front of her with the famous hat on his head. Mariana thought it really did make him look coarse, commonplace, vulgar, not at all serious. Conrado said a ceremonious goodbye and left.

The lady's irritation had subsided a good deal; but the feeling of humiliation was still there. Mariana didn't weep or scream, as she thought she was going to; but in her thoughts she remembered her simple request, Conrado's sarcastic comments, and even though she recognised she had been a little demanding, she could find no excuse for such excesses. She paced up and down, unable to keep still; she went into the sitting room, approached the half-open window, and saw her husband again, in the street waiting for the tram, with his back to the house, and the eternal, disgusting, crass hat on his head. Mariana felt possessed by hatred of that ridiculous article; she didn't understand how she'd been able to put up with it for so many years. And she thought back over those years, thought of her docile ways, her acquiescence to all her husband's wishes and whims, and asked herself if that might not actually be the cause of that morning's outburst. She called herself foolish, a pushover; if she'd been like so many others, Clara or Sophia, for instance, who treated their husbands as they should be treated, nothing remotely like this would have happened. One thought led to another, and she thought of going out. She got dressed, and went round to see Sophia, an old schoolfriend, just to get some fresh air, not to tell her anything.

Sophia was thirty, two years older than Mariana. She was tall, robust and very much her own mistress. She greeted her friend in her usual enthusiastic manner; and even though Mariana said nothing, she guessed she was nursing a considerable grievance. Goodbye to Mariana's intentions! Twenty minutes later, she was telling her all. Sophia laughed at her, shrugged her shoulders, and told her it wasn't her husband's fault.

'Oh of course, it's mine,' Mariana concurred.

'Don't be so silly, my girl! You've been too soft with him. But this time you must be strong; pay no attention; don't speak to him too soon; and if he wants to make it up, tell him to change his hat first.'

'Just think, such a trivial thing . . .'

'At bottom, he's quite right; just like a lot of other men. Look at that booby Beatriz; hasn't she just gone into the country, only because her husband took against an Englishman who used to go by their house in the afternoons, on horseback? Poor Englishman! Naturally, he didn't even notice she'd gone. We women can live quite well with our husbands, with mutual respect, nobody treading on anyone else's toes, with no fits of pique and no overbearing ways. Look – I live very happily with my Ricardo; we're in complete harmony. I never ask him anything but he does it straight away; even when he's not at all in the mood, all I have to do is frown, and he obeys in no time. He'd not be one to dig his heels in! What? Not likely! Where would that lead us! He'd change his hat whether he liked it or not.'

Mariana listened enviously to this delightful definition of conjugal bliss. Eve's rebellion was just putting the trumpet to her lips, ready for a fanfare; and being with her friend gave her an itch for independence and self-assertion. Just to round the situation off, Sophia was not only very much mistress of herself, but of others too; she had eyes for any Englishman, on horseback or on foot. She was virtuous, but a flirt; perhaps the word is a bit crude, and there's no time to find another, more polite one. She flirted with anyone, left, right and centre, out of a natural need, a habit from before she was married. It was the small change of love, which she distributed to all the poor people who knocked at her door – a penny to one, another to another; never a five-pound note, much less a share certificate. This same charitable feeling now led her to propose to her friend that they should go out, see the shops and have a good look at some other handsome, dignified hats. Mariana accepted; some devil was stoking up the fires of vengeance inside her. Moreover, her friend, like Bonaparte, had the gift of seduction, and gave her no time to reflect. Yes, she would go, she was tired of living like a captive. She had the right to some fun too, etc., etc.

While Sophia went to get dressed, Mariana stayed in the drawing room, restless and pleased with herself. She planned her whole week ahead, fixing the day and time for each thing, as if she was on an official trip. She got up, sat down, went to the window, waiting for her friend.

'Is Sophia dead, or what?' she said from time to time.

Once when she went to the window, she saw a young man pass by on horseback. He wasn't English, but she was reminded of that other woman, whose husband had taken her into the country because he was suspicious of an Englishman, and she began to feel hatred for the whole masculine race — except, perhaps, for young men on horseback. In all honesty, this one was too affected; he stuck his legs out in the stirrups, obviously vain about his boots, and stuck his hand in his belt as if in a fashion plate. Mariana did note those two defects, but she thought his hat made up for them; not that it was a top hat: it was flat, but it fitted in with his riding gear. It wasn't sitting on the head of a lawyer going gravely to his office, but on that of a man who was amusing himself or passing the time of day.

Sophia's heels came unhurriedly down the stairs. 'Ready!' she said a little later, as she came into the room. She was pretty, without a word of a lie. We already know she was tall. Her hat made her look more imperious; and a wicked black silk dress, moulding her breasts, made her look even more striking. Next to her, Mariana was somewhat in the shade. You had to look at her first to notice that she had very attractive features, a pair of very pretty eyes, and a great deal of natural elegance. The worst of it was that Sophia took over from the start; and if there was only a brief moment available, she took it all for herself. This comment would be incomplete, if I didn't add that Sophia was aware of her superiority, and for this very reason appreciated beauties of Mariana's type, less flamboyant and obvious. If this is a defect, it's not my duty to correct it.

'Where are we going?' asked Mariana.

'Don't be silly! For a trip into town . . . Now I remember, I'm going to have my photograph taken; then I'm going to the dentist. No; let's go to the dentist first. You don't have to go the dentist?'

'No.'

'Nor have your photograph taken?'

'I've got lots already. And what for? To give it to "him"?'

Sophia realised that her friend's resentment was still there, and on the way, was careful to spice things up a bit. She told her that, difficult though it might be, there was still time to break free. And she showed her the method for escaping tyranny. The best thing was not to do it all at once, but slowly, surely, so that he would only come to when she already had her foot on his neck: a few weeks' work, three or four, no more than that. Sophia herself was quite ready to help her. And she repeated that she mustn't be too soft, she was no one's slave, and so on. Mariana, in her heart, was intoning the Marseillaise of matrimony.

They reached the Rua do Ouvidor. It was a little after midday. There were lots of people, walking or standing, the usual hustle and bustle. Mariana felt a little dizzy, as she always did. Uniformity and placidity, the basis of her character and life, got the usual knocks from all this agitation. She could hardly find her way between the groups of people, even less did she know where to fix her gaze, such was the confusion of the crowds, the variety of the shops. She kept close to her friend, and without noticing that they had already passed the dentist's surgery, was anxious to get there. It would be a resting place; it was something better than this tumult.

'Oh, this street!' she was saying.

'Uh-huh?' Sophia replied, turning her head towards her and the eyes of a young man on the opposite pavement.

Sophia, a frequent traveller on these turbulent seas, made her way through the crowd, passing round people skilfully and calmly. She had an imposing figure; those who knew her were pleased to see her again; those who didn't, stopped or turned round to admire her panache. And the good lady, overflowing with charity, spread her eyes to right and left, causing no great scandal, for Mariana served to lend respectability to her movements. Her sentences were often curtailed; in fact, it seemed as if she hardly heard her friend's replies; but she talked about everything, about other people coming and going, about a shop, a hat . . . And in fact, there were lots of hats – ladies' and gentlemen's hats – as people gathered on the Rua do Ouvidor.

'Look at this one,' Sophia said to her.

And Mariana obediently looked at them, feminine or masculine, without knowing where to put herself, for these accursed hats milled around as if in a kaleidoscope. Where is the dentist? she asked her friend. Only when she asked her a second time did Sophia reply that they'd already passed the surgery; but now they were going on to the end of the street; they'd come back later. Finally, they did so.

'Oh!' Mariana let out a sigh of relief as they entered the corridor.

'Good heavens, what's this? Look at you! You'd think you'd just come in from the country.'

There were some customers already in the dentist's waiting room. Mariana saw not a single face she recognised, and so as not to be inspected by strangers, she went over to the window. From the window she could enjoy looking at the street, without being jostled. She leaned back; Sophia came over. Some male hats, standing in the street, began to look at them; others did the same as they passed by. Mariana was annoyed by their insistence; but when she saw that they were mostly looking at her friend, her boredom dissolved into a kind of envy. Sophia, meanwhile, was telling the stories attached to some of the hats – or their adventures, more accurately. One of them was seldom out of the thoughts of So-and-so, another was head over heels in love with Such-and-such, and she with him, so much so that they were always to be seen on the Rua do Ouvidor on Wednesdays and Saturdays between two and three in the afternoon. Mariana listened in amazement. It was a handsome hat, in fact, with a lovely tie, and had a look somewhere between elegance and roguishness, but . . .

'I can't swear, mind,' Sophia was saying, 'but that's what they say.'

Mariana stared thoughtfully at the hat under inspection. Now there were three more, as elegant and charming, and the four were probably talking about them, and flatteringly too. Mariana blushed to her roots, turned her head away, then back again, and finally left the window. As she did so, she saw two ladies who'd just arrived, and with them a young man who got up and greeted her very ceremoniously. It was her first suitor.

This first suitor would now be thirty-three. He'd been away, in the country, in Europe, and had lately had a spell as president of one of the southern provinces. He was of medium height, pale, with a thin, full beard, and wore very tight clothes. In his right hand he had a new top hat, black, grave, presidential, administrative, a hat suited to the person and his ambitions. Mariana, however, was almost blind to it. She was so confused, so disoriented by the presence of a man she'd known in somewhat exceptional circumstances, and hadn't seen since 1877, that she couldn't fix her eyes on anything. She held her fingers out; it seems she even murmured some kind of reply, and was just going back to the window, when her friend turned from the window towards her and came over.

Sophia also knew the new arrival. They exchanged some words. Mariana asked her in an impatient whisper if it wouldn't be better to put the teeth off for another day; but her friend said no; it was only a matter of half or three-quarters of an hour. Mariana felt oppressed: the presence of a man like this inhibited her, threw her into a state of conflict and confusion. It was all her husband's fault. If he hadn't been so stubborn, and made fun of her on top of that, nothing would have happened. As she thought this, Mariana swore she'd have her vengeance. In her memory she looked longingly at her house, so quiet, so pretty, where she might still have been, as usual, without the pushing and shoving in the street, without her dependence on her friend . . .

'Mariana,' said Sophia, 'Dr Viçoso insists he's quite thin. Don't you think he's put on weight since last year? . . . Don't you remember him last year?'

Dr Viçoso was the ex-suitor; he was chatting with her, frequently casting his gaze in Mariana's direction. She replied in the negative. He took advantage of this opportunity to pull her into the conversation, saying that, as a matter of fact, he

hadn't seen her for some years. And he underlined his words
with a certain sad, profound look. Then he opened up his box
of topics, and pulled out the opera. What did they think of the
company? In his opinion it was excellent, except for the
baritone; the baritone seemed to be suffering from fatigue.
Sophia protested at the baritone's fatigue, but he insisted,
adding that, in London, where he'd heard him for the first
time, he'd already struck him the same way. But the ladies
were a different matter; the soprano and the contralto were of
the first order. He talked about the operas, praised the
orchestra, especially in *Les Huguenots* . . .[4] He'd seen Mariana
on the last night, in the fourth or fifth box on the left, wasn't
that right?

'Yes, we were there,' she murmured, underlining the plural
pronoun.

'I haven't seen you at the Cassino though,'[5] he went on.

'She's turning into a recluse,' said Sophia, laughing.

Viçoso had enjoyed the last ball a great deal, and enum-
erated his reminiscences of it; Sophia did the same. The best
toilettes were described by both in some detail; then came the
people, their characters, with two or three malicious digs, so
anodyne, however, as not to harm anyone. Mariana listened
without interest; two or three times she even got up to go to
the window; but the hats were so many, and they looked at
her with such curiosity, that she went to sit down again. Just to
herself, she called her friend nasty names; I won't quote any of
them here – it's unnecessary, and moreover it would be in bad
taste to reveal what one young lady thought about another
during a few minutes' irritation.

'And the races at the Jockey Club?' asked the ex-president.

Mariana shook her head again. She hadn't gone to the races this year at all. Well, she'd missed a great deal; the meeting before last, in particular; it was very lively, and the horses were of the first order. The horses at Epsom, which he'd seen when he was in England, were no better than those at the meeting before last at the Prado Fluminense. Sophia was in total agreement, the meeting before last was a feather in the Jockey Club's cap. She confessed she'd enjoyed it a lot; it gave her quite a thrill. The conversation moved on to two concerts taking place that week; then it took the ferry, and went up the mountainside to Petrópolis, where two diplomats had put him up at their expense. When he mentioned a minister's wife, it occurred to Sophia to be agreeable to the ex-president, declaring that he must marry too, for he would soon be a member of the cabinet. Viçoso squirmed with pleasure, smiled, and protested; then, with his eyes on Mariana, said that probably he would never marry . . . Mariana blushed deeply and got up.

'You're in a hurry,' said Sophia. 'What time is it?' she went on, turning to Viçoso.

'Nearly three!' he exclaimed.

Time was getting on; he had to go to the Chamber of Deputies. He went over to speak to the two ladies whom he'd accompanied, cousins of his, and said goodbye to them; he was going to say goodbye to our friends as well, but Sophia said she too was leaving. She wasn't waiting any longer. The truth is that the idea of going to the Chamber of Deputies had begun to set off sparks in her mind.

'Shall we go to the Chamber?' she proposed to her friend.

'No, no,' said Mariana; 'I can't, I'm very tired.'

'Come on, just for a short while; I'm very tired too . . .'

Mariana resisted for a little; but resisting Sophia – a dove arguing with a hawk – was a pointless occupation. There was no choice, and she went. The street was busier now; people were coming and going along both pavements, and getting in each others' way at the street corners. What was more, the obliging ex-president walked between the two ladies, having offered to find them a seat to watch the proceedings.

Mariana felt her soul increasingly torn apart by all this confusion. She had lost her original interest; and her vexation, which had provided the strength for her audacious, ephemeral flight, felt its wings weakening – or rather, she felt they had lost all their strength. And again she thought back to her house, so tranquil, with all her things each in their place, methodical, respectful of one another, everything happening unhurriedly, and, above all, with no unforeseen changes. And her soul began to tap its foot, angrily . . . She wasn't listening to anything Viçoso was saying, even though he was talking in a loud voice, and many of his statements were addressed to her. She heard nothing, didn't want to hear anything. She merely asked God to make the time go quickly. They got to the Chamber and went to a seat. The rustle of skirts drew the attention of some twenty deputies, who were still there, listening to a speech on the budget. As soon as Viçoso begged leave and left, Mariana quickly asked her friend not to play another one on her.

'What other?' Sophia asked.

'Don't play another trick on me, having me rushing round from one place to another like a madwoman. What's the Chamber got to do with me? Why should I listen to speeches I don't understand?'

Sophia smiled, fanned herself, and got an outright stare from one of the secretaries. There were many eyes fixed on her when she went into the Chamber, but this secretary's had a special, warm, pleading expression. We can understand, then, that she didn't acknowledge the stare straight away; we can even understand that she sought it out with some curiosity. As she was taking in this legislative gaze, she went on mildly answering her friend, telling her that it was her own fault, and that she, Sophia, had set out with the best of intentions, to restore her to herself.

'But if I'm getting on your nerves you needn't come with me again,' Sophia concluded.

Then, leaning over a little: 'Look at the justice minister.'

Mariana had no alternative but to look at the justice minister. He was putting up as well as he could with a speech by a government supporter, who was proving the importance of the minor criminal courts, and, on the way, providing a summary of the colonial legislation on the matter. No interruptions: a resigned, polite, discreet and cautious silence. Mariana's eyes wandered from one side to another, without interest; Sophia was talking a lot, so as to give occasion for various elegant gestures. After fifteen minutes the Chamber livened up, thanks to one of the orator's expressions and a challenge from the opposition. There was some heckling, which became more and more heated, and then there was an uproar, which lasted nearly a quarter of an hour.

This diversion provided no amusement to Mariana, whose placid, unvarying spirit was bewildered at so much unexpected agitation. She even got up to go, but sat down again. Now she made up her mind to go on to the end, repentant and resolved to weep over her conjugal sorrows on her own. Doubt was beginning to enter, even. She was right to ask her husband what she did; but should she have been so upset? Was it reasonable to make so much fuss? Certainly, his ironies were cruel; but, after all, it was the first time she'd stamped her foot, and naturally, the novelty had irritated him. Whichever way you looked at it, it had been a mistake to reveal everything to her friend. Sophia might well tell others . . . This notion made Mariana go cold; her friend was sure to be indiscreet; she'd heard a lot of stories from her about male and female hats, things rather more serious than just a marital tiff. Mariana felt the need to flatter her, and covered up her impatience and anger with a mask of hypocritical docility. She began to smile too, to make some observations about this or that deputy, and so they reached the end of the speech and the session.

The clocks had already struck four. 'Time to be off,' said Sophia; and Mariana agreed, but without impatience, and both of them went back up the Rua do Ouvidor. Walking along the street and getting into the tram put the finishing touches to the exhaustion of Mariana's spirit; she gave a sigh of relief when she saw she was finally on her way home. A little before her friend got off, she asked her to keep what had happened to herself; Sophia promised she would.

Mariana breathed easily. The dove was free of the hawk. Her soul was bruised from pushing and shoving, dizzy from the variety of things and people. She needed harmony and well-being. The house was nearby; as she saw the other houses with their gardens, Mariana felt restored to her former self. Finally, she got home; she went into the garden, and breathed deeply. That was her world; apart from a flowerpot, which the gardener had moved.

'João, put that pot back where it was,' she said.

Everything else was in order, the hall, the drawing room, the dining room, the bedrooms, everything. Mariana sat down first, in a few different places, looking at all the objects, so still and ordered. After a whole day of variety and disturbance, monotony did her a great deal of good, and had never seemed so delicious to her. It was true, she'd made a mistake . . . She tried to go back over events and couldn't; her soul was stretching its arms and yawning in this homely uniformity. If anything, she thought about the figure of Viçoso, whom she now thought ridiculous, which was unjust. She slowly undressed, lovingly, picking every object up with precision. Once this was done, she thought again about the quarrel with her husband. She thought, when all was said and done, that she was mainly to blame. Why on earth make such a fuss about a hat that her husband had worn for so many years? And her father was too demanding . . .

'I'll wait and see his face when he comes back,' she thought.

It was half past five; he'd not be long. Mariana went to the front room, looked through the glass, listened for the tram – nothing. She sat down right there with *Ivanhoe* in her hands, trying to read, and reading nothing. Her eyes went to the bottom of the page, and back to the top, in the first place because she couldn't grasp the meaning, and in the second place because they kept being diverted, to savour the correct drop of the curtains, or some other feature in the room. Holy Monotony, you cradled her in your eternal bosom.

Finally, a tram stopped; her husband got off; the garden's metal gate creaked. Mariana went to the window and peeped out. Conrado was coming slowly in, looking to right and left, with the hat on his head – not the famous hat he'd been used to wearing, but another, the one his wife had asked him to wear that morning. Mariana's spirit received a violent shock, similar to the one she'd got from the changed flowerpot – or would have got from a sheet of Voltaire encountered among the pages of *Moreninha* or *Ivanhoe* . . . It was a discordant note in the middle of the harmonious sonata of life. No, that hat was impossible. Really, what kind of lunacy was this, demanding he stop wearing the other, which fitted him so well? And even if it wasn't the most appropriate, he'd worn it for many years; it went with her husband's face . . . Conrado came in by a side door. Mariana received him in her arms.

'Well, is it over?' he asked, finally, holding her by the waist.

'Listen,' she said with a divine caress, 'chuck that one out; I'd rather have the other.'

Those Cousins from Sapucaia!

SOMETIMES A HAPPY OPPORTUNITY comes our way, but mischance then lands two or three cousins from Sapucaia on us; at other times, however, these same cousins are more of a blessing than a misfortune.

It happened at a church doorway. I was waiting for my cousins Claudina and Rosa to take holy water, so I could conduct them to our house, where they were staying. They had come from Sapucaia at around carnival time, and had stayed on in Rio for two months. It was I who accompanied them everywhere, to Mass, the theatres, the Rua do Ouvidor, because my mother, with her rheumatism, could hardly move around the house, and they weren't used to going out alone. Sapucaia was where our family came from. Though our relatives were scattered about all over the place, that was where the family tree had first taken root. My uncle, José Ribeiro, father to these cousins, was the only one of five brothers who stayed there farming the land and playing his part in local politics. I came to Rio early on, and went on from there to study and graduate in São Paulo. I only went back to Sapucaia once, to fight an election, and lost.

Strictly speaking, all this information is unnecessary to the understanding of my adventure; but it's a way of saying something before I get to the real story, since I can't find an entrance for it, large or small; the best solution is to loosen the reins on my pen, and let it wander on till it finds a way in. There must be one; everything depends on circumstances – a rule as valid for one's style as it is for life; one word leads to another, and that's the way books, governments and revolutions happen; some even say that's the way nature put the species together.

So then, where were we? – the holy water and the church doorway. It was the church of São José. Mass was over; Claudina and Rosa made the sign of the cross on their foreheads with their thumbs, dipping them in the water, the glove removed expressly for that purpose. Then they adjusted their capes, while, in the doorway, I stood looking at the ladies as they came out. Suddenly, I shuddered, leaned out, and even took a couple of steps towards the street.

'What was that, cousin?'

'Nothing, nothing.'

It was a lady, who'd passed by right next to the church, slowly, her head bowed, leaning on her parasol; she was going up the Rua da Misericórdia. To explain my agitation, it has to be said that this was the second time I'd seen her. The first was at the races, two months before, with a man who, to all appearances, was her husband, but could just as easily have been her father. She was a bit of a spectacle, dressed in scarlet, with big showy trimmings, and a pair of earrings that were too large; but her eyes and mouth made up for the rest. We flirted outrageously. If I say I left there head over heels in love, I'll not put my soul in hell – it's the simple truth. I was giddy, but frustrated too, for I lost sight of her in the crowd. I never managed to see her again, nor could anyone tell me who she was.

Imagine my vexation when chance brought her my way again and these accidental cousins didn't let me get my hands on her. It'll not be hard to imagine, because these cousins from Sapucaia take all kinds of different guises, and in one shape or another my reader must have come across them. Sometimes they take the form of the gentleman who knows everything about the latest ministerial crisis, and who in the greatest confidence expatiates on all the overt and secret elements in play, conflicts new or old, the interests at stake, conspiracies, crises, etc. At others, they're dressed like that immortal citizen who states in a ponderous, buttoned-up tone that laws depend on customs, *nisi lege sine moribus*. Others slip on the mask of the bore at the tram stop, who recounts every detail of the ribbons and lace worn by some lady or other to a ball or the theatre. Meanwhile, Opportunity passes by, slowly, head bowed, leaning on her parasol; she passes, turns the corner, and goodbye . . . The ministry's on the point of collapse; real Belgian lace, mind you; *nisi lege sine moribus* . . .

It was on the tip of my tongue to tell my cousins to take their own way home; we lived not far off, in the Rua do Carmo – but I gave up on the idea. Once we were in the street, I thought of leaving them to wait for me at the church and going to see if I could catch Opportunity by the coat-tails. I think I even stopped for a moment, but I rejected that option too and went on my way.

I went on my way with them, going in the opposite direction from my mystery lady. I looked back over and over again, until round a curve in the street I lost sight of her, with her eyes on the ground, as if she was reflecting, daydreaming or on her way to a rendezvous. I'd be lying if I didn't say that this last idea gave me a twinge of jealousy. I'm possessive and take things personally; I'd be useless as a lover for a married woman. No matter that all there was between me and the lady was a fleeting dalliance lasting a few hours; since I was so bound up with her, sharing her became unbearable. I'm imaginative too; I soon dreamed up an adventure, with an adventurer to go with it, and gave myself over to the morbid pleasure of tormenting myself for no good reason at all. My cousins walked ahead, and spoke to me from time to time; I gave brief answers, if I answered at all. In my heart, I detested them.

When I got home, I looked at my watch, as if I had something to do; then I told my cousins to go in and start lunch. I ran to the Rua da Misericórdia. First I went to the School of Medicine; then I turned and came back as far as the Chamber of Deputies, then walked slower, hoping to see her at every turn in the street; not a sign. Stupid, wasn't it? Still, I went up the street once more, for I realised that, on foot and walking slowly, she'd hardly have had time to get halfway along Santa Luzia beach – that is, if she'd not stopped before; and on I went, up the street and along the beach, as far as the Ajuda convent. I found nothing, nothing at all. Even so I didn't lose hope; I turned back on myself and walked, slowly or quickly, depending on whether I might catch up with her in front of me or give her time to emerge from somewhere. As I pictured the lady in my imagination, I felt in a state of shock, as if I might see her any minute. I understood what it must feel like to be mad.

However, there was nothing to be seen. I went down the street, but found not the least vestige of my mystery lady. Dogs are lucky; they find their friends by their sense of smell! Who knows if she wasn't there, close by, inside some house, maybe even her own? I thought of enquiring; but who, and how? A baker, leaning in a doorway, was watching me; some women were peeping through the shutters, doing the same thing. Naturally, they were suspicious of this passer-by, his step slow or hurried by turns, his inquisitive look, his restless manner. I went as far as the Chamber of Deputies and stopped for about five minutes, unsure what to do. It was nearly midday. I waited another ten minutes, then five more, standing there in the hope of seeing her; finally I gave up and went to have lunch.

I didn't lunch at home. I didn't want to see those damned cousins, who'd stopped me following the unknown lady. I went to a hotel. I chose a table at the back of the room, and sat with my back turned; I didn't want to be seen or spoken to. I began to eat what they brought me. I asked for some papers, but I confess I read nothing through, and scarcely understood three-quarters of what I did. In the middle of a news item or an article, my mind slipped and fell into the Rua da Misericórdia, at the church door, watching the mystery lady pass by, slowly, her head bowed, and leaning on her parasol.

The final time this separation of mind and the lower instincts happened, I was already at the coffee stage, and had a parliamentary speech in front of me. I found myself once more at the church door; I imagined my cousins weren't there, and that I was walking behind the lovely lady. That's how those who lose in the lottery console themselves; that's how thwarted ambitions are satisfied.

Don't ask for the details or the preliminaries of this encounter. Dreams scorn the delicate lines and the finish of a landscape; they're happy with four or five rough but representative strokes. My imagination leaped over the difficulties of the opening words, and went straight to the Rua do Lavradio, or Inválidos, to Adriana's own house. Her name is Adriana. She hadn't come to the Rua da Misericórdia for an amorous encounter, but to see someone, a relative or a close friend, or a seamstress. She saw me, and felt the same agitation. I wrote to her; she wrote back. We were everything to each other, far above all the decrees of morality and the dangers threatening us. Adriana's married; her husband is fifty-two; she's not yet thirty. She's never been in love, not even with her husband, whom she married to obey her family. I taught her love and betrayal at the same time; that's what she's telling me in this little house I've rented outside the city, just for us.

Intoxicated, I listen to her. I wasn't mistaken; she's the ardent, loving woman her eyes already told me of, the eyes of a bull, like those of Juno, large and round. She lives through me and for me. We write to each other every day; and in spite of that, when we meet in the little house, it's as if a century had gone by. I think her heart has taught me something, though she is so innocent – or maybe for that very reason. In matters like these custom stales, and ignorance is the best teacher. Adriana doesn't disguise her happiness or her tears: she writes as she thinks, and says what she feels; she shows me that we are not two people, but one, simply one universal being, for whom God created the sun and the flowers, paper and ink, the mail system and carriages with their curtains down.

While I was sketching this picture, I believe I finished drinking my coffee; I remember a waiter came to the table and removed the cup and the sugar bowl. I don't know if I asked him for a light – probably he saw me cigar in hand and brought me matches.

I can't swear it, but I think I lit the cigar, because an instant later, through a veil of smoke, I saw the sweet, vibrant face of my lovely Adriana, stretched out on a sofa. I'm on my knees, listening to her recounting her latest tiff with her husband. For he's already suspicious; she goes out a lot, she's distraite, absorbed in her thoughts, seems sad or happy for no reason, and her husband is beginning to threaten her. What with? I tell her that, before anything serious happens, it would be better to leave him, and come to live with me, publicly, only for each other. Adriana listens to me, pensive, looking just like Eve, listening to the devil's words as he whispers in her ear what her heart is already telling her. Her fingers are stroking my hair.

'Yes, yes!'

She came the next day, all alone, no husband, no social ties, no scruples, just herself, and from that moment on we lived together. We did it without ostentation, but without secrecy. We thought of ourselves as foreigners, and in truth that was what we were; we spoke a language no one had ever heard or spoken before. Other love affairs, for centuries, had been counterfeits; ours was the only authentic edition. For the first time, the divine manuscript was printed, a large volume we divided into as many chapters and paragraphs as there were hours in the day or days in the week. The style was a weave of sunshine and music; the language was made up of the choicest parts of other languages. Everything sweet or vibrant that was to be found in them was distilled by the author to make this unique book, which lacked an index, for it was infinite; it had no margins, so that boredom couldn't scribble in them; and it lacked a bookmark, for we no longer needed to interrupt our reading.

A voice called me back to reality. It was a friend who had got up late, and come for his lunch. I couldn't even dream without this cousin from Sapucaia appearing! Five minutes later I said goodbye and left; it was after two.

I'm ashamed to say that I went back to the Rua da Misericórdia, but I must tell all: I went, and found nothing. I went again during the next few days and got nothing further out of it but the time I wasted. I resigned myself to giving up on the adventure, or waiting for chance to bring a solution. My cousins thought I was irritated or ill; I didn't deny it. A week later, they left, and I didn't miss them for a moment; I said farewell to them as one might to a bout of malignant fever.

The image of my mystery lady didn't leave me for many weeks. Several times in the street, I made mistakes. I discerned a figure far off, just like her; I took to my heels till I caught up with her, and was disappointed. I began to think myself ridiculous; but then came another hour or a minute, a shadow in the distance, and the obsession revived. Finally, other concerns took over, and I thought no more about it.

At the beginning of the following year, I went to Petrópolis; I made the journey with an old friend from student days,

Oliveira, who had been a barrister in Minas Gerais but had lately inherited some money and given up the career. He was cheery, as he had been when we were younger; but from time to time he went quiet, looking out from the boat or the carriage with an empty stare, as if his soul was preoccupied with some memory, hope or desire. When we reached the top of the climb I asked him which hotel he was going to; he answered that he was going to a private house, but didn't tell me where; he even changed the subject. I thought he might visit me the next day, but he didn't, nor did I see him anywhere. Another acquaintance of ours had heard tell he had a house over in the Renânia neighbourhood somewhere.

None of these incidentals would have come to my mind if it weren't for the information I was given days later. Oliveira had taken a woman from her husband, and taken refuge in Petró-polis. They gave me the husband's name and hers. Hers was Adriana. I confess that, though the other woman's name was purely an invention of mine, I shivered as I heard it; mightn't it be the same woman? Straight away, I realised that this was asking a great deal of Chance. This poor disposer of human affairs already does enough, pulling one or two loose threads together; to demand that he tie them all up and give them the same titles is to move from reality to the novel. Thus spoke my good sense, and it never said anything so solemnly foolish, for the two women were the very same, no more, no less.

I saw her three weeks later, when I went to visit Oliveira, who'd left Rio unwell. We'd come up together the previous day; halfway up the mountain he began to feel discomfort; by the time we got to the top he was feverish. I accompanied him in the carriage as far as his house, and didn't go in, because he

didn't want to put me to any more trouble. But the next day I
went to see him, partly out of friendship, and partly too
because I was eager to meet the mystery woman. I saw her; it
was her, the one and only, my own Adriana.

Oliveira soon recovered, and in spite of my regular visits he
didn't offer me his hospitality; he limited himself to coming to
see me in my hotel. I respected his motives; but that was just
what brought back my old obsession. I thought that, apart
from reasons of decorum, there was jealousy on his part, itself
the product of love, and that both might prove the existence
of fine, noble qualities in the woman. This was enough to
unsettle me; but the idea that her passion was no less intense
than his, the picture of this couple who were one single soul,
one single person, excited every envious nerve in my body. I
spared no effort to get my foot inside the house; I even told
him of the rumour that was going the rounds; he smiled and
talked about something else.

The Petrópolis season ended, and he stayed on. I believe he
came down to Rio in July or August. At the end of the year
we met by chance; I found him somewhat taciturn and
preoccupied. I saw him a few times more, and he seemed
no different, unless, to go with the taciturnity, he had a long
furrow of unhappiness in his features. I imagined it was the
consequence of the adventure, and, since I'm not here to pull
the wool over anyone's eyes, I can add that I felt a sensation of
pleasure. It didn't last long; it was the devil I have inside me,
who has a habit of making rude gestures. But I soon chastised
him, and replaced him with an angel I also have at my
command for such moments, and who took pity on the poor
lad, whatever the cause of his sadness.

A neighbour of Oliveira, a friend of ours, told me something which confirmed my suspicion of domestic troubles; but
it was he himself who told me everything, one day when I
asked him, rashly, what was the matter with him; why had he
changed so much?

'What do you think's the matter? Imagine I bought a
lottery ticket, and I didn't even have the pleasure of getting
no prize at all; what I got was a scorpion.'

Then, as I raised my eyebrows interrogatively:

'Ah! If you knew half the things that have happened to me!
Have you got time? Let's go over here to the promenade.'

We went into the gardens, and along one of the avenues.
He told me everything. He spent two hours telling the beads
of an infinite rosary of misery. As he talked, I discerned two
incompatible natures, united by love or by sin, sated with each
other, but condemned to live together in hatred. He couldn't
leave her; but neither could he bear her. There was no esteem,
no respect, happiness was rare and tarnished; a life ruined.

'Ruined,' he repeated, vigorously nodding his head.
'There's nothing to be done; my life's ruined. You remember
the plans we made at college, when we decided that you
would be Interior Minister, I Minister of Justice. You can
have both portfolios; I'll never be anything, anything at all.
The egg, which should have produced an eagle, hasn't even
brought forth a chicken. It's completely addled. For a year and
a half now I've been like this, and I can find no way out; I've
lost my energy . . .'

Six months later, I came across him in a worried, frantic
state. Adriana had left him to go and study geometry with a
student from the old Central Engineering School. 'So much

the better,' I said to him. Oliveira looked at the ground in shame; he excused himself, and ran off in search of her. He found her some weeks later; they said unforgivable things to each other, and then at the end were reconciled. I began to visit them, with the idea of separating them from each other. She was still pretty and fascinating; she had delicate, soft manners, but they were obviously put on, accompanied by attitudes and gestures whose latent intent was to attract me and drag me in.

I took fright and drew back. She wasn't bothered; she threw her lace cape aside, and returned to her real self. Then I saw that she was iron-willed, cunning, spiteful and often vulgar; in some situations I noticed a streak of perversity. At first, Oliveira put up with everything, laughing, to make me believe he'd lied or exaggerated; it was shame at his own weakness. But he couldn't keep the mask on; one day she ripped it off him, pitilessly revealing the humiliation he put up with when I wasn't there. I felt disgust at her, and pity for the poor fellow. I openly encouraged him to leave her; he hesitated, but promised he would.

'It's true, I can't take it any longer . . .'

We planned everything; but at the moment of separation, he couldn't do it. She enveloped him once more in her big eyes, like those of a bull or a basilisk, and this time – oh my beloved cousins from Sapucaia! – this time only to leave him exhausted and dead.

Admiral's Night

DEOLINDO NOSTRILS (a shipboard nickname of his) left the
Navy Arsenal and set off up the Rua de Bragança. The
clock was striking three. He was the *crème de la crème* of sailors
and, what's more, his eyes were brimming with happiness. His
corvette had just come back from a long training cruise, and
Deolindo came on land as soon as he got leave. His mates had
said to him, laughing:

'Hey, Nostrils! What an admiral's night you're going to
have! Dinner, music and Genoveva's arms. A little cuddle
from Genoveva . . .'

Deolindo smiled. That hit the nail on the head; an admiral's
night, as the saying goes, a wonderful admiral's night lay in wait
for him on land. The passion had begun three months before
the corvette left. The name of the girl was Genoveva, and she
was from up-country, twenty years old, clever, with mischievous black eyes. They'd met at a friend's house and fallen head
over heels for one another, so much so that they almost decided
to do something silly – he'd abscond from the Navy and she'd
go with him to some town hidden away in the backlands.

Old Ignacia, who lived with her, dissuaded them; Deolindo
had no option but to go on the training cruise. He'd be eight

or ten months away. To commit themselves, they thought
they should swear an oath of fidelity.

'I swear by God in heaven. And you?'

'Me too.'

'Say it out loud then.'

'I swear by God in heaven; may the light fail me at the hour
of death.'

They had made their contract. You had to believe in their
sincerity; she was weeping uncontrollably, he was biting his
lip to disguise his feelings. Finally they parted. Genoveva went
to see the corvette leave, with her chest so tight she thought
she was 'going to have a turn'. Nothing happened, luckily;
days, weeks, months went by, ten months in all. Finally the
corvette came back, and Deolindo with it.

Here he goes then, up the Rua de Bragança, through
Prainha and Saúde, as far as Gamboa, where Genoveva lives.
The house is a wooden shack, its door cracked by the sun, just
beyond the Cemetery of the English; Genoveva's bound to be
there, leaning out of the window, waiting for him. Deolindo's
prepared something to say to her. Here's what he's composed:
'I swore an oath and I kept it,' but he's trying to find
something better. At the same time he remembers the women
he's seen in God's wide world, Italians, Marseillaises and
Turks, lots of them pretty, or he thought they were anyway.
All right, not all of them might be his type; some were,
though, but that didn't mean he paid any attention. He
thought only of Genoveva. Even her house, so tiny, with
its rickety furniture, all old and not much of it either – he
remembered it when he saw palaces in faraway lands. It was
only by saving every penny that he'd bought a pair of earrings

in Trieste, which he was carrying in his pocket with some other trinkets. And what would she have ready for him? Maybe a neckerchief with his name and an anchor in the corner, for she was very good at embroidery. At this point he reached Gamboa, went past the cemetery and found the house with the door shut. He knocked, and a familiar voice answered, old Ignacia, who came to open the door with loud exclamations of delight. Deolindo impatiently asked about Genoveva.

'Don't talk to me about that flibbertigibbet,' the old woman burst out. 'I'm really glad I gave you that piece of advice. Just think, if you'd run away. You'd be in a fine pickle.'

'But what happened? What happened?'

The old woman told him to calm down, it was nothing, one of those things that happen in life; there was no point in getting worked up. Genoveva's head had been turned . . .

'Turned, how?'

'She's taken up with a peddler, José Diogo. Did you ever meet José Diogo, the one that sells cuts of cloth? She's with him. You can't imagine how much in love they are. She's mad about him. That was why we had a fight. José Diogo wouldn't keep away from my door; they were forever whispering to each other, till one day I said I didn't want my house to get a bad name. Oh, God in heaven! It was like the day of judgement. Genoveva took off at me, her eyes bursting out of her head, saying she'd never cast aspersions on anyone and she didn't need my charity. What d'you mean, charity, Genoveva? All I'm saying is I don't want this whispering at my door, from noon till night . . .

Two days later she'd moved and we were no longer speaking.'

'Where does she live?'

'On Formosa beach, before you get to the quarry, in a house with the door freshly painted.'

Deolindo wouldn't listen to any more. Old Ignacia, a bit sorry she'd spoken, gave him some prudent bits of advice, but he wouldn't listen and went on his way. I'll not say what his thoughts were on the way; he had none. Ideas were clambering about in his head, as if in a storm at sea, amid a confusion of howling winds and ships' whistles. His sailor's knife flashed out in the chaos, bloody and vengeful. He'd passed Gamboa and the Alferes inlet, and got to Formosa beach. He didn't know the house number, but it was near the quarry, freshly painted, and with help from the people in the neighbourhood he'd find it. He couldn't have foreseen that, as chance would have it, Genoveva was sitting at her window sewing at the moment Deolindo was going by. He recognised her and stopped; she, seeing the figure of a man, lifted her eyes and recognised the sailor.

'What's this?' she exclaimed in astonishment. 'When did you get in? Come in, Deolindo.'

She got up, opened the door and brought him in. Another man would have been buoyed up with hope, so open was the girl's manner. Maybe the old woman had been wrong or lied; maybe the peddler's serenade had reached its final refrain. All this passed through his head, though not in a reasoned or reflective form, but in a flash, and in a jumble. Genoveva left the door open; she had him sit down, asked about his voyage and said she thought he'd put on weight; no emotion or intimacy. Deolindo lost his last hope. Without his knife, he still had hands to strangle Genoveva, who was a slip of a thing, and for the first few minutes he thought of nothing else.

'I know everything,' he said.

'Who told you?'

Deolindo shrugged his shoulders.

'Whoever it was,' she replied, 'did they say I was in love with someone?'

'Yes.'

'What they said was true.'

Deolindo started forward; she made him stop just with her eyes. Then she said that, if she'd opened the door to him, it was because she thought he was a sensible man. Then she told him everything, how much she'd missed him, the peddler's courting, her refusals, until one day, without knowing why, she'd got up one morning in love with him.

'You can believe I thought about you an awful lot. Sinhá Ignacia'll tell you how much I cried . . . But my heart's changed . . . It's changed . . . I'm telling you all this like I would to a priest,' she ended with a smile.

It wasn't a mocking smile. The tone behind her words was a real mixture of candour and cynicism, simplicity and insolence, and I give up on defining it any better. In fact, I think cynicism and insolence are the wrong words. Genoveva wasn't defending herself for some mistake, or for breaking an oath; she had no moral measure for her actions. What she was saying, summing it up, was that it would have been better not to have changed, she had been quite happy with Deolindo's affection, and the proof of that is that she would have run away with him. But now that the peddler had won out over the sailor, the peddler was in the right, and it might as well be admitted. What do you think? The poor sailor cited the oath they'd sworn when they parted, as an eternal obligation, which had made him agree to not running away, and sent him back to his ship: 'I swear by God in heaven; may the light fail me at the hour of death.' If he'd gone on board, it was because she'd sworn that. With these words he'd departed, travelled, hoped and returned; they had given him the strength to go on living. I swear by God in heaven; may the light fail me at the hour of death . . .

'Yes, Deolindo, it was true. When I swore it, it was true. It was so true, I wanted to run away with you into the back-lands. God alone knows it was the truth! But other things came along . . . This lad appeared, and I began to fall for him . . .'

'But that's just why people swear; so they don't fall for anyone else . . .'

'Give over, Deolindo. Did you never think of anyone else? Don't be silly . . .'

'What time does José Diogo get back?'

'He's not coming back today.'

'Isn't he?'

'No; he's over around Guaratiba with his wares; he should be back on Friday or Saturday . . . And why do you want to know? What harm's he done you?'

Other women might have spoken those words; not many would have expressed it so openly, and not out of guile, but quite unintentionally. Note that we're very close to nature in this case. What harm had he done him? What harm's that stone done, the one that's just fallen on your head? Any physicist could explain the falling stone. Deolindo declared, with a gesture, that he wanted to kill him. Genoveva looked at him with contempt, gave a little smile, tossed her head and tutted; when he started talking about ingratitude and broken vows, she couldn't disguise her amazement. What broken vows? What ingratitude? She'd already said over and over that when she swore it, it was true. Our Lady, there on the dresser, she knew if it was true or not. Was this a way to pay her for what she'd been through? And as for him, so full of talk about being faithful, had he remembered her where he'd been?

His reply was to put his hand in his pocket and pull out the packet he'd brought for her. She opened it, looked at the trinkets one by one, and finally came across the earrings. They weren't expensive, there was no chance of that; they were in bad taste, even, but they twinkled like nothing on earth. Genoveva picked them up, happy, dazzled, looked at them from both sides, close up and far off, and finally put them in her ears; then she went to the cheap mirror hanging on the wall between the door and the window, to see how they looked on her. She stood back, went closer, turned her head from left to right, and from right to left.

'Yes, sir, very pretty,' she said, curtseying to thank him. Where had he bought them?

He said nothing in reply, I think – there was no time, because she fired two or three more questions, one after the other, so confused was she at receiving a gift in exchange for ditching someone. There was confusion for four or five minutes – two, maybe. She soon took the earrings off, looked at them again and put them in the little box on the round table in the middle of the room. He, for his part, began to think

that, just as he'd lost her when he was away, now that his rival
was away, maybe he too might lose her; probably, too, she'd
sworn him nothing.

'Here we are chatting, and it'll soon be night,' said Genoveva.

It was true, night was falling fast. They could no longer see
the Lepers' Hospital and you could hardly make out Melon
Island; the boats and canoes pulled out of the water opposite
the house blended into the earth and mud of the beach.
Genoveva lit a candle. Then she went to sit on the threshold
and asked him to tell her something about the countries he'd
seen. Deolindo refused at first; he said he was going, got up
and took a few steps. But hope kept gnawing at him and
flattering the poor devil's heart, and he sat down to tell two or
three stories about the voyage. Genoveva listened attentively.
Interrupted by a woman from the neighbourhood who came
round, Genoveva made her sit down to listen to 'the lovely
stories Senhor Deolindo's telling'. That was all she said by way
of introduction. The great lady who stays awake to finish her
reading of a book or a chapter feels no closer to its characters
than the sailor's ex-lover who lived through the scenes he
recounted, so freely interested she was, captivated as if there
were nothing more between them than this narration of a few
episodes from the past. What does the great lady care about
the book's author? What did the girl care about the person
relating the events?

Hope, meanwhile, was beginning to forsake him, and he
got up finally to leave. Genoveva didn't want him to go
before her friend had seen the earrings, and showed them to
her with much acclaim. The neighbour was enchanted,

praised them to the skies, asked if he'd bought them in France and asked Genoveva to put them on.

'They're really lovely.'

I'd like to think the sailor himself agreed with this opinion. He liked to look at them, thought they were made for her, and for a brief moment tasted the exclusive, delicious sensation of having given a welcome present; but it was just a few seconds.

As he was going, Genoveva went to the door with him to thank him again for his gift, and probably to say a few sweet, useless words to him. Her friend, whom she'd left in the room, only heard these words: 'Don't be silly, Deolindo,' and this from the sailor, 'You'll see.' She couldn't hear the rest, which was no more than a whisper.

Deolindo went slowly along the beach, downcast, no longer the impetuous fellow he was that afternoon, but with a look that was aged, sad or, to use another nautical metaphor, of a man 'who's halfway back to land'. Genoveva soon went in, happy and boisterous. She told her friend the story of her maritime loves, praised Deolindo's character and his agreeable manners; her friend said she thought he was very charming.

'A really nice lad,' Genoveva agreed. 'D'you know what he said to me just now?'

'What?'

'That he's going to kill himself.'

'Good Jesus!'

'Forget it! He'll not kill himself. That's Deolindo; he says things, but he doesn't do them. You'll see, he'll not kill himself. It's jealousy, poor lad. But the earrings are really gorgeous.'

'I've never seen any like them here.'

'Nor me,' Genoveva agreed, looking at them in the light. Then she put them away and invited her friend to come in and sew. 'Let's sew for a little while, I want to finish my blue top . . .'

The truth is that the seaman didn't kill himself. The next day, some of his mates clapped him on the shoulder, congratulating him on his admiral's night, and asked for news of Genoveva, if she was even prettier, if she'd cried a lot while he was away, etc. He answered everything with a discreet, satisfied smile, the smile of a person who's had a great night. It seems he was ashamed of the truth, and preferred to lie.

Evolution

MY NAME'S IGNACIO; his is Benedito. I'll not give the rest of our names, out of a sense of propriety, something every person of discretion will appreciate. Just Ignacio. Make do with Benedito. It's not much, but it's something, and it goes with Juliet's philosophy: 'What's in a name?' she asked her lover. 'A rose, by any other name, would smell as sweet.' Let's see what kind of a scent Benedito had.

First of all, let's agree that he could hardly be less like Romeo. He was forty-five, when I first met him; I'll not say when, because everything in this story will be mysterious and elliptical. Forty-five, then, and with a lot of black hair; for the ones that weren't that colour, he used a chemical process so effective you couldn't tell which were black and which weren't — except when he got out of bed; but when he got out of bed there was no one to see him. Everything else was natural: legs, arms, head, eyes, clothes, shoes, watch chain and walking stick. Even the diamond pin he wore in his tie, one of the loveliest I've ever seen, was natural and genuine; it cost him a fair sum; I myself saw him buy it at . . . the jeweller's name was on the tip of my tongue; let's just say it was on the Rua do Ouvidor.

Morally, he was what he was. No one can change their character, and Benedito's was good – or, to put it another way, easy-going. Intellectually, however, he was less original. We might compare him to an inn with plenty of guests, where ideas of all kinds from all over the place resorted; they sat down at table with the innkeeper's family. Sometimes two enemies, or just people who didn't much like one another, met up; no one quarrelled, and mine host imposed a mutual forbearance. This was how he managed to combine a kind of vague atheism with two religious brotherhoods he founded, in Gávea, Tijuca or Engenho Velho, I can't recall which. That's how he managed to sport a mixture of devotion, irreligion and silk stockings. I never saw his stockings, be it said; but he had no secrets from his friends.

We met on a journey to Vassouras. We'd got out of the train and into the coach taking us from the station to the town. We exchanged a few words, and in no time we were having a frank and free conversation, in tune with the circumstances that had brought us together, even before either of us knew who the other was.

Naturally, our first topic was the progress brought by the railways. Benedito could still remember the time when the whole journey was made on mule-back. We recounted a few anecdotes, mentioned a few names, and agreed that railways were a condition of progress for the country. Those who don't travel have no idea how useful one of these solid, serious banalities is to dispel the boredom of the journey. The mind gets a breath of fresh air, even the muscles get an agreeable message, the blood flows as it should, and we are at peace with God and our fellow men.

'Our children won't live to see the whole country criss-crossed with railways,' he said.

'No, certainly not. Have you any children?'

'None.'

'Nor I. It won't happen in fifty years, but it's our most urgent need. I compare Brazil to a child crawling on all fours; it'll only begin to walk when it's got lots of railways.'

'A delightful idea!' Benedito exclaimed, and his eyes sparkled.

'I'm not worried whether it's delightful, so long as it's true.'

'Delightful and true,' he amiably replied. 'Yes, sir, you're right: Brazil is a child crawling on all fours; it'll only begin to walk when it's got lots of railways.'

We got to Vassouras; I went to the house of the local judge, an old friend; he stayed for a day and went on, further inland. Eight days thereafter, I returned to Rio de Janeiro, but on my own. A week later, he came back to town; we met at the theatre, talked a lot and exchanged news. Benedito ended up asking me to lunch with him the next day. I went; he gave me a lunch fit for a king, with good cigars and lively talk. I noticed that his conversation had had more effect when we were travelling – airing the mind and leaving us at peace with God and our fellow men; but I should say that maybe the lunch got in the way. It really was magnificent; and it would be a historical solecism to set the table for Lucullus in Plato's house. Between the coffee and the brandy, leaning his elbow on the edge of the table, and looking at his burning cigar, he said to me:

'Just now, on my trip, I had occasion to see how right you were, with that idea about Brazil crawling on all fours.'

'Oh?'

'Oh, yes; it's just what *you were saying* in the coach to Vassouras. We'll only begin to walk when we've got lots of railways. You've no idea how true that is.'

He told me lots of things, making observations on the customs of the interior of the country, the hard life they led, their backwardness, insisting, however, on the goodwill of the local population and their desire for progress. Unfortunately, the government didn't respond to the country's needs; it even seemed as if it wanted to keep us behind other American nations. But it was indispensable for us to realise that principles are everything, and men nothing. People are not made for governments, but governments for people: and *abyssus abyssum invocat.*[1] Then he showed me the other rooms. They were all tastefully furnished. He showed me his collections of pictures, coins, old books, seals, arms; he had swords and foils, but admitted he didn't know how to fence. Among the pictures I saw a beautiful portrait of a woman; I asked him who it was. Benedito smiled.

'I shall say no more,' I said, smiling too.

'No, there's nothing to deny,' he rejoined, 'she was a girl I was very fond of. Pretty, isn't she? You've no idea how lovely she was. Her lips were scarlet, her cheeks like roses; she had black eyes, the colour of night. And what teeth! Veritable pearls. A gift from nature.'

We then passed into his study. It was vast, elegant, a little unoriginal, but nothing was missing. There were two bookcases, full of handsomely bound books, a world map and two maps of Brazil. The writing desk was ebony – beautiful workmanship; on top, casually open, was a Laemmert almanac.[2] The

inkstand was crystal – 'rock crystal', he said, explaining the
inkstand as he explained the other things. In the room next door
was an organ. He played the organ, and was very fond of music,
speaking about it enthusiastically, quoting from the operas, all
the best passages, and informed me that when he was a child
he'd begun to learn the flute; he soon abandoned it – which was
a pity, he concluded, for it is a truly poignant instrument. He
showed me other rooms; we went into the garden, which was
splendid, for art assisted nature, just as nature crowned art.
Roses, for example – there's no denying that the rose is the
queen of flowers, he said – he had roses of all kinds and from
every region.

I was delighted with the visit. We met a few times, in the
street, at the theatre, at the houses of mutual friends, and I was
able to take the measure of him. Four months later I went to
Europe, on business that meant I had to be away for a year. He
stayed at home, involved in the election; he wanted to be a
deputy. It was I who had led him to this, without the least
political aim, only wishing to be agreeable to him; you could
perhaps say it was like complimenting him on the cut of his
waistcoat. He took the idea up, and put himself forward. One
day, as I was crossing a street in Paris, I suddenly ran into him.

'What's this?' I exclaimed.

'I lost the election,' Benedito said, 'and I've come on a trip
to Europe.'

He stayed with me from then on; we travelled together. He
confessed that losing the election hadn't stopped him wanting
to get into parliament. On the contrary, it had spurred him
on. He spoke of a grand plan he had.

'I'll see you a minister yet,' I said.

Benedito hadn't reckoned on these words, and his face lit up; but he disguised his feelings.

'I wouldn't go that far,' he replied. 'But if I were to be a minister, I would only be Minister for Industry. We are tired of political parties; we need to develop the nation's true energies, its enormous resources. Do you remember what *we were saying* in the coach to Vassouras? Brazil is crawling on all fours; it'll only walk when it's got railways.'

'You're right,' I agreed, a little astonished. 'And why have I come to Europe myself? To lay plans for a railway. I've left it all set up in London.'

'Have you?'

'Certainly.'

I showed him the papers; he looked at them, dazzled. Since I had gathered a few notes, statistical data, leaflets, reports, copies of contracts, all of this referring to industrial matters, I showed them to him, and Benedito said he too was going to collect some things like that. In fact, I watched as he went round ministries, banks, associations, asking for all kinds of notes and pamphlets, which he piled up in his cases; but his enthusiasm, while it was intense, was short; it was borrowed. Benedito collected political sayings and parliamentary for-mulae. He had a vast arsenal of them in his head. In con-versations with me he often repeated them, as if trying them out; he thought them very impressive, of inestimable value. Many were of English origin, and he preferred them to the others, as if they had something of the House of Commons about them. He savoured them so much that I don't know if he'd have accepted true liberty without these verbal trappings; I think not. I even think that, if he'd had to choose between the two, he'd have opted for these short phrases, so convenient, some beautiful, some sonorous, all of them axiomatically true, which don't force one to think; they fill any gaps, and leave one at peace with God and our fellow men.

We came back together; but I stayed in Pernambuco and later went back to London, returning to Rio de Janeiro from there, a year later. At this stage, Benedito was a deputy. I went to visit him; I found him preparing his maiden speech. He showed me some of the notes, passages from reports, books on political economy, some with the pages marked with strips of paper entitled: *Exchange Rate, Land Tax, The Corn Law Problem in England, The Opinion of Stuart Mill, Adolphe Thiers Mistaken on Railways*, etc. He was sincere, thorough and impassioned. He told me about these things as if he'd just discovered them, expounding everything, *ab ovo*; he was determined to show practical men in the Chamber that he was practical too. Then he asked about my company; I told him what was going on.

'In two years I expect to open the first stretch of line.'

'And the English financiers?'

'What about them?'

'Are they happy, hopeful?'

'Oh yes; you've no idea.'

I told him a few technical particulars, which he listened to a little half-heartedly – either because my narration was extremely complicated, or for some other reason. When I had finished, he told me how pleased he was to see me giving my energies to the movement for industry; that was what we needed, and on just this subject he did me the kindness of reading the first part of the speech he was going to deliver a few days later.

'It's still a rough draft,' he explained; 'but the central ideas won't change.' And he began: 'In the midst of the growing confusion in men's minds, the partisan uproar which drowns the voices of legitimate interests, allow someone to bring the nation's plea to your ears. Gentlemen, it is time for us to give our exclusive attention – I say again, exclusive – to the material improvement of our country. I am not unaware that some will object; you will say that a nation does not just consist of a stomach to digest, but of a head to think and a heart to feel. I reply in my turn that all this will be of little or no value if it has no legs to walk; and here I will repeat what, some years ago, *I said* to a friend during a journey in the interior: Brazil is a child crawling on all fours; it'll only begin to walk when it's criss-crossed by railways.'

I couldn't listen to any more, and became immersed in thought. More than that, I was astonished, aghast in the face of the abyss that psychology opened up beneath my feet. 'This is a sincere man,' I thought to myself, 'he is quite convinced of what he's written.' And down I went to see if I could find the explanation for the processes that the memory of the coach to Vassouras had passed through. I found (and forgive me if this seems pretentious), there I found one more effect of the law of evolution, as Spencer defined it – Spencer or Benedito, one or the other.

A Schoolboy's Story

THE SCHOOL WAS IN the Rua do Costa, a little two-storey house with wooden railings. The year was 1840. That day – a Monday in May – I lingered for a moment in the Rua da Princesa to see where I might go and play that morning, I hesitated between Diogo hill and the Campo de Sant'ana, which wasn't yet the polite park it is today, but a more or less infinite rustic space, full of washerwomen, grass and loose donkeys. The hill or the Campo? That was the problem. Suddenly I said to myself that school was the best notion. I made my way towards school. Here's the reason.

The previous week I'd played truant twice, and when I was found out got due recompense from my father – a hiding with a quince rod. My father's hidings hurt for a long time. He was an old employee of the Arsenal, severe and intolerant. He dreamed of an important position in commerce for me, and wanted me to get the elements of bookkeeping, reading, writing and arithmetic, so I could get work as a cashier. He cited names of rich men who'd begun serving behind the counter. So it was the memory of the latest punishment that took me to school that morning. Virtue wasn't my strong suit.

I stole up the stairs so the master wouldn't hear me, and got in in time; he entered the room three or four minutes later. He came in with his usual soft step, his leather slippers, a light canvas jacket, washed and faded, white trousers and a big floppy collar. His name was Policarpo and he was around fifty years of age, or more. He sat down, extracted a snuffbox and a red handkerchief from his jacket and put them in a drawer; then he cast his eyes around the room. The boys, who had stood up as he entered, sat down again. All was in order; work began.

'Hey, Pilar, I want to speak to you,' the master's son whispered in my ear.

This young fellow was called Raimundo, and he was slow, hardworking and not very bright. Raimundo took two hours to learn what took others only thirty or fifty minutes; that was his way of mastering what his brain couldn't take in straight away. He was a thin, pale child, with a sickly face; he was hardly ever cheerful. He came to the school after his father, and left before him. The master was harsher with him than with us.

'What do you want?'

'Later,' he replied with a shaky voice.

The writing lesson began. I'm embarrassed to say I was one of the more advanced pupils; but I was. A scruple that will be easily understood also prevents me from saying I was one of the most intelligent, but that's my firm conviction. Be it noted that I wasn't pallid or frail: I had a good complexion and good strong muscles. In the writing lessons, for example, I always finished before the others, but I filled the time drawing noses or carving them on the desk – not a noble or profound occupation I admit, but innocent, none the less. That day was like any other; as soon as I'd finished, I started drawing the master's nose, giving it five or six different expressions, of which I recall the interrogative, the appreciative, the dubitative, and the meditative. Poor beginner in the art of letters that I was, I didn't give them these names; but instinctively I gave them these expressions. Slowly, the others finished; the time came for me to finish too, give my work in and go back to my place.

Frankly, I was sorry I'd come. Now I was a prisoner, I was dying to be outside, and thought back to the hill and the Campo, and the other idle kids, Chico Telha, Américo, Carlos das Escadinhas, the cream of the neighbourhood and of the human race. Just to complete my despair, through the school windows, in the clear blue sky, above Livramento hill, I saw a paper kite, a big one high up in the sky, attached to an endless string, billowing in the wind, a wonderful sight. And there I was in the school, sitting with my legs together, and my reading book and grammar on my knees.

'What an idiot I was to come,' I said to Raimundo.

'Don't say that,' he whispered.

I looked at him; he'd gone paler. Then I remembered another time he'd wanted to ask me something, and I asked him what it was. Raimundo shivered again, and quickly asked me to wait a little; it was a very particular thing.

'Pilar . . .' he whispered some minutes later.

'What is it?'

'You . . .'

'You what?'

He looked towards his father, and then at some of the other boys. One of them, Curvelo, looked suspiciously at him, and

Raimundo, noticing this, asked me to wait for a few more minutes. I confess I was beginning to burn with curiosity. I glanced at Curvelo – it looked as if he was watching. It might be simple vague curiosity, a natural lack of discretion; but there might be something between them. This Curvelo was a mischievous rascal. He was eleven, older than us.

What might Raimundo want of me? I was still uneasy, fidgeting in my seat, asking insistently, in a low voice, for him to tell me – nobody was looking at him or me. Or later on, in the afternoon . . .

'Not this afternoon,' he interrupted; 'it can't be this afternoon.'

'Now, then . . .'

'Papa's looking.'

It was true, the master was looking at us. As he was stricter with his son, he often sought him out with his eyes, to keep him on a short leash. But we were cunning too; we stuck our noses in our books, and went on reading. Finally he gave up, and picked up the daily papers, three or four of them, which he read slowly, chewing over his ideas and his emotions. Don't forget we were at the end of Regency, and public excitement was running high.[1] Policarpo certainly supported some party or other, but I could never find out which. The worst thing he could threaten us with was the *palmatória*, a piece of wood with holes drilled in its flat, round end. And there it was, hanging from the window frame, looking at us with its five deadly eyes. All he had to do was lift his hand, take it down and wield it with his usual vigour, which was considerable. Then again, maybe his political emotions sometimes took over to the point of sparing us some punishment or other. That day, at any rate, it seemed he was reading the papers with interest; he lifted his eyes from time to time, took a pinch of snuff, and went back to the papers, devouring them with a passion.

After some time – ten or twelve minutes – Raimundo put his hand into his trouser pocket and looked at me.

'D'you know what I've got here?'

'No.'

'A silver coin Mama gave me.'

'Today?'

'No, the other day, when it was my birthday . . .'

'Real silver?'

'Real.'

Slowly he took it out, and showed it to me from a distance. It was a coin from thirty years back, when the Portuguese king lived in Rio,[2] a dozen *vinténs* or two *tostões*, I can't remember; but it was a coin, a real coin, and it made my heart beat faster. Raimundo rolled his pale gaze in my direction; then he asked me if I wanted it for myself. I said he was joking, but he swore he wasn't.

'But would you give it up?'

'Mama'll get me another. She has a lot that Granny left her, in a little box; some are gold. Do you want this one?'

In reply, I surreptitiously stretched out my hand, after a look at the master's desk. Raimundo withdrew his hand and gave an unconvincing twist to his mouth, an attempt at a smile. Then he proposed a deal, an exchange of services; he'd give me the coin, and I would explain a passage in the syntax lesson. He couldn't remember a thing from the book, and he was afraid of his father. He concluded the proposal by rubbing the little silver coin on his knees . . .

I felt a strange sensation. It wasn't that I had an idea of virtue more appropriate to a grown man; nor was I averse to telling a few childish lies. Both of us knew how to trick the master. The novelty was in the terms of the proposal, the exchange of lesson and money, an overt, explicit deal – you scratch my back, I'll scratch yours; that was the cause of the sensation. I stared at him aimlessly, unable to say a word.

You'll understand that it was a difficult passage, and that Raimundo, who'd failed to learn it, was resorting to this way of escaping his father's punishment. If he'd asked me as a favour, he'd have got what he wanted just the same, as he had at other times; but it seems that the memory of these other times, the fear of finding me weak-willed or tired of being asked, and not getting the lesson right – and it may be that the odd time I'd given him the wrong answer – it seems that was the cause of the proposal. The poor devil was counting on my doing him the favour – but he wanted to make sure of its efficacy, and so resorted to the coin his mother had given him, which he kept like a relic or a toy; he took it and rubbed it on his knees, so I could see, to tempt me . . . and, truly, it was pretty, thin, white, very white; imagine the effect on a lad who only ever carried copper in his pocket, when I carried anything at all – thick, ugly, tarnished copper coins . . .

I didn't want to take it, and it was hard to refuse. I looked at the master, who was still reading, so involved that the snuff was dropping out of his nose. 'Come on, take it,' said his son, in a low voice. And the coin glinted between his fingers, like a diamond . . . Really, as long as the master saw nothing, what harm was done? And he could see nothing; he was gripping the newspapers, reading with fury and indignation . . .

'Take it, take it.'

I cast a quick glance round the room, and saw that Curvelo was looking at us; I told Raimundo to wait. It seemed to me he was observing us, so I acted as if nothing was happening; but a little later, I looked over at him again, and – see how desire leads to self-deceit! – he looked no different from usual. I got my courage back.

'Give it here . . .'

Raimundo slyly gave me the little coin; I put it in my trouser pocket, with a thrill I'm unable to define. There it was, mine, right next to my leg. All that was left was to provide the service, tell him the answer, and I took no time doing it, nor did I give the wrong answer, at least consciously; I passed the explanation over on a scrap of paper which he took carefully, paying close attention. You could feel him taking five or six times the effort to learn something trifling; but so long as he escaped punishment, everything would be all right.

Suddenly, I looked at Curvelo and shuddered; his eyes were on us, with what looked like malicious mockery. I dissembled; but a little later, turning round to him again, I found he had the same look, the same air about him, and he was beginning to fidget impatiently on his seat. I smiled at him and he didn't smile; on the contrary, he frowned, which gave him a menacing aspect. My heart started beating fast.

'We've got to be very careful,' I said to Raimundo.

'Just tell me this,' he murmured.

I signalled to him to be quiet; but he insisted, and the coin, right there in my pocket, reminded me of the contract I'd made. I gave him the answer as surreptitiously as I could; then I looked at Curvelo again, who seemed even more restless, and his mockery, which before looked malicious, now looked worse. There's no need to say that I was on hot coals, desperate for the lesson to finish; but the clock didn't move as it usually did, nor was the master paying any attention to the class; he was reading the papers, article by article, punctuating them with exclamations, shrugs of the shoulders, one or two taps on the table. And there outside, above the hill, the same eternal kite, swinging from side to side as ever, calling me to go and play with it. I imagined myself there, with my books and my slate, under the mango tree, with the silver coin in my trouser pocket; I'd not give it to anyone, for all the tea in China; I'd keep it at home, telling Mama I'd found it in the street. So it couldn't escape, I kept touching it, running my fingers over the marks, almost reading the inscription by touch, and hugely tempted to take a look at it.

'Oi! Pilar!' shouted the master with a voice like thunder.

I shook as if awaking from a dream, and got up in a hurry. I found the master looking at me with a scowl, his newspapers scattered, and next to the desk stood Curvelo. I sensed everything.

'Come here!' the master shouted.

I went and stood before him. He burrowed a pair of pointed eyes right into my conscience; then he called his son. The whole class had stopped; no one was reading any longer, nobody made the least movement. Though I couldn't take my eyes off the master, I felt everyone's curiosity and fear.

'So you receive money to do others' lessons for them?'

'I . . .'

'Give me the coin your schoolmate gave you!' he exclaimed.

I didn't obey straight away, but I could deny nothing. I was still trembling a great deal. Policarpo shouted again for me to give him the coin, and I resisted no longer, I put my hand in my pocket slowly, took it out and gave it to him. He examined it on both sides, snorting with rage; then he stretched his arm out and flung it into the street. He said all kinds of harsh things, that both I and his son had just committed a base, unworthy, vile act, a villainy, and we were to be punished as an example and a lesson.

'Forgive me, master . . .' I sobbed.

'There's no forgiveness! Hold out your hand! Hold it out! Come on! You shameless scoundrel! Hold out your hand!'

'But, master . . .'

'It'll be worse if you don't!'

I held my right hand out, then the left, and took the blows one on top of the other, twelve in all, leaving me with my palms red and swollen. Then it was the son's turn, and the same thing happened; he spared him nothing, two, four, eight, twelve blows. When he'd finished, he preached us another sermon. He called us shameless, insolent, and swore that if we did the same thing again, we'd be punished so we'd remember it for ever more. And again he exclaimed: Swine! crooks! cowards!

For my part, I was staring at the floor. I dared not look at anyone, and felt as if everyone's eyes were on me. I went back to my bench, sobbing, crushed by the teacher's insults. In the classroom, terror reigned; no one would do anything like that again that day. I think even Curvelo had blenched with fear. I didn't look at him straight away, but in my mind I swore I'd smash his face in in the street as soon as we got out, as sure as two and three are five.

A little later I looked at him; he was looking at me too, but he turned his face away, and I think he went pale. He pulled himself together and began to read out loud; he was afraid. He began to change his posture, fidgeting for no reason, scratching his knees or his nose. Maybe he was sorry he'd informed on us; and, in fact, why had he done it? What harm were we doing him?

'You'll pay for this! You'll get it in the neck!' I said under my breath.

The class came to an end, and we went out; he went ahead, in a hurry, and I didn't want to fight him right there, in the Rua do Costa, near the school; I'd catch him in the Rua Larga de São Joaquim. However, when I got to the corner, I couldn't see him any more; probably he'd hidden in some shop or entrance-way; I went into a chemist's, peeped into other houses, asked a few people if they'd seen him, but no one could tell me anything. In the afternoon, he didn't come to school.

At home I said nothing, of course; but to explain my swollen hands I lied to my mother, and said I'd not learned the lesson properly. I slept that night wishing both boys, the informer and the tempter, to the devil. And I dreamed of the coin; I dreamed that, when I came back to the school the next day, I'd come across it in the street and picked it up, without fear or scruple . . .

In the morning I woke early. The idea of going to look for the coin made me dress in a hurry. It was a splendid May day, with magnificent sunshine, soft air, not counting the new trousers my mother had given me – yellow, they were. All this, and the silver coin . . . I left the house as if I was stepping up to a throne. I hastened so no one would get to school before me; even so, I took care not to crumple my trousers. They were far too handsome! I kept looking at them, taking care not to bump into people or touch the rubbish in the street . . .

In the street I met a company of fusiliers, with a drum beating at their head. I couldn't resist it. The soldiers were marching rapidly, in step, left, right, to the drum's rhythm; they came, passed by me and went on their way. I felt an itch in my feet, and an urge to go after them. I've already said it was a beautiful day, and the beating of that drum . . . I looked to one side and another; in the end, I don't know how it was, I started marching to the beat too; I think I was humming something: *Rato na casaca* . . .[3] I didn't go to school, I went along with the fusiliers, then off to Saúde, and ended the morning on Gamboa beach. I got back home with my trousers dirtied, no silver coin in my pocket or resentment in my soul. Still, the coin was pretty, and it was they, Raimundo and Curvelo, who gave me my first taste of corruption in one case, of betrayal in the other; but the beat of that drum . . .

Dona Paula

S HE COULDN'T HAVE COME at a better moment. Dona
Paula came into the room, just as her niece was drying
her eyes, worn out with crying. We can understand her
aunt's astonishment – the niece's, too, when we realise that
Dona Paula lives up in Tijuca,[1] and seldom comes down to
town. The last time was at Christmas, and it's now May
1882. She came down yesterday afternoon, and went to her
sister's house on the Rua do Lavradio. Today, as soon as
she'd had lunch, she dressed and hurried to visit her niece.
The first slave she saw was going to let her mistress know,
but Dona Paula told her not to, and went on tiptoes, very
slowly so her dress wouldn't rustle, opened the drawing-
room door and went in.

'What's this?' she exclaimed.

Venancinha threw herself into her arms, and her tears burst
out again. Her aunt kissed her over and over, embraced her,
spoke words of comfort, and begged her to tell her what the
matter was, if it was an illness . . .

'I wish it was! I wish I was dead!' the girl interrupted.

'Don't be so silly; what's the matter? Come on, what's
happened?'

Venancinha dried her eyes and began to speak. At the fifth or sixth word, she had to stop; the tears came back, so abundant and unrestrained that Dona Paula thought it best to let them have their way first. Meanwhile, she started taking off her black lace cape and removing her gloves. She was an attractive lady, elegantly dressed, proud owner of a large pair of eyes, which once upon a time must have been infinite. While her niece was crying, she carefully went to shut the door and returned to the sofa. After a few minutes Venancinha stopped, and told her aunt what the matter was.

It was nothing less than a quarrel with her husband, violent enough for them to have talked about separation. The cause was jealousy. Her husband had taken a dislike to a certain individual; but the previous evening, in C——'s house, seeing her dance with him twice and converse for a few minutes, he'd concluded they were flirting. He'd been sullen on the way home; in the morning, after breakfast, his anger exploded and he said harsh, cruel things to her, which she rebuffed with others equally harsh.

'Where is your husband?' asked the aunt.

'He's gone out; to his office, I think.'

Dona Paula asked if it was still the same one, and told her to relax, it was nothing; two hours from now it would all be over. She quickly put her gloves on.

'Are you going there, Auntie?'

'Of course I'm going. Your husband's a good man; this is just a tiff. Number 104? I'm off; wait for me, and don't let the slaves see you.'

All this was said rapidly, confidently and gently. Once her gloves were on, she got her cape, and her niece helped her, talking as well, and swearing that, in spite of everything, she adored Conrado. Conrado was the husband; he'd been a lawyer since 1874. As Dona Paula left, the girl showered her with kisses. It was true: she couldn't have come at a better moment. On the way, however, it seems Dona Paula, not exactly mistrustful, but a bit concerned about what might really be happening, began to look at the incident a little sceptically; in any event, she was determined to re-establish domestic harmony.

She got there; Conrado wasn't in, but he soon came back, and once the first surprise was over Dona Paula didn't have to tell him what the object of the visit was: he guessed everything. He admitted he'd overstepped the mark in some ways; in any case, he wasn't saying his wife was at all perverse or vicious. That much was true; but she was a giddy creature, who loved idle chatter, tender looks and words softly spoken, and frivolity is one of the doors leading to sin. As far as the person in question was concerned, he had no doubt they were flirting. Venancinha had only recounted yesterday's events; she'd said nothing about the other four or five times, the last one at the theatre, when they'd even created a bit of a scandal. He wasn't about to cover up for his wife's ineptitude. If she wanted to flirt, she'd have to reckon on doing it on her own.

Dona Paula listened to all this in silence; then she spoke in her turn. She agreed that her niece was frivolous; it was natural at her age. A pretty girl can't go out in the street without attracting attention, and it's only natural she should be flattered by the admiration of others. It's also natural that her reaction should look to others, and to her husband, like the beginning of an affair: foolishness on the one side, jealousy on the other, and everything's explained. For her part, she'd just seen the girl weeping genuine tears; she'd left her inconsolable, saying she wanted to die, devastated by what he'd said to her. If, even, he only thought her frivolous, why not proceed with caution and tact, using advice and observation, sparing her the opportunities for temptation, pointing out how much damage is done to a lady's reputation by appearing to be pleasant and affable with other men?

The good lady spent fully twenty minutes saying these gentle words, so agreeably, that Conrado felt less agitated. True, he did resist: two or three times, so as not to slip too easily into forgiveness, he told Dona Paula it was all over between him and Venancinha. And, to spur himself on, he brought to mind all the reasons he had to mistrust his wife. Her aunt, however, ducked her head to let the wave pass, then surfaced again with her large, wise, insistent eyes. Conrado gave way reluctantly, little by little. Then Dona Paula proposed a compromise.

'You forgive her, make it up between you, and she can come and stay with me, in Tijuca, for a month or two: a kind of exile. During that time, I'll take it upon myself to put her mind in order. Agreed?'

Conrado accepted. Dona Paula, as soon as she had his word, took her leave to go and convey the good news to her niece; Conrado escorted her as far as the stairs. They shook hands; Dona Paula didn't let go of his until she'd repeated her advice to be gentle and prudent; then she made this comment, natural enough in the circumstances:

'You'll see the man in question isn't worth a moment of our thoughts . . .'

'He's one Vasco Maria Portela . . .'

Dona Paula went pale. What Vasco Maria Portela? An old man, an ex-diplomat, who . . . No, he's in Europe, has been for a few years, retired, and he's just been made a baron. It's his son, recently come back, a scoundrel . . . Dona Paula grasped his hand and hurried downstairs. In the corridor, though she didn't have to adjust her cape, she did so for some minutes, her hand trembling and her features somewhat perturbed. She even stopped and stared reflectively at the floor. She left; she went to see her niece, bringing the reconciliation and its extra clause with her. Venancinha accepted everything.

Two days later they went to Tijuca. Venancinha wasn't as happy as she'd promised she'd be, probably it was the exile, or maybe she felt a bit of nostalgia. In any case, Vasco's name came up to Tijuca, if not in both their heads, at least in the aunt's, where it was a kind of echo, a distant, soft sound, something that seemed to come from the times of Rosina Stoltz and the Paraná ministry.[2] The diva and the minister, fragile things, were no less fragile than the happiness of youth itself – where had those three eternities gone? Ruins, nothing more, these thirty years. That was all Dona Paula had inside her, all she could see in front of her.

It's no secret, then, that the other Vasco, the older one, was once young too, and in love. They fell in love and got their fill of each other, in the protective shadow of marriage, for some years, and as the passing breeze keeps no record of men's words, there's no way of telling what was said of the affair in those days. The affair ended; it was a succession of sweet and bitter moments, of delights, of tears, of anger and ecstasy, various potions that filled the lady's cup of passion to the brim.

Dona Paula drank it dry and then turned it over so she could drink no more. Satiety brought abstinence, and with time, it was this last phase that left its mark on public opinion. Her husband died, and the years came and went. Dona Paula was now an austere, pious person, well respected and esteemed.

It was her niece that took her thoughts back to the past. It was the analogous situation, together with the name and the blood of the same man, that brought some old memories back. Don't forget they were in Tijuca, they were going to live together for a few weeks, and the one had to obey the other; it was a temptation, and a challenge to the memory.

'Is it really true we're not going back to town for a while?' Venancinha asked, laughing, the next morning.

'Are you bored already?'

'No, no, of course not, I'm just asking . . .'

Dona Paula, laughing too, said no with her finger; then she asked her if she was missing the city below. Venancinha said no, not at all; and to underline her answer, she let the corners of her mouth drop, as if in indifference or disdain. This was insisting too much. Dona Paula had the good habit of not reading in a hurry, as if her life depended on it, but slowly, her eyes burrowing between the syllables and the letters, so as not to miss a thing – she thought her niece's gesture too emphatic.

'They're in love!' she thought.

The discovery brought the spirit of the past back to life. Dona Paula struggled to shake off these importunate memories; but they came back, surreptitious or impetuous, just like the young girls they were, singing, dancing, up to all kinds of tricks. Dona Paula went back to the dances of old, to the endless waltzes that had everyone gasping in astonishment, to the mazurkas, which she insisted to her niece were the most graceful thing in the world, and to the theatre, the letters, and, vaguely, to the kisses; but – in all honesty – all this was like a dead chronicle, the skeleton of the story, without its soul. It all took place in her head. Dona Paula tried to bring her heart in tune with her head, to see if she could still feel something beyond pure mental repetition, but, however much she evoked these extinct passions, none of them came back to her. They were dead and gone.

If she could spy into her niece's heart, maybe she'd see her own image, and then . . . When this idea penetrated Dona Paula's mind, it complicated the business of repair and cure somewhat. She was sincere, and her care was for the girl's soul; she wanted her restored to her husband. Sinners might well want others to sin too, so as to have company on the way down to purgatory; but in this case the sin was over. Dona Paula stressed Conrado's superiority, his virtues, but also his passions, which could lead the marriage to a bad – worse than tragic – end: he might disown her.

Conrado, on the first visit he made to them, nine days later, confirmed the aunt's warning; he was cold when he came in and left the same way. Venancinha was terrified. She'd hoped that the nine days of the separation might have softened him, as, in fact, they had; but he put on a mask when he came in and held back, so as not to give way too soon. And this was more salutary than anything else. The terror of losing her husband was the main element in her restoration. Even exile had less effect.

And lo and behold, two days after the visit, when both of them were at the garden gate, ready for their usual walk, they saw a horseman approaching. Venancinha stared, gave a little cry, and ran to hide behind the wall. Dona Paula understood, and stayed where she was. She wanted to see the horseman closer to; she saw him two or three minutes later, a gallant young man, well dressed with his elegant shiny boots, dashing, upright in the saddle. He had the same face as the other Vasco; the same turn of the head, a little to the right, the same wide shoulders, the same round, deep eyes.

That same night, Venancinha told her everything, after the first word had been dragged from her. They'd first seen one another at the races, soon after he'd arrived from Europe. Two weeks later, he was introduced to her at a dance, and he looked so handsome, with that Parisian air about him, that she mentioned him to her husband the next morning. Conrado frowned, and this was the gesture that gave her an idea she hadn't had till then. She began to enjoy seeing him; soon after, she felt a certain agitation. He spoke respectfully to her, said nice things, that she was the prettiest young lady in Rio and the most elegant, that he'd heard her praises already in Paris, from some of the ladies of the Alvarenga family. He was amusing when he criticised others, and knew how to say things with feeling, like no one else. He didn't speak of love, but he followed her with his eyes, and she, much as she tried to remove hers, couldn't do it altogether. She began to think of him, repeatedly, with a certain interest, and when they met her heart beat faster; perhaps he saw the impression he was making on her in her face.

Dona Paula, leaning towards her, listened to this account, of which this is just a coherent summary. All her life was in her eyes; her mouth half open, she seemed to drink her niece's words, eagerly, as if they were a cordial. She asked for more, for her to tell her all, absolutely everything. Venancinha became more assured. Her aunt looked so young, her encouragement was so gentle, as if she were forgiving her beforehand; she found a confidante and a friend, in spite of some severe words mixed in with the others, motivated by an unconscious hypocrisy. I won't call it calculation; Dona Paula was deluding herself. We might compare her to a retired general, struggling to find a little of his old ardour by listening to accounts of others' campaigns.

'Now you see your husband was right,' she said, 'you've been rash, very rash . . .'

Venancinha agreed, but swore it was all over.

'I'm not so sure. Did you really come to love him?'

'Auntie . . .'

'You still do!'

'I swear I don't. I don't like him; but I confess . . . yes . . . I confess that I did . . . Forgive me; don't say anything to Conrado; I'm repentant . . . at the beginning, like I said, I was a bit fascinated . . . But what do you expect?'

'Did he say anything to you?'

'Yes; it was at the theatre, one night, at the Teatro Lirico, as we were coming out. He used to come by our box and accompany me to the carriage; it was as we were coming out . . . three words . . .'

Out of modesty, Dona Paula didn't ask what the suitor's actual words were, but she imagined the circumstances, the corridor, the couples leaving, the lights, the crowd, the noise of voices, and with this picture, she could experience a little of her niece's sensations; and she asked about them cunningly, with interest.

'I don't know what I felt,' the girl rejoined, as her feelings loosened her tongue, 'I don't remember the first five minutes. I think I looked serious; in any case, I didn't say anything to him. It seemed as if everyone was looking at us, they might have heard, and when someone greeted me with a smile, I had the idea they were laughing at me. I've no idea how I got down the stairs; I got into the carriage without knowing what I was doing; when I shook his hand, I let my fingers go limp. I swear to you I wished I hadn't heard anything. Conrado told me he felt sleepy, and leaned back in the carriage; it was better that way, because I don't know what I'd have said, if we'd had to go on talking. I leaned back too, but not for long; I couldn't keep still. I looked out of the windows, and all I could see was the glare from the street lamps, and after a while not even that; I saw the corridors at the theatre, the stairs, all the people, and him right next to me, whispering those words, just three words, and I can't say what I thought all that time; my ideas were mixed up, shaken, a revolution going on inside me . . .'

'But when you got home?'

'At home, while I was undressing, I could think a little, but only a little. I got to sleep late, and slept badly. In the morning, my head was confused. I can't say if I was happy or sad; I remember I was thinking about him a lot, and to put him out of my mind I promised myself I'd tell Conrado everything; but the thoughts came back again. From time to time, I thought I could hear his voice, and shuddered. I even remembered that when I was leaving I'd let my fingers go limp, and I felt, I don't know how to put it, a kind of regret, a fear I'd offended him . . . then the desire to see him again came back . . . I'm sorry, Auntie; you want me to tell you everything.'

In reply, Dona Paula squeezed her hand hard and nodded her head. At last, she'd found something of times past as she came into contact with these sensations, naïvely recounted as they were. Her eyes were half shut at one minute, as her memories lulled her – then, the next instant, sharpened with curiosity and warmth, and she listened to everything, day by day, meeting by meeting, the scene at the theatre itself, which her niece had at first hidden from her. And then everything else came along: hours of anxiety, of longing, of fear, hope, despondency, duplicity, sudden urges, all the turmoil of a young woman in circumstances like this – the aunt's insatiable curiosity let nothing pass. It wasn't a whole adultery novel, not even a chapter, just a prologue – but it was interesting and violent.

Venancinha ended. Her aunt said nothing, withdrew into herself for a moment; then she awoke, took her niece's hand and pulled it towards her. She didn't speak at once; first she looked closely at all that restless, palpitating girlhood, her fresh mouth, her eyes still infinite, and only came to herself when her niece asked pardon of her once more. Dona Paula said everything that a gentle, severe mother might have said, talked of chastity, of love for her husband, of public reputation; she was so eloquent that Venancinha couldn't hold back, and began to cry.

Tea arrived, but there are some confidences that make tea impossible. Venancinha soon retired, and as the lights were now brighter, she went out of the room with her eyes lowered, so the servant wouldn't see how upset she was.

Dona Paula stayed, facing the table and the servant. She spent twenty minutes, not much less, drinking a cup of tea and nibbling a biscuit, and as soon as she was alone, she went to lean against the window, looking out over the garden.

There was a little wind, the leaves moved and whispered, and even though they weren't the same ones as years back, they still asked her: 'Paula, do you remember the old days?' Leaves have this particularity, you see – past generations tell the succeeding ones the things they've seen, so that they know everything and ask about everything. Do you remember the old days?

She did remember, yes; but that sensation she'd just had, a mere reflection, had stopped now. In vain she repeated her niece's words, breathing in the raw night air: it was only in her mind that she found some vestige, memories, ruins. Her heart had slowed down again; the blood was flowing at its usual rate. She missed the contact with her niece. And she stayed there, in spite of everything, looking out at the night, which was no different from any other, and had nothing in common with those of the time of Stoltz and the Marquis of Paraná; but there she stayed, and indoors the slaves kept sleep at bay by telling stories, saying, over and again, in their impatience:

'Ol' missy's off to bed real late tonight!'

The Diplomat

T HE BLACK GIRL CAME into the dining room and over to
the crowded table, to whisper in her mistress's ear. It
must have been something urgent, because her mistress got up
straight away.

'Shall we wait, Dona Adelaide?'

'Don't wait for me, Senhor Rangel; you carry on, I'll take
my turn later.'

Rangel was the reader of the fortune-book. He turned the
page, and read out a question: 'Does someone love you secretly?'
General excitement; the girls and the young men smiled at each
other. It is St John's Night, 1854; the house is in the Rua das
Mangueiras. João is the host's name, João Viegas, and he has a
daughter, Joaninha. This same party takes place every year, with
relatives and friends; there's a bonfire in the garden, they roast
potatoes as usual, and tell fortunes. There's a dinner too, dancing
sometimes, and a game of forfeits, just a family affair. João Viegas
is a clerk in a public notary's office in Rio.

'Off we go. Who's going to start?' he said. 'Come on, Dona
Felismina. Let's see if anyone secretly loves you.'

Dona Felismina gave a forced smile. She was a good lady, in
her forties, neither rich nor gifted, but still looking for a

husband out of the corner of her eye as she kneeled to pray. It was a cruel joke, but understandable. Dona Felismina was a perfect example of those indulgent, gentle creatures who seem to be born to amuse others. She picked the dice up and threw them with a look of incredulous compliance. Number ten, two voices cried out. Rangel's eyes went to the bottom of the page, looked at the item with that number, and read what it said: yes, it said, there was someone, and she should look for him next Sunday at Mass. Everyone round the table congratulated Dona Felismina, who smiled disdainfully, though secretly hopeful.

Others picked up the dice, and Rangel went on reading everyone's fortunes. He read in an affected voice. From time to time, he took his glasses off and wiped them very slowly with the corner of his cambric handkerchief – either because it was cambric, or because it gave off a delicate jasmine scent. He put on airs, and the others called him 'the diplomat'.

'Come on, Mr Diplomat, on you go.'

Rangel woke up with a start; engrossed in perusing the line of girls on the other side of the table, he'd forgotten to read one of the fortunes. Was he courting one of them? Let's take this step by step.

He was a bachelor, but not because he wanted to be. As a young man, he'd had a few passing dalliances, but time brought with it an obsession with rank and status, and it was this that prolonged his bachelorhood till the age of forty-one, which is where we are now. He wanted a wife superior to him and his social circle, and he spent his time waiting for her. He even went to dances given by a rich, famous lawyer for whom he copied papers, and who favoured him with his protection. At the dances, he occupied the same subordinate position as he did at the office; he spent the evening wandering around the corridors, peeping into the ballroom, watching the ladies pass, devouring a multitude of magnificent shoulders and shapely figures with his eyes. He envied the men, and copied them. He would come out full of excitement and determination. When there were no balls, he went to church festivals where he could see some of the most eligible girls in the city. He was a regular too in the courtyard of the imperial palace on gala days, in order to watch the great ladies and gentlemen of the court, ministers, generals, diplomats, high court judges, and he could identify them all, the people themselves and their carriages. He came back, from church or palace, just as he came back from the ball, impetuous and impassioned, ready to pluck fortune's laurels at a single stroke.

The worst of it is that between the hand and the fruit there's often a wall, and Rangel was not the sort to jump over walls. In his imagination he did everything, carrying off women and pillaging cities. More than once, in his own mind, he was a minister of state, and got his fill of bowing and scraping and issuing decrees. He even went as far as proclaiming himself Emperor, one day on 2 December,[1] as he was coming back from the parade in the palace square; to this end, he imagined a revolution, in which he spilled some blood, not very much, and a benevolent dictatorship, in which he did no more than avenge a few minor contretemps he'd suffered at work. Here outside, however, all these feats were mere fables. In reality, he was good-natured and discreet.

At the age of forty, he'd given up on his ambitions; but his nature remained the same, and in spite of his vocation for marriage, he'd still not found a bride. More than one would have accepted him with pleasure; his circumspection made him lose them all. One day, he noticed Joaninha, who would soon be nineteen and had a lovely tranquil pair of eyes – a virgin, what's more, of all commerce with men. Rangel had known her since she was a child, had carried her in his arms to the Passeio Público[2] or to see the fireworks at Lapa; how could he speak to her of love? But, on the other hand, he was so well accepted in the household that it would ease his way to marriage; anyway, it was this or nothing.

This time the wall wasn't high, and the fruit hung low; all he needed to do was stretch his arm out with a bit of effort, and pick it from the branch. For some months, Rangel had been engaged in this enterprise. He wouldn't stretch his arm out without looking all around to see if anyone was coming, and, if there was, he pretended nothing was happening and went on his way. When he did stretch it out, a gust of wind moved the branch, or a bird rustled in the fallen leaves, and that was all it took to make him withdraw his hand. Time went by and this passion got into his system, bringing with it many hours of anguish, always followed by greater hopes. At this very moment, he's brought his first love letter with him, and is ready to hand it over. He's already had two or three good opportunities, but still he puts it off; there's a long night ahead! Meanwhile, he continues reading out the fortunes, solemn as a high priest.

There's happiness all around. They whisper, laughing and talking at the same time. Uncle Rufino, who's the family joker, goes round the table with a feather, tickling the girls behind the ears. João Viegas is anxiously awaiting Calisto, a friend who's late. Where can Calisto have got to?

'Out of the way! I need the table; let's go into the drawing room.'

Dona Adelaide was back; they were going to lay the table for dinner. Everyone moved away and, as she walked, you could see how delightful the notary's daughter was. Rangel followed her, his eyes wide with passion. She went to the window for a few moments, while a game of forfeits was being set up, and he went too; it was an opportunity to slip her the letter.

On the other side of the street, in a grand house, there was a ball, and people were dancing. She was looking, and he looked too. In the windows they could see the partners pass, swaying to the rhythm, the ladies with their silks and lace, the gentlemen refined and elegant, some with medals on their chests. From time to time, there was a flash of diamonds, swift and fleeting, in the whirl of the dance. Couples talking, gleaming epaulettes, the men leaning towards the women, fluttering fans, all this in brief glimpses through the windows, which didn't reveal the whole of the ballroom; but the rest could be imagined. He, at least, knew it all, and conveyed it all to the notary's daughter. The obsession with rank, which had seemed dormant, began to perform cartwheels in our friend's heart, and here he was trying to seduce the girl's heart too.

'I know someone who'd be in their element in there,' murmured Rangel.

'You,' said Joaninha, naïvely.

Rangel smiled, flattered, and could find nothing to say. He looked at the lackeys and the coachmen in livery in the street, chatting in groups or leaning over the roofs of the coaches. He began to point some of them out: this is Olinda's, that's Maranguape; but another wheels in from the Rua da Lapa into the Rua das Mangueiras. It stops opposite; the lackey jumps down, opens the carriage door, takes his hat off and stands to attention. There comes out a bald pate, a head, a man, a couple of medals, then a richly dressed lady; they go into the foyer, and up the stairs, carpeted and flanked at the bottom by two large vases.

'Joaninha, Senhor Rangel . . .'

Damn the game of forfeits! Just as he was putting a suggestive phrase together in his head about the couple going up the stairs, intending to pass naturally on to handing over the letter . . . Rangel obeyed, and sat down opposite the girl. Dona Adelaide, who was presiding over the game of forfeits, was collecting names; each person was to take the name of a flower. Uncle Rufino, of course, always the clown, chose the pumpkin flower. As for Rangel – trying to avoid being common, he mentally compared flowers, and when the lady of the house asked him for his, he answered, gently and slowly:

'The forget-me-not, madam.'

'What a pity Calisto isn't here!' the notary sighed.

'Did he really say he'd come?'

'He did; only yesterday he came by the office, on purpose to tell me he'd come late, but he'd be here; he had to go to a do in the Rua da Carioca . . .'

'Room for two more?!' shouted a voice in the corridor.

'Thank goodness for that! Here he comes!'

João Viegas went to open the door; it was Calisto, accompanied by an unknown young man, whom he introduced to everybody in general: 'This is Queiroz, he works in the Santa Casa hospital; he's not a relative, though he looks a lot like me: two peas in a pod . . .' Everyone laughed; it was Calisto's joke, for he was ugly as sin – whereas Queiroz was a handsome lad of twenty-six or twenty-seven, with black hair, black eyes, and extraordinarily slim. The girls drew back a little; Dona Felismina put on full sail.

'We were playing forfeits; d'you want to join in?' said the lady of the house. 'Will you play, Senhor Queiroz?'

Queiroz said he would and started to survey the other guests. He knew some, and exchanged two or three words with them. He told João Viegas that he'd wanted to meet him for a long time, because of a favour he'd done his father a while back, in a court case. João Viegas didn't remember a thing about it, even after he told him what the favour was; but he was pleased to hear of it, and in public too; he looked round at everyone, and took a few minutes for silent gratification.

Queiroz entered the game with a will. After half an hour, he was at home. He was lively and voluble; his manners were spontaneous and natural. He had a huge repertory of penalties for the game of forfeits, which delighted everyone, and no one could impose them better. He was so vivacious and animated, going hither and thither, putting groups together, moving chairs, talking to the girls as if he'd been their playmate when they were children.

'Dona Joaninha here, in this chair; Dona Cesária, over here, standing, and Senhor Camilo comes in by that door . . . No, no: look, like this, so as to . . .'

Stiff in his chair, Rangel was dumbfounded. Where had this hurricane come from? And on the hurricane went, lifting the hats off the men and shaking the girls' hair loose, as they laughed happily: Queiroz here, Queiroz there, Queiroz everywhere. Rangel was stupefied, then mortified. His sceptre was falling from his hands. He didn't look at the intruder, laughed at nothing he said, and answered him curtly. Inside, he was riddled with envy, wished him to the devil, called him a halfwit, good for amusing people and making them laugh – that's parties for you. But, as he repeated these things and worse, he couldn't get back his peace of mind. He was really suffering, in the heart of his self-esteem; worse, Queiroz could see all this agitation, and worst of all, Rangel saw that he was seen.

Just as he dreamed of glory, so Rangel imagined revenge. In his head, he smashed Queiroz to smithereens; then he thought of some disaster or other, an ache would do, but something really painful that would remove the intruder from the scene. But nothing happened; the devil was more and more sprightly, and the whole room was spellbound, fascinated. Even Joaninha, timid as she was, came to life in Queiroz's hands, as did the other girls; everyone, men and women, seemed eager to obey him. He mentioned dancing, and the girls went over to Uncle Rufino, to ask him to play a quadrille on the flute – just one, that was all they wanted.

'I can't, I've got a corn.'

'Flute?' shouted Calisto. 'Ask Queiroz to play something for us, and you'll see what flute-playing is . . . Go and get the flute, Rufino. Listen to Queiroz. You've no idea how tenderly he plays!'

Queiroz played 'Casta Diva'. How ridiculous! Rangel said to himself – a tune even the kids in the street can whistle. He looked at him askance, asking himself if a serious person would be seen dead doing that; and came to the conclusion that the flute was a grotesque instrument. He looked at Joaninha too, and saw that, like everyone else, she was watching Queiroz, enthralled, enamoured of the sound of the music, and he shuddered, uncertain why. The other faces had the same expression, but even so, he felt something which complicated his aversion for the intruder. When the flute finished, Joaninha applauded less than the others, and Rangel began to wonder if it was her usual shyness, or if something else was affecting her . . . He must give her the letter without delay.

Dinner was served. Everyone went into the dining room, and happily for Rangel, he was placed opposite Joaninha, whose eyes were more beautiful than ever, and so liquid they looked changed. Rangel savoured them in silence, and reconstructed the entire dream that Queiroz had demolished with a flick of his fingers. Thus it was that he saw himself by her side, in the house he'd rent – a love-nest he gilded with his imagination. He even won a lottery prize and spent it all on silks and jewels for his wife, lovely Joaninha – Joaninha Rangel – Dona Joaninha Rangel – Dona Joana Viegas Rangel – or Dona Joana Cândida Viegas Rangel . . . He couldn't leave the Cândida out . . .

'Come on, Mr Diplomat; give us one of those toasts of yours . . .'

Rangel woke up; the whole table was seconding Uncle Rufino's suggestion; Joaninha herself was asking him to propose a toast, like last year's. Rangel said he would obey; he was just finishing this chicken wing. Nudges, winks and

flattering whispers; Dona Adelaide, when a girl said she'd
never heard Rangel speak:

'Haven't you?' she asked in astonishment. 'You've no idea;
he speaks so well, very clearly, such well-chosen words, and so
beautifully expressed . . .'

As he was eating, he summoned up some memories, shreds
of ideas, for use in putting his sentences and metaphors
together. He finished and got to his feet. He looked happy
and full of himself. At last, they were knocking at his door.
The round robin of silly stories and empty jokes was over, and
they'd come to him to hear something correct and serious. He
looked around, and saw all eyes lifted up in expectation. Not
all; Joaninha's sloped off in Queiroz's direction, and his came
to meet hers halfway, in a regular cavalcade of promises.
Rangel went pale. The words died in his mouth, but he had to
speak; they were waiting for him, in approving silence.

He didn't come up to expectations. It was just a toast to the
host and his daughter. He called her one of God's thoughts,
borne from the immortal realms into reality, a phrase he'd
used three years ago, but which should have been forgotten
by now. He also mentioned the sanctuary of the family, the
altar of friendship, and of gratitude, which is the flower of
pure hearts. The more nonsensical the words, the more
grandiose and resonant they were. All in all, a toast that
should have lasted a good ten minutes he disposed of in five,
and sat down.

Nor was that all. Queiroz soon got up, two or three
minutes later, for another toast, and the silence was even
more sudden and complete. Joaninha stared into her lap,
embarrassed by what he might say; Rangel shivered.

'The illustrious friend of this house, Senhor Rangel,' said Queiroz, 'drank the health of the two people who share the name of the saint whose day we are celebrating; I drink to the one who is a saint every day, to Dona Adelaide.'

Great applause greeted this compliment, and Dona Adelaide, flattered, was congratulated by each and every guest. Her daughter didn't stop there. 'Mama! Mama!' she exclaimed, getting up. She went to embrace her and kiss her three or four times; a sort of letter to be read by two people.

Rangel went from anger to despondency, and when the dinner was over he thought of leaving. But hope, a devil with green eyes, begged him to stay, and he stayed. Who knows? It was all a passing whim, one night only, a flirtation for St John's Night; he, after all, was a friend of the family, and was esteemed by them; he only needed to ask for the girl's hand, and he'd be given it. And anyway, Queiroz might not have the means to marry. What did he do at the Santa Casa? Maybe it was some inferior job . . . At this, he looked sideways at Queiroz's clothes, carefully inspected his seams, scrutinised the embroidery on his shirt, examined his trouser knees to see if they were worn, and his shoes, and concluded that he took pains with the way he dressed, but probably spent everything on himself – marriage, however, is a serious matter. Maybe he had a widowed mother, unmarried sisters . . . Rangel lived on his own.

'Uncle Rufino, play a quadrille.'

'I can't; after a meal the flute gives you indigestion. Let's play lotto.'

Rangel declared he couldn't play, he had a headache; but Joaninha came over and asked him to partner her. 'Half the

winnings for you, half for me,' she said smiling; he smiled too
and accepted. They sat next to one another. Joaninha was
talking to him, laughing, lifting her beautiful eyes to him,
restless, moving her head to one side and another. Rangel felt
better, and in no time he was completely happy. He marked
the numbers at random, missing some, which she pointed out
with her finger – a nymph-like finger, he said to himself; and
he began making mistakes deliberately so as to see her finger,
and hear her scolding him: 'You're very forgetful; if you carry
on like this, we'll lose our money . . .'

Rangel thought of giving her the letter under the table; but
since nothing had been said, she'd be bound to be shocked
and spoil everything; she must be forewarned. He looked
around the table: all the faces were bent over their cards,
attentively following the numbers. Then he leaned over to
the right, and looked down over Joaninha's cards, as if to
check something.

'You've got two lines,' he whispered.

'I haven't, I've got three.'

'Three, yes, three, you're right. Listen . . .'

'And you?'

'I've got two.'

'What d'you mean, two? You've got four.'

There were four; she leaned over to show him them,
almost brushing her ear against his lips; then she looked at
him, laughing and shaking her head: 'Tut, tut, Senhor
Rangel!' Rangel heard this with singular delight; her voice
was so sweet, her expression so friendly, that he forgot
everything, grabbed her by the waist, and threw himself into
an eternal, chimerical waltz. House, table, guests, all disap-

peared, vain products of the imagination, all of them. Nothing was left but a single reality, the two of them whirling in space under a million stars purposely shining to light up their way.

No letter, nothing. When morning was near, they all went to the window to see the guests leaving from the ball opposite. Rangel recoiled in horror. He saw Queiroz gently squeeze the lovely Joaninha's hand. He tried to explain it away, it was just an illusion, but no sooner had he destroyed one than others appeared, like waves breaking over him, one after another. He could barely understand that one single night, a few hours could be enough to join two creatures in this way; but it was the living truth, evident from their gestures, their eyes, their words, their laughter, even from the sadness with which they separated in the early morning.

He left in a state of shock. A single night, just a few hours! When, some time later, he got home, he lay down on the bed, not to sleep, but to burst out sobbing. When he was alone, all his affectation disappeared, no longer was he the diplomat, he was a maniac rolling around on the bed, shouting, crying like a child, truly unhappy, all because of this sad, autumnal passion. This poor soul, this mixture of daydreaming, indolence and affectation, was, in substance, as unhappy as Othello, and his end was even crueller.

Othello kills Desdemona; our lover, whose hidden passion had been suspected by no one, acted as Queiroz's witness when he and Joaninha were married six months later.

The years passed by, and nothing happened to change his nature. When the Paraguayan war broke out[3] he often thought of enlisting as an officer in the volunteer force; he never did; all the same, he won a few battles and ended up as a brigadier.

The Fortune-Teller

HAMLET OBSERVES TO HORATIO that there are more things in heaven and earth than are dreamt of in his philosophy. The lovely Rita gave this same explanation to young Camilo, one Friday in November 1869, when he was laughing at her for having consulted a fortune-teller the day before; the only difference was that she used other words to express the idea.

'Go on, laugh if you want. That's men for you; they don't believe in anything. Well, I did go, and she knew why I was consulting her even before I'd told her. She'd hardly begun to lay out the cards when she said to me, "You're fond of someone . . ." I confessed I was, and then she went on laying out the cards, put them in order, and then told me I was frightened you'd forget me, but there was no need . . .'

'Wrong!' Camilo interrupted, laughing.

'Don't say that, Camilo. If you knew how I've been lately, because of you. You know; I've told you. Don't laugh at me, don't laugh . . .'

Camilo took hold of her hands, and gazed at her with a serious, steady look. He swore he really loved her, that these were childish fears; in any case, if she was at all fearful, he was the best fortune-teller to come to. Then he reproached her, and said it was imprudent to go to houses like that. Vilela might get to know about it, and then . . .

'Not a chance! I took great care as I went in.'

'Where's the house?'

'Near here, in the Rua da Guarda Velha; there was no one in the street at the time. Don't worry; I'm not crazy.'

Camilo laughed again:

'Do you really believe in that kind of thing?' he asked her.

That was when, without knowing she was translating Hamlet into common speech, she told him that there are lots of mysterious things in the world that are true. If he didn't believe her, fine; but the truth is that the fortune-teller had divined everything. What more did he want? The proof is that now she was calm and contented.

I think he was going to say something, but he stopped himself. He didn't want to deprive her of her illusions. He too, when he was a boy, and even later in life, had been superstitious; he'd had a whole arsenal of absurd beliefs impressed on him by his mother, which disappeared when he was twenty. This parasitic vegetation then fell away, leaving only the main trunk of religion; but since he'd received both from his mother, he wrapped them up in the same doubt, and soon afterwards in a single total denial. Camilo believed in nothing. Why? He couldn't say; he didn't have a single argument, and limited himself to denying everything. Even that isn't right, because denying something is still a kind of affirmation, and he didn't put his disbelief into words; faced by life's mystery, he was happy to shrug his shoulders and carry on as before.

They went their separate ways; each of them was happy, he even more than she. Rita was certain she was loved; Camilo not only was sure of that, but saw how she trembled and risked herself for him by going to fortune-tellers – however much he reproached her, he couldn't but feel flattered. The house they'd met in was in the old Rua dos Barbonos, where a friend of Rita's from her home town lived. Rita went off down the Rua das Mangueiras towards her home in Bota-fogo; Camilo went down the Rua da Guarda Velha, looking at the fortune-teller's house as he passed.

Vilela, Camilo and Rita, three names – an affair, then, but what about its origins? Here they are. The first two were childhood friends. Vilela studied to be a lawyer, and became a magistrate. Camilo trained to be a civil servant, against the wishes of his father, who wanted him to be a doctor; but his father died, and Camilo preferred doing nothing, until his mother got him an administrative job. In early 1869, Vilela came back from the provinces, where he'd married a beauti-ful, foolish woman; he abandoned the magistracy and opened a law firm. Camilo got him a house in the Botafogo area, and went on board ship to welcome him.

'Is it you?' Rita had exclaimed, holding out her hand. 'You can't imagine how much my husband thinks of you; he was always talking about you.'

Camilo and Vilela looked at each other affectionately. They were true friends. Then, Camilo confessed to himself that Vilela's wife didn't belie her husband's letters. She really was a lovely, vivacious woman, her eyes were warm, her mouth delicate and inquisitive. She was a little older than either – thirty, while Vilela was twenty-nine and Camilo twenty-six. However, Vilela's air of severity made him look older than his wife, while Camilo was an innocent in the moral and practical sides of life. Time had taught him nothing, and he was not provided with the crystal spectacles nature puts in some people's cradles to foresee the effects of time. He possessed neither experience nor intuition.

The three became fast friends. Daily contact brought on intimacy. A little later, Camilo's mother died, and in this calamity – which was what it was – the other two stuck by him and showed real friendship. Vilela looked after the funeral, the Masses and the inventory; Rita especially looked after the emotional side of things, and no one could have done it better.

How they moved from this stage to love he never knew. The truth is that he liked spending time in her company; she was his moral nurse, almost a sister, but more than anything else she was a woman, and a pretty one. *Odor di femmina*: that was what he scented in her and around her, and it enveloped him. They read the same books, went to the theatre and on trips together. Camilo taught her draughts and chess and they played in the evenings; she played badly – he, to be agreeable to her, a little less badly. So much for the preliminaries: then there was the woman herself, Rita, with her insistent eyes, which often sought his out, which consulted him before her husband, her cold hands, her unexpected attitudes. One day, on his birthday, he got an expensive walking stick from Vilela, from Rita only a card with plain good wishes in pencil, and it was then he started to read his own heart; he couldn't tear his eyes from the words. Common words; but things can be common and sublime or, at least, delicious. The old hired cab in which you first went for a ride with your loved one with the curtains down is worth as much as Apollo's chariot. That's the nature of man, and of the things that surround him.

Camilo sincerely wanted to escape, but he couldn't. Rita, like a snake, moved closer and closer, wrapped herself round him, made his bones crack in a single spasm, and dropped her venom on his lips. He was stunned, and submitted. Embarrassment, fright, remorse, desire – he felt them all, each mixed with the other; but the battle was short and the victory ecstatic. Goodbye to scruples! It didn't take long for the shoe to adjust itself to the foot, and there they went along the high road, arm in arm, happily treading on plants and pebbles, suffering nothing but a little longing when they were apart. Vilela's trust and esteem were the same as ever.

One day, however, Camilo received an anonymous letter, calling him immoral and perfidious, and saying that their adventure was public knowledge. Camilo was afraid, and, to deflect suspicions, began to visit Vilela's house less often. The latter noticed his absences. Camilo replied that the cause was a trivial, youthful love affair. Innocence bred guile. His absences became longer and longer, until the visits came to a complete stop. Maybe a little *amour propre* came into it too, a desire to lessen the husband's favours, and so make the betrayal itself less burdensome.

It was around this time that Rita, suspicious and fearful, had recourse to the fortune-teller to ask her about the real cause of Camilo's behaviour. We have seen that the fortune-teller restored her trust, and that the young man reprimanded her. A few weeks went by. Camilo got two or three more anonymous letters, so heated, that they couldn't have been prompted by a concern for virtue or morality; they were written by some jealous, thwarted lover; this was Rita's opinion, who formulated this thought in other, ill-expressed words: virtue is lazy and stingy, and doesn't waste time or paper; only self-interest is active and spendthrift.

This made Camilo no less anxious; he feared that the anonymous author would go to see Vilela, and then catastrophe would be unavoidable. Rita agreed it was possible.

'Well,' she said, 'I'll take the envelopes to compare the writing with any letters that appear there; if any are the same, I'll take them and tear them up . . .'

None came; but a little time later Vilela began to look morose, saying little, as if he was suspicious. Rita lost no time in telling her lover, and they deliberated on the matter. Her opinion was that Camilo should go back to their house, sound out her husband, and maybe he would confide some private trouble to him. Camilo begged to differ; to appear after so many months was to confirm the suspicion or the accusation. It was better that they should be cautious, and sacrifice themselves for a few weeks. They fixed a way of exchanging news, if they had to, and tearfully separated.

The following day, at work, Camilo got a message from Vilela: 'Come to our house instantly; I need to speak to you without delay.' It was after midday. Camilo left immediately; in the street, he realised it would have been more natural for Vilela to have asked him to come to his office; why at home? Everything pointed to something unusual, and the handwriting, rightly or not, looked shaky to him. He put all these things together with yesterday's news.

'Come to our house instantly; I need to speak to you without delay,' he repeated, staring at the piece of paper.

In his imagination, he saw the tip of a drama – Rita humiliated and in tears, Vilela indignant, taking up the pen, certain he would come, and waiting there to kill him. Camilo shivered, he was frightened; then he smiled nervously – in any case, any idea of going back was repugnant to him, and he went on his way. As he did so, it occurred to him to go home; he might find a message from Rita explaining everything. There was nothing there, nobody. He went back into the street, and the idea that they had been found out began to seem more and more probable; some kind of anonymous accusation was likely, perhaps from the same person who had threatened him before; maybe Vilela now knew everything. The cessation of his visits for no apparent motive, on a feeble pretext, must have confirmed everything else.

Camilo went on his way, worried and nervous. He didn't reread the note, but he had the words by heart, fixed, in front of his eyes; or, what was even worse, they were whispered in his ear, in Vilela's own voice. 'Come to our house instantly; I need to speak to you without delay.' Said in this way, in another's voice, they had a tone of mystery and menace. Come instantly, what for? It was nearly one in the afternoon. He became more and more agitated by the minute. His imagination was so fixed on what might happen that he began to believe it and see it. He was genuinely afraid. He considered taking a weapon with him, thinking that, if there was nothing wrong, nothing would be lost by doing so, and it was a useful precaution. Soon after, he rejected the idea, ashamed of himself, and went on, hurriedly, towards the

Largo da Carioca, to get a cab. He got there, got in, and ordered the driver to go fast.

'The sooner the better,' he thought, 'I can't carry on in this state . . .'

But even the horse's trotting worsened his anxiety. Time was flying, and very soon he'd be face to face with the danger. Almost at the end of the Rua da Guarda Velha the cab had to stop; the street was blocked by an upturned cart. Camilo, at bottom, was glad of the obstacle, and waited. After five minutes, he noticed that at the roadside, on the left, right by the cab, was the fortune-teller's house, the one Rita had once consulted, and never before had he wanted so much to believe in the lessons the cards had to teach. He looked and saw the windows, closed, while all the others were open and jammed with faces looking at the incident in the street. You might have said it was the abode of indifferent Destiny itself.

Camilo leaned back in the cab, so as to see nothing. He was very agitated indeed, extraordinarily so, and from the depths of his moral being emerged ghosts of another time, old beliefs, ancient superstitions. The cab driver suggested that they go back to the first cross-street, and go by another route; he said no, they should wait. And he leaned forward to look at the house . . . Then he made an incredulous gesture: it was the idea of hearing what the fortune-teller had to say, passing by in the distance, far away, with huge grey wings; the idea disappeared, came back again, and once more faded out of his mind; but a little later it flapped its wings again, closer now, sweeping round in concentric circles. In the street, men were shouting, freeing the cart:

'Right now! Push! Come on, come on!'

The obstacle would soon be removed. Camilo shut his eyes, thought about other things; but the husband's voice whispered in his ears the words of the letter: 'Don't delay, come, come . . .' He saw the twists in this drama, he was shaking. The house was looking at him. His legs wanted to get down and go in . . . Camilo found himself in front of a long opaque veil . . . hurriedly, he thought about how so many things are inexplicable. His mother's voice was telling him about a large number of extraordinary happenings, and the Prince of Denmark's very own words echoed inside him: 'There are more things in heaven and earth than are dreamt of in your philosophy.' What was there to lose, if . . .?

He came to on the pavement, right next to the door, told the driver to wait, and quickly slipped into the corridor and up the stairs. There was very little light, the stairs were worn down and the handrail was sticky; but he saw and felt none of this. He ran up and knocked. Nobody came, and he thought of going back down; but it was too late, his heart was beating fast, his temples throbbing; he knocked, once, twice, three times. A woman came; it was the fortune-teller. Camilo said he'd come to consult her, and she asked him in. From there they went up to the attic, by a staircase worse than the first one, and darker. At the top was a little room, badly lit from a window which gave on to the roofs at the back. Old bits of furniture, dark walls, an air of poverty — all of which, far from destroying the impact of the place, increased it.

The fortune-teller asked him to sit on one side of the table, and herself sat down on the other side, her back to the window, so that the little light coming from outside fully illuminated Camilo's face. She opened a drawer and took out a pack of cards, large and soiled. While she shuffled them, quickly, she was looking at him, not full in the face, but from under her lids. She was a woman of forty, Italian, dark and thin, with big, cunning, acute eyes. She turned three cards on the table over, and said to him:

'First, let's see what brings you here. You've had a shock . . .'

Camilo, astonished, gestured that he had.

'And you want to know,' she went on, 'if something is going to happen to you or not . . .'

'To me and her,' he hurriedly explained.

The fortune-teller didn't smile; she only told him to wait. Quickly she picked up the cards again and shuffled them with her long thin fingers, their nails neglected; she shuffled them well, changing the groups of cards once, twice, three times over; then she began to lay them out. Camilo's eyes were fixed on her, curious and anxious.

'The cards are telling me . . .'

Camilo leaned over to drink her words in one by one. Then she told him not to be afraid of anything. Nothing would happen to one or the other; he, the third person, was ignorant of everything. Nevertheless, they must be very cautious; envy and resentment were seething round them. She told him of the love between them, of Rita's beauty. Camilo was amazed. The fortune-teller finished, gathered up the cards and shut them in the drawer.

'You have given me peace of mind,' he said, stretching over the table, and grasping her hand in his.

She got up, laughing.

'Go on,' she said, 'off you go, *ragazzo innamorato*.'

As she stood there, she touched him on the head with her index finger. Camilo trembled, as if it was the hand of the Sibyl herself, and got up too. The fortune-teller went over to the dresser, on which there was a plate with some raisins, picked a bunch, and began to tear them off and eat them, showing two rows of teeth which formed a vivid contrast to her nails. Even in this everyday act, the woman had a peculiar air about her. Camilo, anxious to go, didn't know how to pay; he didn't know what the price was.

'Raisins cost money,' he said finally, taking out his wallet. 'How many do you want to send out for?'

'Ask your heart,' she replied.

Camilo got a ten *mil-reis* note out, and gave it to her. The fortune-teller's eyes flashed. The usual price was two *mil-reis*.

'I see you love her very much . . . and you're right. She loves you very much too. Go with peace of mind. Careful of the staircase, it's dark; put your hat on . . .'

The fortune-teller had already put the note in her pocket, and was going downstairs with him, talking with a slight accent. Camilo said goodbye to her below and went down the stairs leading to the street, while the fortune-teller, happy with her payment, went back up, humming a barcarolle. Camilo found the cab waiting; the street was clear. He got in and went on at a canter.

Everything seemed better now, things had another aspect to them, the sky was clear, and faces were cheery. He began to laugh at his fears, calling them puerile; he remembered the terms of Vilela's letter and had to recognise they were intimate and familiar. What had he found so menacing? He also noted that the terms of the letter were urgent, and he'd done wrong in taking so much time; it might be something really serious.

'Go as fast as you can,' he said to the cab man more than once.

To himself, so as to explain the delay to his friend, he thought up some story; it seems he also devised a plan to take advantage of the incident to return to the frequent visits . . . Along with the plans, the fortune-teller's words echoed in his soul. It was true, she had divined the object of the consultation, his state of mind, the existence of a third person; why should she not divine the rest? Thus it was, slowly and unerringly, that the young man's old beliefs came back to the surface, and mystery gripped him in its nails of steel. Sometimes he wanted to laugh, and laughed at himself, somewhat shamefaced; but the woman, the cards, the dry, confident words, her exhortation: 'Off you go, *ragazzo innamorato*'; and finally, the barcarolle as she said goodbye, slow and graceful – these were the new elements which, together with the old ones, made up a new and vibrant faith.

The truth is that his heart was content and impatient, thinking of happy times in the past and others which were on their way. As he passed Glória, Camilo looked out over the sea, looked far out, at the point where the sea and sky form an infinite embrace, and had the sensation of a long, long, unbroken future.

A little later he got to Vilela's house. He got down, pushed the iron garden gate and went in. The house was silent. He went up the six stone steps, and had hardly had time to knock when the door opened, and Vilela appeared.

'Sorry, I couldn't come any sooner; what's happened?'

Vilela didn't reply; he had a deranged look; he beckoned him in, and they went into a small room inside. Going in, Camilo couldn't suppress a shriek of terror — at the back, on the sofa, was Rita, dead and bloody. Vilela grabbed him by the throat, and with two shots of his revolver, stretched him out dead on the floor.

The Hidden Cause

G ARCIA WAS STANDING, staring at his fingernails and
cracking his knuckles from time to time; Fortunato,
in a rocking chair, looked at the ceiling; Maria Luisa, near the
window, was finishing off some needlework. For five minutes
none of them had said a thing. They'd talked about the
weather, which had been very pleasant – about Catumbi,
where Fortunato and his wife lived, and about a private
hospital, something we'll explain later. As all three characters
here present are now dead and buried, it's time the story was
told with no holds barred.

They had talked about something else too, something so
serious, so nasty, that they hardly had the heart to talk about
the weather, the neighbourhood and the hospital. Embarrassment held them back. Even now, Maria Luisa's fingers look as
if they're trembling, while Garcia's face wears a severe expression, unusually for him. In fact, the nature of what had
happened was such that to understand it we'll have to take the
story back to its beginnings.

Garcia had graduated in medicine in the previous year,
1861. In 1860, when he was still a student, he met Fortunato
for the first time, in the doorway of the Santa Casa hospital; as

he was going in, the other man was coming out. Fortunato's appearance made an impression; even so he would have forgotten him if it hadn't been for the second encounter a few days later. Garcia was living in the Rua de Dom Manuel. One of his few amusements was to go to the São Januário theatre, which was nearby, between the street and the bay; he went once or twice a month – there were never more than forty people in the audience. Only the most intrepid ventured as far as that part of town. One night, when he'd taken his seat, Fortunato came in and sat next to him.

The play was a melodrama, clumsily put together, bristling with daggers, curses and pangs of conscience; but Fortunato watched with a singular interest. At painful moments, he was doubly attentive; his eyes eagerly went from one character to another, so intently that the student thought the play must be stirring personal memories. The melodrama was followed by a farce; but Fortunato didn't see it through; he left, and Garcia went after him. Fortunato went along the Beco do Cotovelo and the Rua de São José, as far as the Largo da Carioca. He walked slowly, head bent, stopping at times to thwack some sleeping dog with his cane; the dog would yelp, and he would go on his way. In the Largo da Carioca he got into a cab and went off towards the Praça da Constituição. Garcia went back home none the wiser.

Some weeks went by. One night, about nine o'clock, he was at home when he heard voices on the stairway; he went down from his lodgings at the top of the house to the first floor, where an employee of the Arsenal lived. The man was being carried up the stairs, covered in blood. His black servant hurried to open the door; he was groaning, and there was a confusion of voices in the semi-darkness. Once he'd been laid out on the bed, Garcia said they should call a doctor.

'Here's one,' someone volunteered.

Garcia looked: it was the man from the Santa Casa and the theatre. He thought he might be a relative or a friend of the patient; but discarded the notion when he heard him ask if the man had any family or a close friend nearby. The servant said not. He then took charge of affairs, asked the strangers to leave, paid the people who had carried the man, and gave preliminary orders. Knowing Garcia was a neighbour and a medical student, he asked him to stay and help the doctor. Then he recounted what had happened.

'It was a *capoeira* gang.[1] I was coming from the Moura barracks where I'd been to visit a cousin when I heard shouting, and then a loud commotion. It seems they'd attacked another passer-by too, who disappeared up one of those alleyways; but I only saw this man – he was crossing the street when one of the gang brushed past, and knifed him. He didn't fall to the ground straight away; he said where he lived, and as it was no distance away I thought it best to bring him back.'

'Did you know who he was?'

'No, I've never seen him. Who is he?'

'He's a good fellow, an employee at the Arsenal. His name's Gouveia.'

'I don't know him.'

A doctor and a policeman arrived a short time later; his wounds were dressed, and information was taken. The unknown man said his name was Fortunato Gomes da Silveira; he was a bachelor, living off his investments, and came from Catumbi. They agreed the wound was serious. While the doctor was putting the dressings on, assisted by the student, Fortunato acted as servant, holding the bowl, the candle, the cloths, keeping out of the way, looking coldly at the patient, who was groaning out loud. In the end, he had a private conversation with the doctor, accompanied him to the door-way leading to the staircase, and again told the officer he was ready to help the police with their investigation. The doctor and the policeman left, and Fortunato and the student stayed in the room.

Garcia was astonished. He looked at him, saw him calmly sit down, stretch out his legs, put his hands in his trouser pockets, and stare at the sick man. His eyes were pale, the colour of lead; they moved slowly, and had a hard, dry, cold expression. His face was thin and pallid; there was a narrow strip of beard under the chin and from one temple to the other, short, reddish and sparse. He'd be about forty. From time to time, he turned round to the student and asked him something about the patient; but he soon turned back to look at him, in the middle of the young man's answer. Garcia felt repelled as well as curious; there was no denying he was witnessing an act of rare dedication, and if Fortunato was as disinterested as he seemed, the conclusion seemed to be that the human heart is a well of mysteries.

Fortunato left a little before one in the morning; he came back during the next few days, but the recovery was quick, and before it was complete he disappeared without telling the man where he lived. It was Garcia who gave him the name, the street and the number.

'I'll go and thank him for his kindness as soon as I can get out,' said the convalescent.

Six days later, he hurried to Catumbi. Fortunato greeted him with embarrassment, listened impatiently to his words of thanks, replied in an offhand manner and ended up tapping the tassels of his dressing gown on his knee. Gouveia sat silently opposite him and smoothed his hat with his fingers, lifting his eyes from time to time, finding nothing else to say. After ten minutes, he begged leave, and left.

'Steer clear of the *capoeiras*!' Fortunato said, laughing.

The poor fellow came away exasperated, humiliated, chewing over the contempt he'd been treated with, struggling to forget it, explain it or forgive it, and let the favour itself dwell alone in his memory; but all in vain. Resentment, a new and exclusive lodger, moved in, and threw the favour out – all it could do was hide itself at the back of his brain, reduced to a mere idea. Thus it was that the benefactor himself prompted the feeling of ingratitude the man felt.

All this astonished Garcia. The young man had the beginnings of a capacity to decipher men's characters and examine them; he was fond of analysing, and enjoyed the pleasure, than which he knew no greater, of cutting through many moral layers till he felt the living heart of an organism. His curiosity was aroused, and he thought of going to Catumbi to see the man, but then he remembered he hadn't even been formally invited. At the least he needed a pretext, and he couldn't find one.

Some time later, after he'd graduated, and was living on the Rua de Mata-Cavalos, near the Rua do Conde, he met Fortunato on a horse-drawn bus, then ran into him a few more times, until they became familiar with one another. One day Fortunato invited him to go and visit him nearby, in Catumbi.

'You know I've married?'

'No, I didn't know.'

'I got married four months ago; it seems like four days. Come and have dinner with us on Sunday.'

'Sunday?'

'Don't be making up excuses; I'll have none of it. Come on Sunday.'

Garcia went on the Sunday. Fortunato gave him a good dinner, good cigars and good conversation, in the company of his wife, who was an interesting woman. His appearance hadn't changed; his eyes were the same tin plates, hard and cold; his other features were no more attractive than before. However, if the welcome didn't exactly compensate for the nature of the man, it made up for it somewhat, and made a difference. Maria Luisa charmed him, both in her manners and in herself. She was slim, graceful, with soft, submissive eyes; she was twenty-five, but looked no more than nineteen. Garcia, the second time he went there, saw that there was a kind of lack of harmony in their characters, little or no moral affinity, and on the woman's side there were some signs of feelings that went beyond respect, and looked more like resignation or fear. One day, when the three of them were together, Garcia asked Maria Luisa if she'd been informed of how he had met her husband.

'No,' the young woman replied.

'Get ready to hear about a good deed.'

'It's not worth telling,' Fortunato interrupted.

'You'll see whether it's worth telling or not,' the doctor insisted.

He told the story of the Rua de Dom Manuel. She listened, astonished. Instinctively, she stretched out her hand and grasped her husband's wrist, grateful and smiling, as if she'd just discovered his heart. Fortunato shrugged his shoulders, but he wasn't unmoved. He himself then told the story of Gouveia's visit, with all the details of his appearance, his gestures, the words struggling to get out, the silences – he was a halfwit, in fact. He laughed a lot as he told the story. It wasn't false laughter either. Falsity is evasive and oblique; his laughter was jovial and open.

'Strange man!' thought Garcia.

Maria Luisa was upset by her husband's raillery; but the doctor brought back her previous happiness by retelling the story of Fortunato's dedication, and his rare qualities as a nurse; such a good nurse, he concluded, that if one day I set up a private hospital, I'll take him on.

'Shall we?' asked Fortunato.

'Shall we what?'

'Let's set up a hospital.'

'No, no, I'm only joking.'

'We could do something; and for you, just starting out on your career, I think it'd be ideal. I've got a house that's coming vacant, just the thing.'

Garcia refused then, and the next day; but the idea had got into Fortunato's head, and there was no going back. True, it was a good start for him, and might be a money-maker for both. Finally, a few days later, he accepted, to Maria Luisa's disappointment. A nervous, fragile creature, she suffered at the mere notion of her husband being in daily contact with human disease, but she dared not oppose him, and bowed

to the inevitable. The plans were quickly laid and carried out.
It must be said that Fortunato thought about nothing else,
then or later. When the hospital was open he was the
administrator and chief nurse, inspected everything, organised
everything, stores and soups, pills and accounts.

Then Garcia was able to observe that the dedication to
Gouveia was not an isolated case; it was inherent in the man's
very nature. He watched him carry out his duties with more
dedication than the servants themselves. He flinched at nothing; there was no disease too painful or repellent; he was ready
for anything, at any time of the day or night. Everyone was
amazed and delighted. Fortunato studied and followed the
operations, and no one else was allowed to apply the caustics.
'I've a lot of faith in caustics,' he'd say.

Their common interest brought them closer together. Garcia was always at their house; he dined there almost every day,
observing Maria Luisa's character and her life, as her moral
solitude became more obvious. The solitude only seemed to
double her charms. Garcia began to notice that he felt uneasy
when she appeared, when she spoke, when she was silently
working by the window, or playing some sad tune on the piano.
Softly, slowly, love entered his heart. When he realised what
was happening he tried to blot it out, so there should be nothing
other than friendship between him and Fortunato: but he
couldn't. All he could do was shut it in; Maria Luisa saw both
the affection and the silence, but she didn't let it show.

At the beginning of October something happened that
made the young woman's situation even clearer to Garcia.
Fortunato had started studying anatomy and physiology, and
spent his spare time poisoning cats and dogs and cutting them

up. As the animals' squeals unnerved the patients, he moved his laboratory to their house, and his wife, with her nervous disposition, had to put up with them. One day, however, unable to bear it any longer, she went to Garcia and asked him, as a favour to her, to get her husband to stop these experiments.

'But you yourself . . .'

Maria Luisa replied with a smile:

'Of course, he'd say I'm a child. What I want is for you, as a doctor, to tell him that it's doing me harm; and it is, believe me . . .'

Garcia easily got Fortunato to give up these studies. If he continued them elsewhere, nobody found out; maybe he did. Maria Luisa thanked the doctor, for her own sake and that of the animals, for she couldn't bear to see suffering. She coughed from time to time; Garcia asked if there was anything wrong with her; she said no.

'Hold out your wrist.'

'There's nothing the matter.'

She didn't give him her wrist, and left the room. Garcia felt concerned. On the contrary, he thought, maybe there was something wrong, and her husband ought to be warned in time.

Two days later – just the day we first came across them, in fact – Garcia went there to dine. In the parlour, they told him Fortunato was in the study, and he headed that way; as he got near the door, Maria Luisa was coming out, in distress.

'What is it?' he asked.

'The mouse! the mouse!' the young woman exclaimed in a stifled voice, leaving hurriedly.

Garcia remembered that, the day before, he'd heard Fortunato complaining about a mouse that had chewed some
important piece of paper; but he was far from expecting what
he saw. He saw Fortunato sitting at the table, in the middle of
the study, on which he had placed a saucer filled with alcohol.
The burning liquid flickered. Between his thumb and index
finger he held a piece of string, tied round the mouse's tail. In
his right hand he held a pair of scissors. At the moment Garcia
came in, Fortunato cut one of the mouse's legs off; then he
lowered the poor beast into the flame, quickly, so as not to kill
it, and started to do the same with the third leg; he'd already
cut one off. Garcia stopped in his tracks, horrified.

'Kill it at once!' he said.

'Any minute now.'

And with an inimitable smile, the true reflection of a
contented soul as it savoured inwardly the most delicious
of sensations, Fortunate cut the third leg off the mouse, and
for the third time lowered it into the flame. The miserable
animal twisted this way and that, squealing, bleeding,
scorched, and still it didn't die. Garcia averted his eyes, then
looked again, and held out his hand to stop the torture, but he
couldn't, because this man, with the radiant serenity of his
features, inspired fear. There was one leg left; Fortunato cut it
very slowly, following the scissors with his eyes; the leg fell
off, and he stopped to look at the half-dead mouse. As he
lowered it for the fourth time to the flame, he did it deftly, so
as to save, if possible, any shred of life.

Garcia, facing him, managed to control his disgust at the
spectacle and observe the man's expression. No anger, no
hatred; just a vast pleasure, quiet and profound; what you

might get from hearing a beautiful sonata, or looking at a perfect piece of sculpture – something like a pure aesthetic sensation. It seemed to him, rightly, that Fortunato had completely forgotten he was there. If that was true, he couldn't be play-acting – this was the real thing. The flame was dying, the mouse might possibly have a little life left in it, the shadow of a shade; Fortunato turned it to good account by cutting off its nose and again lowering the flesh to the fire. Finally, he let the body drop into the saucer, and pushed the mixture of blood and burned skin away.

When he got up, he saw the doctor and got a shock. He made a show of anger at the animal that had eaten his piece of paper, but it was obviously put on.

'There's no anger in the punishment,' the doctor thought, 'he does it out of the need for a pleasurable sensation, which can only be provided by another creature's pain; that's the man's secret.'

Fortunato laid great stress on the importance of the piece of paper and what he'd lost – only time, admittedly, but time was very precious to him these days. Garcia just listened to him, not saying a word; he didn't believe him for a moment. He remembered his actions, trivial or not, and found the same explanation for all of them. It was as if the man's sensibility had gone through a key-change, to a peculiar kind of dilettantism – he was a Caligula in miniature.

When Maria Luisa came back into the study, a little bit later, her husband went to her, took her hands and quietly said: 'Such a delicate little thing!'

And, turning to the doctor, he said: 'Can you believe she nearly fainted?'

Maria Luisa timidly defended herself, saying she was nervous and a woman, then went and sat by the window with her wool and her needles, her fingers still trembling, just as we found her at the beginning of the story. You'll recall that, after they'd talked about other things, the three of them went quiet, the husband sitting and looking at the ceiling, the doctor cracking his knuckles. A little later they went to have dinner – but it wasn't a happy occasion. Maria Luisa was brooding and coughing; the doctor was wondering if she might not be in some danger in the company of such a man. It was only a possibility; but love turned it into a certainty; he feared for her and determined to keep an eye on them.

She coughed and coughed, and it wasn't long before the disease unmasked itself. It was tuberculosis, that insatiable old hag that sucks life away and leaves only the bones. It was a blow to Fortunato; he really loved his wife in his way, he was used to her, and losing her was a wrench. He spared no effort, doctors, medicines, a change of air, every possible expedient and palliative. But it was all in vain. She was mortally ill.

In the final days, as he watched the girl's final struggle, her husband's nature subdued any other passion. He never left her side; he fixed his cold, dull eyes on the slow, painful decomposition of life, drank in the beautiful creature's afflictions one by one. She was thin, transparent, devoured by fever and riddled with death itself. His exacerbated egotism, hungry for sensations, made him hang on every minute of her agony, nor did he pay for this with a single tear, public or private. Only when she died was he stunned. When he came back to his senses, he saw he was alone again.

At night, when a relative of Maria Luisa's, who had assisted her while she was dying, went to rest, Fortunato and Garcia stayed in the room, keeping vigil, both of them lost in thought; but the husband was tired, and the doctor told him to go and rest awhile.

'Go and lie down, have a couple of hours' sleep: I'll go later.'

Fortunato went out, lay down on the sofa in the next room, and soon went to sleep. Twenty minutes later he woke up, tried to go to sleep again, nodded off for a few minutes, then got up and went back to the sitting room. He went on tiptoes, so as not to wake the relative, who was sleeping nearby. When he got to the door, he stopped short, astonished.

Garcia had approached the body, lifted the veil and looked at her dead features for a few moments. Then, as if death had spiritualised everything, he bent over and kissed her on the forehead. That was when Fortunato came to the door. He stopped short, astonished; it wasn't a kiss of friendship – it might even be the epilogue of an adultery novel. He wasn't jealous, be it noted; nature had made him in such a way that he was neither jealous nor envious, but it had made him vain, and no less subject to resentment than the next man. He looked on in shock, biting his lip.

Meanwhile, Garcia leaned over to kiss the dead body again, but he could control himself no longer. The kiss burst into sobs, the eyes couldn't hold back the tears, which flowed thick and fast; the tears of silent love and irremediable despair. Fortunato, at the door, where he had stopped, quietly savoured this explosion of moral pain, which lasted a long, long, deliciously long time.

A Pair of Arms

I GNACIO TREMBLED AS HE heard the lawyer's shouts, took the plate he was given and tried to eat under a cloudburst of names: layabout, day-dreamer, fool, nutcase.

'Where's your brain gone? Why do you never hear a word I say? I'll tell your father everything, so he can beat the laziness out of your body with a good quince cane or a stick; yes, you're not too old for a beating, don't think you are! Fool! Nutcase!'

'He's just the same out there as he is here,' he went on, turning to Dona Severina, a lady who'd been living with him, maritally so to speak, for years. 'He gets all my papers mixed up, goes to the wrong addresses, goes to one notary when he should go to another, mixes up lawyers' names – it's murder! It's this doze he's in all the time. In the mornings, that's the way it is; you need to break his bones to wake him up . . . leave it to me; tomorrow I'll wake him with a broomstick!'

Dona Severina prodded Borges gently with her foot, as if asking him to stop. He spat out a few more insults, then settled down, at peace with man and God.

I'll not say he was at peace with children, because our friend Ignacio was not exactly a child. He was fifteen, and looked every bit of it. The head was handsome, with its dishevelled hair and the dreamy, inquisitive eyes of a lad who questions, searches and never quite finds – all this crowning a body not without charm, even if it was badly dressed. His father's a barber in Cidade Nova, and placed him as an agent, scribe, clerk, or something of the sort with Borges the lawyer, hoping he'd rise in the world, because he thought barristers got a lot of money. All this took place in the Rua da Lapa, in 1870.

For some minutes there was nothing more than the clink of knives and forks and the noise of chewing. Borges stuffed himself with beef and lettuce; he punctuated the flow with a slug of wine, and carried on in silence.

Ignacio went on eating slowly, not daring to lift his eyes from the plate or put them where they were at the moment the terrible Borges took off at him. The truth is that at this moment it would be very risky. If he so much as let his eyes wander to Dona Severina's arms he'd forget himself, and everything else too.

It was, truly, Dona Severina's fault, going round with them bare all the time. All her indoor dresses had short sleeves, which stopped a few inches below her shoulder; from that point on her arms were on show. They really were lovely and rounded, in harmony with the lady herself, more plump than she was thin, and they lost none of their colour or softness by exposure to the open air; but it is fair to explain that she didn't wear them that way to show off, but because she'd already worn out all her long-sleeved dresses. When she was standing she was very striking; when she walked she swayed in a funny way; Ignacio, however, almost never saw her except at table, where, beyond her arms, he could hardly even see her bust.

You can't say she was pretty; but she wasn't ugly either. She wore no ornament; even her hair was simply arranged; she smoothed, gathered, and tied and fixed it on top of her head with the tortoiseshell comb her mother had left her. At her throat was a dark neckerchief; in her ears, nothing. Her twenty-seven years were solid and in full bloom.

They finished dining. Borges, when the coffee came, took four cigars out of his pocket, compared them, pressed them between his fingers, chose one and put the others back. With his cigar lit, he placed his elbows on the table and spoke to Dona Severina of thirty thousand things that had no interest for our young friend; but while Borges was speaking, he wasn't lambasting him, and he could dream at leisure.

Ignacio made the coffee last as long as he could. Between one sip and the next, he smoothed the cloth down, picked imaginary pieces of skin off his fingers, or let his eyes wander round the pictures in the dining room, which were two, one of St Peter, the other of St John, devotional pictures bought at festival time and framed at home. We can believe he could disguise his thoughts with St John, whose young head brings cheer to Catholic imaginations; but with the austere St Peter it is going a bit far. Ignacio's only defence is that he saw neither one nor the other. All he saw was Dona Severina's arms – either because he took a sly look at them, or because they were imprinted on his memory.

'Come on, man! Are you never going to finish?' the lawyer shouted suddenly.

There was no help for it; Ignacio drank the last cold drop and retired, as usual, to his room at the back of the house. As he went in he made a gesture of anger and despair, and later went to lean out of one of the two windows looking over the sea. Five minutes later, the sight of the water nearby and the far-off mountains gave him a confused, vague, restless feeling, painful and pleasurable at the same time, like something a plant must feel when its first flower comes into bud. He wanted to leave, and he wanted to stay. He'd been there for five weeks, and life was the same every day, out in the morning with Borges, going round courts and notaries, running round, taking papers to be stamped, to the post, to scribes and officials. He came back in the afternoon, had lunch and went to his room until supper-time; he had his supper and went to bed. Borges didn't admit him into the family circle, which consisted only of Dona Severina, and Ignacio saw her no more than three times a day, at meals. Five weeks of solitude, of drudgery, far from his mother and sisters; five weeks of silence, because he only said anything once or twice in the street; in the house, he never said a word.

'You'll see,' he thought one day, 'I'll run away from here and not come back.'

He didn't; he felt bound and chained to Dona Severina's arms. He'd never seen any as pretty and as fresh. His upbringing didn't allow him to look at them openly; it seems, in fact, that at the beginning he withdrew his eyes in embarrassment. He began to look little by little, once he saw that they never had sleeves to cover them, and he gradually discovered them, looking and loving. At the end of three weeks they were, morally speaking, the tents where he took his repose. He put up with all the work in town, all the melancholy of solitude and silence, and all his boss's rude abuse, just for the reward of seeing, three times a day, the famous pair of arms.

That day, when night was falling and Ignacio was stretching out in his hammock (he had no other bed), Dona Severina, in the front room, was thinking over the dinner episode and, for the first time, she suspected something. She rejected the idea immediately – he was only a boy! But there are ideas akin to insistent flies: the more we beat them off, the more they come back and alight on us. A boy? He was fifteen; and she noticed that between the lad's nose and mouth there was the beginning of a sketch of fuzz. Was it so astonishing that he was beginning to fall in love? And wasn't she pretty? This last idea wasn't rejected; rather it was caressed and kissed. Then she remembered his demeanour, his distracted air, his oversights – one incident after another; these were all symptoms, and she thought yes, it was true.

'What's the matter with you?' said the lawyer to her, stretching out on the settee, after a few minutes' silence.

'Me? Nothing.'

'Nothing? It seems everything's asleep in this house! Leave it to me, I know a good medicine for waking sleepyheads . . .'

And so he went on, in the same angry tone, firing off threats, but in fact incapable of carrying them out, for he was more of a loudmouth than a truly nasty man. Dona Severina kept telling him no, he was mistaken, she wasn't asleep, she was thinking about her good friend Fortunata. They hadn't been to see her since Christmas; why didn't they go over there some night soon? Borges replied that he was tired all the time, working like a black man, and he'd no time for idle chat; and he attacked Fortunata, her husband, and their son, who wasn't going to school, at the age of ten! He, Borges, when he was ten, already knew how to read, write and do his sums, not very well, it's true, but at least he knew. Ten! He'd come to a good end: a good-for-nothing, he'd be press-ganged in no time. Life in the army would teach him a lesson.

Dona Severina soothed him with excuses, Fortunata's poverty, her husband's bad luck, and caressed him a little fearfully, in case the caresses irritated him some more. It was completely dark; she heard the click of the gas lamp, which had just come on, and saw its glimmer in the windows of the house over the street. Borges, tired out after his day, for he really did work very hard, closed his eyes and started to drop off. He left her in the room, in the dark, alone with herself and the discovery she'd just made.

Everything seemed to tell the lady it was true; but this truth, once she'd got over the surprise, brought with it a moral complication, which she only recognised by its effects; she couldn't put her finger on what it was. She couldn't understand herself or settle down, and even thought of telling the lawyer everything, so that he would send the youngster away. But what did it all amount to? Here she stopped in her tracks: in reality, there was nothing more than supposition, coincidence and possibly illusion. No, no, it wasn't an illusion. Then she started piecing together the vague clues, the lad's attitudes, his shyness, his distractedness, till she rejected the idea that she was mistaken. In a short while (O perfidious nature!), reflecting that it would be wrong to accuse him baselessly, she admitted she might be deluded, with the single aim of observing him better and seeing what was really going on.

That very night, Dona Severina looked from under her eyelids at Ignacio's gestures; she saw nothing, because tea didn't take long, and the lad didn't take his eyes off the cup. The next day she was able to observe him better, and later still, extremely well. She saw it was true, she was loved and feared, with an adolescent, virginal love, held back by social ties and a feeling of inferiority which prevented him from understanding himself. Dona Severina realised that she need fear no misdemeanour, and concluded it was better to say nothing to the lawyer; she would save him from one nasty surprise, and the poor child from another. She was already persuading herself that he was a child, and determined to treat him as coolly as she had done till now, or even more so. So she did; Ignacio began to feel that her eyes avoided his, or she spoke sharply, almost as much so as Borges himself. It is true that at other times her tone of voice came out quite soft and even gentle, very gentle; in just the same way her look, generally elusive, wandered elsewhere so much that, just to find some rest, it would sometimes alight on his head; but all this was fleeting.

'I'm going to leave,' he repeated in the street, as he had when he was first there.

But he'd come back to the house, and he didn't leave. Dona Severina's arms formed a parenthesis in the middle of the long and tedious sentence of the life he was leading, and this inserted phrase had an original and profound idea embedded in it, invented by Heaven only for him. He stayed and carried on as before. In the end, however, he had to leave, and for good; here's how and why.

Dona Severina had been treating him with some benevolence. The roughness in her voice seemed to have disappeared, and there was more than softness, there was care and affection. One day she would tell him to keep out of draughts, another that he shouldn't drink cold water after hot coffee, reminders, advice, the considerate thoughts of a friend and mother, which threw his soul into even greater anxiety and confusion. Ignacio grew so confident of himself that he laughed one day at the table, something he'd never done; and the lawyer didn't berate him this time, because it was he who was telling a funny story, and no one punishes anyone for applauding them. It was then that Dona Severina saw that the boy's mouth, charming when he was silent, was no less charming when he laughed.

Ignacio's agitation grew; he couldn't keep calm or understand what was happening to him. Nowhere did he feel easy. He'd wake up at night, thinking about Dona Severina. In the street, he would take wrong turnings, go to the wrong doors, much more than before, and he couldn't set eyes on a woman, nearby or far off, who didn't remind him of her. When he entered the house along the corridor as he returned from work, he always felt some excitement; sometimes a great deal, when he saw her at the top of the stairs, looking at him through the wooden slats of the door, as if having come to see who it was.

One Sunday – he never forgot that Sunday – he was alone in his room, at the window, looking at the sea, which was whispering the same obscure new language as Dona Severina. He amused himself watching the gulls describing circles in the air, alighting on the water or simply fluttering round. It was a beautiful day. It wasn't just a Christian Sunday; it was an immense, universal Sunday.

Ignacio always spent these days there in his room or looking out of the window, or rereading one of the three little books he'd brought with him, stories of times past, bought for next to nothing under the archway in the Largo do Paço. It was two in the afternoon. He was tired, he'd slept badly, having walked around a great deal the previous day; he stretched out in the hammock, picked up one of the books, *Princess Magalona*, and began reading. He'd never been able to understand why all the heroines in these old stories had the same face and figure as Dona Severina, but the fact was that they had. After half an hour, he let the book drop and stared at the wall, from where, five minutes later, he saw the mistress of his thoughts emerge. He should have been astonished; but he wasn't. Even though his lids were shut, he saw her detach herself completely, stop, smile, and walk towards the hammock. It was she; those were her arms.

The truth is, however, that not only could Dona Severina not have emerged from the wall, supposing there to have been a door or a fissure there – but she was in the front room, listening to the lawyer's footsteps as he went downstairs. She heard him go down; she went to the window and only came back when he'd disappeared into the distance, on his way to the Rua das Mangueiras. Then she came in and went to sit on the settee. She seemed out of sorts, restless, almost manic; getting up, she went to pick up a jar on the sideboard and put it back where it had been; then she walked as far as the door, stopped and turned back, for no reason at all, it seems. She sat down again, for five or ten minutes. Suddenly, she remembered that Ignacio hadn't eaten much at breakfast and looked a bit downcast. It occurred to her he might be ill – maybe he was very ill indeed.

She went out of the door, hurriedly crossed the corridor and went to the lad's room, finding the door wide open. Dona Severina stopped, peeped in, and saw him in the hammock, asleep, with his arm hanging down and the book on the floor. His head was turned a little towards the door, so one could see his eyes were closed; his hair was tousled and he had a smiling, blissful look about him.

Dona Severina's heart beat violently, and she drew back. She had dreamed of him the previous night; maybe he was dreaming about her now. Since daybreak, the lad's image had been floating in front of her eyes like a temptation of the devil. She drew back further, then came forward again, and looked for two, three, five minutes or more. It seems sleep gave an emphasis to Ignacio's adolescence, an almost feminine, child-like expression. A child! she said to herself, in that wordless language we all have within us. This idea slowed the rush of blood to her heart and partially calmed her agitated feelings.

'A child!'

She looked him over slowly, surfeited herself with looking at him, with his head bent to one side, his arm drooping; but, at the same time as she found him childlike, she found him handsome, much more than when he was awake, and one of these notions corrected or corrupted the other. Suddenly she shuddered and drew back in shock: she'd heard a noise nearby, in the ironing closet. She went to look – a cat had knocked a bowl on to the floor. Slowly, quietly coming back to look at him, she saw he was in a deep sleep. How soundly the boy slept! The noise that had given her such a fright hadn't even made him change position. And she went on looking at him sleeping – sleeping, dreaming, who knows?

How sad we can't see each other's dreams! Dona Severina would have seen herself in the boy's imagination; she would have seen herself standing by the hammock, smiling and motionless; then leaning over, taking his hands, lifting them to her chest and enfolding them in her arms, her wondrous arms. Ignacio, fond as he was of her arms, even so heard her words, which were beautiful, warm, and above all new – or, at least, they belonged to some language he didn't know, even though he understood it. Two, three, four times the figure faded away, only to return, coming from the sea or somewhere else, flying with the gulls, and crossing the corridor, with all the robust charm she was capable of. And coming back, she leaned over, took his hands in hers again and folded her arms across her chest, until, leaning over further, much further, she pursed her lips and gave him a kiss on the mouth.

Here the dream coincided with reality, and the same mouths were united in the imagination and outside it. The difference is that the vision did not draw back, and the real person had no sooner completed this movement than she fled to the door, ashamed and afraid. From there she went to the front room, stunned by what she had done, unable to fix her eyes on anything. Her ears were on stalks, she went to the end of the corridor to see if she could hear any noise that might tell her he was awake, and only after a long time did the fear begin to subside. It really was true that the lad slept soundly; nothing would open his eyes, whether it was a nearby crash, or a real kiss. But, if the fear faded, her shame stayed and grew. Dona Severina couldn't believe she'd done a thing like that; it seems she'd wrapped up her desires in the idea that in front of her was an adoring child, unconscious and blameless; and half-mother, half-friend, she had leaned over and kissed him. However that may be, she was confused, irritated, annoyed at herself and at him. The fear that he might be pretending he was asleep surfaced in her soul and made her shiver.

But the truth is that he slept for much longer, and only woke for supper. He sat eagerly down at the table. Although he found Dona Severina silent and severe and the lawyer as sharp as ever, neither the sharpness nor the severity could dissolve the charming scene he still had in his mind, nor could they dull the sensation of the kiss. He didn't notice that Dona Severina was wearing a shawl covering her arms; he noticed later, on the Monday, and the Tuesday, and until the Saturday, when Borges sent to tell his father that he couldn't keep him any longer. He didn't do it angrily, treating him relatively well, and even saying as he left:

'If you need me for anything, look me up.'

'Yes, sir. Senhora Dona Severina . . .'

'She's in her room, with a bad headache. Come back tomorrow or the next day to say goodbye to her.'

Ignacio left without understanding a thing. The dismissal, the complete change in Dona Severina's attitude towards him, the shawl, it was all a mystery to him. She seemed so content! She spoke to him so kindly! How, so suddenly . . . He thought about it so much that he ended up surmising that some indiscreet look or a momentary distraction had offended her. That must be it; that explained the frowning face and the shawl covering those beautiful arms . . . Never mind; he took the taste of the dream away with him. And for many years, passing through other love affairs, more tangible and longer, he never found a sensation like the one he felt that Sunday, in the Rua da Lapa, when he was fifteen years old. Sometimes, unaware of his mistake, he himself exclaims:

'And it was a dream! No more than a dream!'

The Cynosure of All Eyes

'C OME, COME, COUNSELLOR, you're beginning to talk in verse.'

'All men should have their lyrical side – without it, they're not men. I'm not saying it should surface all the time, or for just any reason; but now and then, for some particular memory . . . Do you know why I sound like a poet, in spite of my grey hairs and my lawyer's training? It's because we're walking along here by Glória, by the foreign ministry . . . There's the famous hill . . . Just ahead there, there's a house . . .'

'Let's walk on.'

'Let's go . . . Divine Quintilia! All these faces passing by have changed, but they speak to me of that time, as if they were just the same; it's that lyrical side again, and my imagination does the rest. Divine Quintilia!'

'Was that her name? When I was a medical student, I knew a lovely girl called that, though only by sight. They said she was the most beautiful girl in town.'

'It'll be the same one, because she had that reputation. Tall and thin, was she?'

'That's the one. What became of her?'

'She died in 1859. The twentieth of April. I'll never forget the day. I'll tell you what I think is an interesting story, and I think you'll find it interesting too. Look, that's the house . . . She lived with an uncle, a retired naval commander; she had another house in Cosme Velho. When I met Quintilia . . . How old do you think she was when I met her?'

'If it was in 1855 . . .'

'It was.'

'She must have been twenty.'

'She was thirty.'

'Thirty?'

'Thirty. She didn't look it, but it wasn't just said by some rival. She admitted to it herself, even insisted on it. In point of fact, one of her friends said that Quintilia was no older than twenty-seven; but since both of them were born on the same day, she said it to make herself look younger.'

'Now, now, less of the irony; you can't be ironic *and* nostalgic.'

'What is nostalgia but an irony of time and fortune? There you are; I'm beginning to sound pompous. Thirty; but she really didn't look it. Remember too that she was tall and thin; as I used to say back then, she had eyes that seemed as if they'd just been plucked from the night sky, but though they were dark, they had no mysteries, no depths. Her voice was very soft, with a bit of a São Paulo accent, and an ample mouth; she only had to talk, and her teeth made it seem she was laughing. She laughed, too, and it was her laughter, together with her eyes, that caused me a great deal of pain for a long while.'

'But if her eyes had no mysteries . . .'

'It's true; so much so that I thought they were the open doors to the castle, and her laughter the clarion summoning the knights to combat. We already knew her, my colleague João Nóbrega and I, when we were both beginning our careers and were very close friends; but it never occurred to us to woo her. She was on the top rung; she was beautiful, rich, elegant and a member of high society. But one day, in the old Pedro II theatre, between two acts of *I Puritani*,[1] when I was in the corridor, I heard a group of young men talking about her, referring to her as an impregnable fortress. Two of them confessed they'd tried something on, but had got nowhere; and all of them were amazed by the girl's aloofness, for which they could find no explanation. And they joked about it: one said that it was a vow, and she wanted to see if she could get fat first; another that she was waiting for her uncle's second childhood so she could marry him; another that she'd probably had a guardian angel specially sent from heaven – childish comments that annoyed me a good deal. Coming from people who admitted they'd wooed her or fallen for her, I thought they were appalling. What they did all agree on was that she was extraordinarily beautiful; on that point, they were enthusiastic and sincere.'

'Oh! I can still remember! . . . She was very pretty.'

'The next day, when I got to the office, in between two of our non-existent cases, I told Nóbrega what I'd heard the day before. Nóbrega laughed, went thoughtful, paced around a bit and stopped in front of me, silently staring. "I bet you're in love with her?" I asked. "No," he said, "nor you? I've had an idea: let's see if we can take the fortress. What have we got to lose? Nothing; either she sends us packing, as is only to be expected, or she accepts one of us, and all the better for the loser, who'll see his friend happy." "Are you serious?" "Very." Nóbrega added that it wasn't just her beauty that made her attractive. It's as well to say that he prided himself on being the practical sort, but in fact he was a dreamer who spent all his time reading and constructing social and political systems. In his opinion, what those lads in the theatre had avoided mentioning was the girl's wealth, which was one of her charms, and one of the probable causes of the distress some suffered, and the sarcasm they all dispensed. He said: "Listen, money isn't everything, but you can't ignore it; we shouldn't think it's the be-all and end-all, but we should admit it provides something – quite a lot, in fact: this watch, for example. Let's fight for our Quintilia, mine or yours, but probably mine, because I'm the more handsome of the two." '

'Counsellor, this is a serious thing to confess to; was this the way it began, just a joke . . . ?'

'Just a joke; like a couple of foolish students, we entered on such an important matter – it might have ended in nothing, but it had consequences. It was a silly beginning, like a children's game, with nothing sincere about it; but man proposes and the species disposes. We knew her, though we'd not met her often; once we'd started on this common enterprise, a new element came into our life, and in a month we'd fallen out.'

'Fallen out?'

'Or almost. We hadn't reckoned on her, and she cast a powerful spell on us. Within a few weeks we hardly mentioned Quintilia, and then it was with indifference; we were trying to dupe one another, and hide what we were feeling.

That was how our friendship collapsed, after six months, with no hatred or quarrels, nothing overtly said, because we still spoke to each other, when we met accidentally; but we had separate offices.'

'I'm beginning to see the beginnings of a drama . . .'

'Tragedy, rather, call it a tragedy; because a little time later, either because she had told him to desist, or because he gave up hope, Nóbrega left the field to me. He got himself appointed as a judge in a small town in the backlands of Bahia, where he pined away and died before he was forty. And I swear to you it wasn't Nóbrega's vaunted practical sense that separated us; he, who used to talk so much about the importance of having money, died of love like Werther.'

'Without the pistol.'

'Poison kills too; and love for Quintilia could be said to be something like that; it killed him, and still gives me pain . . . But I see I'm getting on your nerves . . .'

'Not for the world. No, I swear to you; it was just a stupid wisecrack. Go on, Counsellor; you were alone in the field.'

'Quintilia never left anyone alone in the field – not that it was her doing; others answered for that. Many came to drink a hopeful little aperitif, and then went off to dine elsewhere. She showed no particular favours to anyone; but she was affable, charming, and her eyes had a liquid quality about them not made for the jealous among us. I was bitterly, sometimes violently jealous. I thought every mote a beam, and every beam the devil incarnate. In the end, I got used to the idea that they only lasted a day or two. Others gave me more cause for alarm; they were the ones introduced by lady friends. I think these led to one or two attempts at negotiation, but nothing came of it. Quintilia said she would do nothing without consulting her uncle, and the uncle advised refusal – something she knew would happen. The good old fellow never liked men visiting, out of fear his niece would choose one and marry. He was so used to having her by him; it was as if he needed a crutch for his soul, and was afraid of losing her altogether.'

'Maybe that was the cause of the girl's systematic coldness?'

'You'll see not.'

'What I can see is that you were more stubborn than the rest . . .'

'. . . Deluded, at first, because in the midst of so many failed candidates, Quintilia preferred me to all other men, and spoke to me more openly and intimately, so much so that the rumour got around that we were to be married.'

'But what did you talk about?'

'About everything she didn't talk to others about; and it was astonishing how a person who loved balls and excursions, waltzing and laughing, was so serious and earnest with me, so different from what she was, or seemed to be.'

'It's obvious why: she found your conversation less trivial than that of other men.'

'Thank you; the cause of the difference was deeper than that, and it grew over time. When life here in town got on her nerves she went up to Cosme Velho, and there our conversations became longer and more frequent. I can't tell you – you wouldn't understand anyway – what the hours I spent there were like; all the life bursting out of her blended into mine. Often I wanted to tell her what I felt, but the words took fright and stayed in my heart. I wrote one letter after another; all of them seemed cold, wordy or pompous. What's more, she never gave any opening; she seemed like an old friend. At the beginning of 1857 my father fell ill in Itaboraí; I hurried to his bedside, and found him dying. This kept me away from Rio for some four months. I came back around the end of May. When I visited Quintilia, she seemed affected by my sadness, and I saw clearly that my mourning had migrated to her eyes . . .'

'But surely that could only be love?'

'That's what I thought, and I organised my effects as if to marry her. At that point, her uncle fell seriously ill. Quintilia wouldn't be left alone if he died, because, as well as a lot of other relatives she had here and there, there was a cousin living with her now, in the Catete house, Dona Ana, a widow; still, it is true that her principal companion would no longer be there, and in this transition from the present life to the future, I might get what I wanted. The uncle's illness was short; old age contributed, and it took him in a space of two weeks. I can tell you that his death reminded me of my father's, and I felt almost the same grief. Quintilia saw my suffering, understood the double cause, and, so she told me later, she was glad of the coincidence, since it had to happen anyway, and it happened quickly. These words seemed to me like an invitation to marriage; two months later I decided to ask for her hand. Dona Ana was now living with her, and they were up in Cosme Velho. I went there, and found them both on the terrace, which was close to the mountain. It was four o'clock on a Sunday afternoon. Dona Ana, who thought we were in love, left the field open.'

'At last!'

'The terrace was a solitary place, even a bit wild – it was there I said the first word. My plan was to precipitate everything, afraid that after five minutes of conversation my strength would fail me. Even so, you've no idea what it cost me; a real battle would have been less effort, and I swear to you I wasn't born for war. But that thin delicate woman held more sway over me than any other, before or after . . .'

'Well then?'

'Quintilia had gathered what I was going to ask her by the strength of feeling evident in my face, and let me speak so she could prepare her reply. Her reply was interrogative and negative. Marry, what for? It was better for us to remain friends. I answered that friendship had been for me, for a long time, the mere sentinel of love; now love could no longer be contained, I'd let it come out in the open. Quintilia smiled at the metaphor, which hurt me, needlessly; seeing the effect she'd had, she became serious again, and set out to persuade me that it was better not to marry. "I'm old," she said; "nearly thirty-three." "But I love you just the same," I replied, and said a whole lot of things I can't possibly repeat now. Quintilia reflected for a moment; then she insisted again on feelings of friendship; she said that, though I was younger than her, I had the dignity of an older man, and inspired confidence in her as no one else did. I paced around a bit in despair, then sat down again and recounted everything. When she heard about my fight with my friend and fellow student, and the way we had separated, she felt upset or irritated, I'm not sure which is the right word. She blamed us both; we should never have gone so far. "You say that," I said, "because you don't feel the same." "But is it some kind of delirium?" "I think so; what I

can swear to you is that still now, if I had to, I'd break with
him a hundred times over; and I think I can say he would do
the same thing." Here she looked at me in shock as one might
at someone no longer in charge of his faculties; then she shook
her head, and repeated that it had been a mistake; it wasn't
worth it. "Let's stay friends," she said, holding out her hand.
"It's impossible," I said, "you're asking something beyond my
power to give, I can never see you as just a friend; I don't want
to impose anything on you; I'll even say that I'll insist no
longer, because no other reply would satisfy me now." We
exchanged a few more words, and I left . . . Look at my
hand.'

'It's still shaking . . .'

'And I've still not told you everything. I won't tell about
the distress I underwent, nor the pain and resentment I was
left with. I was angry, sorry I'd done what I had – I should
have provoked her to it in the early weeks; but hope was to
blame – it's a weed, and it took over the space occupied by
other, more useful plants. After five days, I left for Itaboraí to
attend to some business connected with my father's will.
When I came back, three weeks later, I found a letter from
Quintilia waiting for me at home.'

'Oh!'

'I opened it with my heart in turmoil: it was four days old.
It was long; it alluded to recent events, and its tone was tender
and serious. Quintilia said she had waited for me every day,
not thinking I could be so egotistical as never to go back, and
for that reason she was writing to me, to ask me to make my
personal, unrequited feelings history; to be a friend, and go
and see her as a friend. She ended with these strange words:

"Do you want a guarantee? I swear to you that I will never marry." I realised that a bond of moral sympathy linked us; with the difference that what for me was a physical passion was for her simply an elective affinity. We were two partners, entering the business of life with different capital: I with everything I had; she with barely more than a shilling. That's how I answered her letter; and I declared that my obedience and my love were such that I gave way, but unwillingly, because after what had happened between us, I would feel humiliated. I crossed out "ridiculous", which I'd already written, so that I could go and see her without that embarrassment – the other word was enough.'

'I bet you followed soon after the letter? That's what I'd do, because either I'm much mistaken or that girl was dying to marry you.'

'Forget your usual psychological theories; this is a very individual case.'

'Let me guess the rest; the oath was a sublime stratagem; later, you, the recipient, could release her from it, so long as you got the benefits of your own absolution. But, anyway, you hurried to her house.'

'I didn't; I went two days later. In the meantime, she replied to my letter with an affectionate note, which concluded with this argument: "Don't speak of humiliation, where there were no witnesses." I went, returned a few times, and we re-established our relationship. Nothing was said; at first, it was a great effort to pretend I was as I had been; then, the accursed hope lodged in my heart again; and, saying nothing, I thought that one day, in the future, she'd marry me. It was that hope that made me able to look myself in the eye, in the situation I found myself in. Rumours of impending marriage got around. They reached our ears; I denied them, formally and with a serious look; she shrugged her shoulders and laughed. That was the most serene period of our life for me, except for a brief incident with a diplomat, Austrian or something of the sort, a strapping fellow, elegant, red-haired, large attractive eyes, and a nobleman to boot. Quintilia was so charming with him that he thought he'd found favour, and tried to take the matter further. I think some quite unconscious gesture of mine, or perhaps a little bit of Heaven-sent intuition, soon brought disillusionment to the Austrian legation. A little later she fell ill; and then our friendship grew. She decided she shouldn't go out while she was being treated, and those were the doctors' orders. I spent many hours a day there. Quintilia and her cousin played the piano, or we had a game of cards, or read something; mostly, we just talked. That was when I studied her closely. Listening to her reading, I saw that she found books about love incomprehensible, and if there was violent passion she was bored and put them aside. It wasn't that she was ignorant; she had vaguely heard about passion, and had witnessed it in other cases.'

'What illness did she have?'

'It was in her spinal column. The doctors said that perhaps it had been there for a while, and it was getting dangerous. It was now 1859. From March of that year on, the illness got much worse; it gave a short respite, but towards the end of the month things were in a desperate state. Never since have I seen anyone react with more energy to an imminent catastrophe; she was so thin she was transparent, almost pellucid; she laughed, or rather smiled, and seeing me hiding my tears she gratefully pressed my hands. One day, when I was alone with the doctor, she asked him for the truth; he tried to lie; she said it was useless – there was no hope. "I wouldn't say that," the doctor murmured. "Do you swear?" He hesitated, and she thanked him. Now she was certain she would die, she organised what she'd promised herself.'

'She married you, I'll wager?'

'Don't remind me of that unhappy ceremony; or rather, let me remind myself, because it brings me a breath of the past. She wouldn't accept my refusals or pleas; she married me at the portals of death. It was on the eighteenth of April, 1859. I spent the last days, till the twentieth of April, at my dying bride's bedside, and embraced her for the first time when she was a corpse.'

'It's all very strange.'

'I don't know what your theories would tell you. I'm only a layman in these matters, but I think that girl had a purely physical aversion to marriage. She married when she was half dead, at the edge of the abyss. Call her a monster if you like, but say she was divine too.'

A Famous Man

'OH! ARE YOU PESTANA?' asked Sinhazinha Mota[1], holding up her hands in admiration. And then, correcting herself, in a less familiar tone: 'Excuse my manners, but . . . are you really he?'

Embarrassed and annoyed, Pestana answered yes, it was he. He'd just got up from the piano, and was mopping his brow with a handkerchief as he went over to the window, when the girl made him stop. It wasn't a ball; just an intimate soirée, not many people, twenty in all, who'd come to dine with the widow Camargo, on the Rua do Areal – this was on her birthday, 5 November 1875 . . . What a cheery person she was, the good widow! She enjoyed fun and games, in spite of her sixty years, and it was the last time she enjoyed them, for she died in early 1876. What a cheery person! With what loving care she set up some dancing, right after dinner, asking Pestana to play a quadrille! She didn't have to finish her request; Pestana bowed graciously, and hastened to the piano. When the quadrille was over, they'd hardly had ten minutes' rest when the widow rushed over to Pestana again to ask a very particular favour.

'Just say, madam.'

'It's for you to play that polka of yours, "Don't Meddle with Me, Young Sir".'

Pestana made a face, but soon disguised it, inclined silently, ungraciously, and went unenthusiastically to the piano. As soon as the first measures sounded, a new, different happiness spread through the room, the gentlemen hurried over to the ladies, and they began to shake their hips in time to the latest polka. The latest: it had been published three weeks ago, and there was no corner of the city where it was unknown. It had reached the point where it was being whistled and hummed in the streets at night.

Sinhazinha Mota had been far from surmising that the same Pestana she'd seen at the dining table and later at the piano, in his snuff-coloured frock-coat, with long curly black hair, cautious eyes and shaven chin, was really Pestana the composer; it was a friend who'd told her as she saw him leaving the piano when the polka was done. Hence the admiring question. We've seen his answer was embarrassed and annoyed. Even so, the two girls spared him no flatteries; such they were, and so many, that the most modest of vanities would have been pleased to hear them. He greeted them with growing irritation, until, pleading a headache, he asked to be excused. Nobody, neither the girls nor the lady of the house, could detain him. They offered him home remedies, or a little rest; he accepted nothing, insisted on leaving and left.

In the street he walked fast, fearful they might still call after him; he only slowed down after he'd turned the corner of the Rua Formosa. But even there his famous festive polka lay in wait. From a modest house on the right, a few yards away, came the notes of the latest tune, played on a clarinet. There was dancing. Pestana stopped for a few moments, thought of retracing his steps, but pressed on, quickened his step, crossed the street, and went by on the opposite side from the house with the dancing. Gradually the notes faded away, far off, and our friend went into the Rua do Aterrado, where he lived. When he was getting close to home, he saw two men approaching; one of them, passing right close to Pestana, began to whistle the same polka, vigorously, con brio; the other picked up on the tempo, and off down the street went the two of them, noisy and happy, while the tune's author, in desperation, ran to take shelter at home.

At home, he breathed easier. It was an old house, with an old staircase, and an old black servant, who came to ask if he wanted to have dinner.

'I don't want a thing,' Pestana shouted; 'make me some coffee and go to bed.'

He got undressed, put a nightgown on, and went to the back room. When the servant lit the gas, Pestana smiled and, in his heart, greeted some ten portraits hanging on the wall. Only one was in oils, of a priest who had educated him, taught him Latin and music, and who, according to idle tongues, was Pestana's father. He certainly had left him the old house, with the old furniture, dating from the time of Pedro I.[2] This priest had composed some motets, was mad about music, sacred or profane, and instilled the taste for it in the boy – unless he'd also transmitted it in his blood, that's if the gossips were right. But this is something my story is not concerned with, as you'll see.

The other portraits were of classical composers, Cimarosa, Mozart, Beethoven, Gluck, Bach, Schumann and some three more. Some were engravings, others lithographs, all of them badly framed and of different sizes, but put there like saints in a church. The piano was the altar; the gospel for the night was open: it was a Beethoven sonata.

The coffee came; Pestana swallowed the first cup, and sat down at the piano. He looked at Beethoven's portrait, and began to play the sonata, oblivious to himself, absorbed, as if in a delirium, but with the greatest perfection. He repeated the piece; then stopped for some moments, got up and went to one of the windows. He went back to the piano; it was Mozart's turn – he picked on a passage and played it in the same way, with his soul in another place. Haydn took him up to midnight and the second cup of coffee.

Between midnight and one o'clock, Pestana did little more than stand at the window and stare at the stars, then go back into the room and look at the portraits. From time to time he went to the piano, and, without sitting down, played some disconnected notes, as if searching for some idea; but the idea didn't come and he went back to lean at the window. The stars looked like musical notes fixed in the sky waiting for someone to loosen them; the time would come when the heavens would be empty, but then the earth would be a constellation of musical scores. No image, reverie or reflection had any echo of Sinhazinha Mota, who, however, at this moment was thinking about him as she went to sleep, he, the famous author of so many beloved polkas. Maybe some idea of marriage prevented her sleeping for a little while. What's so surprising? She was nearly twenty, he nearly thirty, a good age. The girl slept to the sound of the polka, which she knew by heart, while the author of the said polka wasn't thinking about it or her, but the old classical works, scanning the night and the heavens, begging the angels, in a last resort the devil himself. Why couldn't he write even one of those immortal pages?

At times, it seemed as if the dawn of an idea was going to arise from the depths of his unconscious; he ran to the piano to try it out entire, to translate it into sounds, but in vain; the idea vanished. At other moments, sitting at the piano, he let his fingers run over the keys, at random, to see if fantasias sprung from them, as they did from Mozart's; but nothing, nothing, inspiration didn't come and his imagination still lay sleeping. If by chance an idea appeared, well-defined and beautiful, it was just the echo of someone else's music, repeated from memory, and that he'd thought he was inventing. Then, irritated, he got up, swore he would give up art and go and plant coffee or push a cart round the streets; but ten minutes later, there he was, with his eyes on Mozart and imitating him at the piano.

Two, three, four o'clock. After four he went to bed; he was tired, despondent, dead with fatigue; he had to give lessons the next day. He didn't sleep much; at seven he was awake. He got up and had breakfast.

'Master, do you want your stick or your umbrella?' asked the servant, following orders, for his master was frequently distrait.

'The stick.'

'But it seems it's going to rain today.'

'Rain,' Pestana repeated mechanically.

'It seems so, sir, the sky's getting darker.'

Pestana stared vacantly at the servant, his mind preoccupied. Suddenly:

'Wait there.'

He ran to the room with the portraits, opened the piano, sat down and spread his hands over the keyboard. He began to play something of his own, with real, immediate inspiration, a polka, a spirited polka as the advertisements say. There was no reluctance on the part of the composer; his fingers drew the notes out, linking them, shaking them about; you'd have said that the muse was composing and dancing at the same time. Pestana had forgotten his pupils, he'd forgotten the servant, who was waiting there with his stick and umbrella; he'd even forgotten the portraits, hanging there on the wall with their serious faces. He was simply composing, at the keyboard or on paper, without yesterday's vain struggle, without the frustration, asking nothing of the heavens, no longer scrutinising Mozart's eyes. No ennui – life, charm and novelty flowed out of his soul as if from a perennial fountain.

In a short time the polka was written. He corrected a few notes when he came back for supper; but he was already humming it as he walked along, out in the street. He liked it; the blood of his paternity and his vocation flowed freely in this recent, unpublished work. Two days later, he went to take it to the publisher of other polkas of his; there must have been about thirty already. The publisher thought it was lovely.

'It'll be a hit.'

The question of the title arose. Pestana, when he'd composed his first polka, in 1871, wanted to give it a poetic title, and chose this: 'Sun-Drops'. The publisher shook his head, and said that the titles ought themselves to appeal to the popular mind, either by alluding to some event of the day – or by the charm of the words themselves. He suggested two:

'The Law of 28 September'[3] or 'You'll Not Get Your Way with Me.'

'But what's the point of "You'll Not Get Your Way with Me"?'

'There isn't one, but it'll spread like wildfire.'

Pestana, a still-unpublished youth, refused either of the titles and kept his polka; but it was no time till he'd composed another, and the itch for publicity made him print the two with whatever titles the publisher thought attractive or appropriate. And that was how he kept on doing things over the years.

Now, when Pestana handed over his new polka and they came to the title, the publisher said that for the last few days he'd had one in his head for the first work that came along, a really terrific title, long and with a swing to it. Here it was: 'Hey Lady, Hang on to That Basket.'

'And for the next time,' he added, 'I've got another in mind.'

The first edition sold out as soon as it was put on display. The composer's fame was enough to make people buy; but the work itself was in keeping with the genre, original, made you want to dance and could be quickly committed to memory. In a week, it was famous. For the first few days, Pestana was truly in love with the composition, liked to hum it under his breath, stopped in the street to hear it being played in some house or other, and got annoyed when it was badly executed. From the start, the orchestras played it in the theatres, and he went to one to hear it. He got some pleasure from hearing it whistled, one night, by a figure going down the Rua do Aterrado.

The moon hadn't had time to wax and wane before the honeymoon was over. As at other times, and sooner still than before, the old masters in the portraits made him bleed with remorse. Irritated and fed up, Pestana took it out on the muse that had come so often to console him, the one with the roguish eyes and seductive gestures, lively and graceful. Then his self-aversion came back, his hatred of anyone who asked him to play the latest polka, and together with it the effort to compose something in classical taste, one page would do, but one that could be printed and bound to stand between Bach and Schumann. But all study was useless, all struggle vain. He plunged into the Jordan, but came back out unbaptised. Night after night he spent in this manner, confident, stubborn, sure that will-power was enough, and that once he gave up the easy music . . .

'The polkas can go to hell for the devil to dance to,' he said to himself one day, at dawn, on his way to bed.

But the polkas didn't want to go that far down. They came to Pestana's house, right into the room with the portraits, and burst in so readily that he barely had the time to compose them, have them printed, enjoy them for a few days, get fed up with them, and go back to the old wellsprings, from whence nothing flowed. He lived this way, between these two options, until he married, and even after.

'Marry who?' asked Sinhazinha Mota of her uncle, a notary, who'd given her this news.

'He's going to marry a widow.'

'Old, is she?'

'Twenty-seven.'

'Pretty?'

'No. She's not ugly either – so-so. I've heard he fell in love with her because he heard her sing in the last festival at St Francis de Paul. But I've also heard she's got another quality, not uncommon, but less attractive: she's consumptive.'

Notaries shouldn't be so witty – or, at any rate, so unkind with it. His niece felt a final drop of balm, which cured the slight sting of envy. It was all true. A few days later, Pestana married a twenty-seven-year-old widow, a good singer and a consumptive. He received her as the spiritual bride of his genius. Doubtless celibacy was the cause of his sterility and his straying from the straight and narrow, he said to himself; artistically, he thought of himself as a late-night reveller – the polkas were the affairs of a habitual roué. Now, however, he would father a family of serious, profound, inspired and polished works.

This hope came to bud in the first hours of their love, and burgeoned in the first dawn of their marriage. 'Maria,' stammered his soul, 'give me what I've not found in nights of solitude, or in the tumult of my days.'

Right at the beginning, to celebrate the marriage, he had the idea of composing a nocturne. He would call it 'Ave, Maria'. Happiness, it seemed, brought him the beginnings of inspiration; not wanting to say anything to his wife before it was ready, he worked in secret. This was difficult, for Maria, who loved music as much as he did, came to play with him, or just to listen to him, hour after hour, in the portrait room. They even put on some weekly concerts, with three artists, friends of Pestana's. One Sunday, however, he could no longer contain himself, and called his wife to play her a part of the nocturne; he didn't tell her what it was nor whom it was by. Suddenly, stopping, he looked at her questioningly.

'Go on,' said Maria; 'isn't it Chopin?'

Pestana went pale, stared into space, repeated one or two passages and got up. Maria sat down at the piano, and after a small effort of memory played the Chopin piece. The idea and the motif were the same; Pestana had found it down some alleyway of his memory, an ancient city full of treacherous turnings. Unhappy, desperate, he left the house, and went towards the bridge on the way to São Cristóvão.

'Why fight it?' he said. 'Let's go with the polkas . . . Hurrah for the polka!'

Men who passed by and heard his words stopped to look, as if he was a madman. He went on his way, delirious, tormented, an eternal shuttlecock between his ambition and his vocation . . . He went past the old slaughterhouse; when he got to the railway crossing gate, he had the notion to walk up the line and wait for the first train to come and crush him. The guard made him turn back. He came to his senses and went home.

A few days later – a clear and fresh morning in May 1876 – it was six o'clock, and Pestana felt in his fingers a peculiar, well-known tremor. He got up slowly, so as not to wake Maria, who had coughed all night and was now in a deep sleep. He went into the portrait room, opened the piano and, as quietly as possible, brought out a polka. He had it published with a pseudonym; in the next two months he composed and published two more. Maria knew nothing of it; she went on coughing and dying, till, one night, she expired in the arms of her terrified and desperate husband.

It was Christmas Night. Pestana's grief was made worse by a dance in the neighbourhood where several of his best polkas were being played. The dance was bad enough; his compositions gave it an ironic, perverse air. He heard the steps, imagined the movements, maybe provocative, which some of his compositions led to; all this right next to the pallid corpse, a bag of bones laid out on the bed . . . Every hour of the night went by like this, slow or fast, wet with tears or sweat, with cheap scent or cologne, ceaselessly frolicking and cavorting, as if to the sound of a polka by a great invisible Pestana.

Once his wife was buried, the widower had a single aim: he would abandon music after composing a requiem, which he'd have played on the first anniversary of Maria's death. He'd choose another occupation, clerk, postman, peddler, anything to make him forget art, murderous and deaf to his pleas.

He began the work; he employed every trick, boldness, patience, meditation, even the caprices of chance, as he'd done in the old days, when he'd imitated Mozart. He reread and studied the composer's Requiem. Weeks and months went by. The work, which first of all went quickly, began to slow its pace. Pestana had ups and downs. He thought it was missing something, that it had no religious feeling, no ideas, no inspiration or method; later, his heart would lift once more and he'd be hard at work. Eight months, nine, ten, eleven, and the requiem wasn't finished. He redoubled his efforts; forgot his teaching and his friends. He'd reworked the piece many times; but now he wanted to finish it, one way or another. Two weeks, one week, five days . . . The dawn of the anniversary found him still at work.

He contented himself with a simple spoken Mass, for himself alone. It's impossible to say if all the tears that came furtively to his eyes belonged to the husband, or if some were the composer's. What's certain is that he never went back to the requiem.

'What for?' he said to himself.

Yet another year went by. At the beginning of 1878, the publisher came by.

'It's been two years since you've given us one of those tunes of yours,' he said. 'Everyone's asking if you've lost your gift. What have you been doing?'

'Nothing.'

'I know you've had a severe blow; but it was two years since. I've come to propose a new contract: twenty polkas in twelve months; the old price, and a bigger percentage on the sales. Then, when the year's up, we can renew it.'

Pestana made a gesture of assent. He didn't have many pupils, he'd sold the house to pay off debts, and his basic needs were eating up what was left, which wasn't very much. He accepted the contract.

'But the first polka must come straight away,' the publisher explained. 'It's urgent. Have you seen the Emperor's letter to Caxias?[4] The liberals have been called on to form a government; they're going to undertake electoral reform. The polka will be called "Hurrah for Direct Elections!" It's not a political statement; just a good topical title.'

Pestana composed the first work for the contract. In spite of the long silence, he hadn't lost his originality or his inspiration. He still had the same touch of genius. The other polkas came, in regular succession. He'd kept the portraits and their works; but he avoided spending every night at the piano, so as not to get caught up in more failed attempts. Now he asked for a free ticket whenever there was a good opera or solo concert; he went and sat in a corner, enjoying all these things which would never sprout from his brain. Once or twice, when he came back home, his head full of music, the unpublished maestro woke again; then, he'd sit down at the piano, and, with no real aim, play a few passages until he went to bed twenty or thirty minutes later.

So the years went by, until 1885. Pestana's fame had given him the undisputed first place among polka composers; but the chief place in the village wasn't enough for this Caesar, who would still have preferred not the second, but the hundredth place in Rome. He still had the mood swings he'd had before about his compositions; the difference was they were less violent now. There was no enthusiasm in the first hours following a new composition, nor was there the horror after the first week; a bit of pleasure and a certain ennui were all.

That year, he picked up a slight fever, which worsened in a few days, and became pernicious. He was already in danger when the publisher appeared; he knew nothing of the illness, and was coming to give him the news of the conservatives' return to power, and to ask him for a topical polka. The nurse, an impoverished clarinet player in a theatre band, told him of Pestana's state, so the publisher thought it better to remain silent. It was the sick man who insisted he should tell him what he'd come for; the publisher obeyed.

'But only when you're completely better,' he concluded.

'As soon as the fever's gone down a bit,' said Pestana.

There was a pause for a few seconds. The clarinettist went on tiptoe to prepare his medicine; the publisher got up and took his leave.

'Goodbye.'

'Look,' said Pestana, 'as it's probable I'll be dying in the next few days, I'll do you two polkas; the other'll serve when the liberals come back again.'

It was the only joke he'd ever cracked in his life, and it was just in time, because he died early the next morning, at five past four, at peace with his fellow men and at war with himself.

The Cane

DAMIÃO RAN AWAY FROM the seminary at eleven in the morning one Friday in August. I don't know what year it was; before 1850, anyhow. A few minutes later he stopped in confusion; he hadn't bargained on the effect on passers-by of a shocked runaway seminarian in a cassock. He wasn't familiar with the streets, and kept losing his way and retracing his steps; finally he stopped. Where was he to go? Not home; his father was there, and he'd send him back to the seminary after a good hiding. He'd not fixed on where he'd go, because he'd planned the escape for later; a chance event had brought it forward. Where could he go? He remembered his godfather, João Carneiro, but his godfather was a gutless lazybones, who'd do nothing unless he was pushed to it. It was he who'd taken him to the seminary and introduced him to the rector:

'Here he is; here's the great man of the future,' he said to the rector.

'Come in,' the rector replied, 'let the great man come in, so long as he's humble and good. True greatness is modest. My lad . . .'

That was when he got there. A little time later he ran away from the seminary. Here he is now, in the street, scared, uncertain, unsure where to go for safe haven or for advice; he searched his memory for the houses of relatives and friends, without settling on any. Suddenly, he exclaimed:

'I'll take refuge with Sinhá Rita! She'll call my godfather over and tell him she wants me out of the seminary . . . Maybe that way . . .'

Sinhá Rita was a widow, João Carneiro's mistress; Damião had some inkling of this situation and thought of using it for his own ends. Where did she live? He was so dazed that it was only a few minutes later that it came to mind; it was in the Largo do Capim.

'Holy name of Jesus! What's this?' shouted Sinhá Rita, sitting up on the settee where she was reclining.

Damião had just entered in terror; at the very moment he got to the house he'd seen a priest go by, and shoved the door open – luckily it wasn't locked or bolted. Once inside, he peeped through the shutters, looking for the priest. He hadn't noticed him, and went on his way.

'What's this, young Senhor Damião?' shouted the lady of the house, again, for she'd only just recognised him. 'What are you doing here?'

Damião, trembling, almost unable to speak, told her not to be afraid, it was nothing; he'd explain everything.

'Calm down, and explain yourself.'

'I'll tell you now; I've not committed a crime, I swear; but wait a moment.'

Sinhá Rita looked at him in shock, and all the girls, both those belonging to the house and those from outside, who were sitting around the room in front of their lace-making cushions, stopped their hands and their bobbins. Sinhá Rita

lived mostly from teaching lace-making, appliqué and embroidery. While the lad was catching his breath, she ordered
the girls to go on working, and waited. In the end, Damião
told her everything, his loathing of the seminary; he was
certain he wouldn't make a good priest; he spoke with
passion, and asked her to save him.

'What do you mean? There's nothing I can do.'

'You can, if you want.'

'No,' she replied, shaking her head; 'I'm not getting involved in your family's business; I hardly know them; and then
there's your father – they say he's got a temper on him!'

Damião thought he was lost. He kneeled at her feet and
kissed her hands in despair.

"There's a lot you can do, Sinhá Rita, for the love of God,
by whatever's most sacred to you, by your husband's soul, save
me from death, because I'll kill myself if I have to go back to
that place.'

Sinhá Rita, flattered by the lad's pleas, tried to persuade him
to change his attitude. A priest's life was holy and beautiful,
she told him; time would show him that it was better to get
over his aversion, and one day . . . No, never, never, Damião
answered, shaking his head and kissing her hands; and again he
said it would kill him. Sinhá Rita hesitated for a long while;
finally she asked him why he didn't go and see his godfather.

'My godfather? He's worse than Papa; he won't listen to
me, I don't think he'd listen to anyone . . .'

'Oh no?' Sinhá Rita interrupted, hit where it hurts. 'I'll
show you if he'll listen or not . . .'

She called a slave-boy and ordered him to go to Senhor
João Carneiro's house and call him over on the instant; and if

he wasn't at home, he should ask where he could be found, and run to tell him she needed to talk to him straight away.

'Go on, boy.'

Damião sighed heavily, out loud. To cover up the imperious way she'd given those orders, she explained to the boy that Senhor João Carneiro had been her late husband's friend and had got her some orphan girls to teach. Later, as he still looked down in the mouth, leaning in a doorway, she laughingly pinched his nose:

'Come on, my young priest, relax, everything'll work out.'

Sinhá Rita was forty on her birth certificate, and twenty-seven in her eyes. She was a handsome woman, lively, jolly, fond of a good laugh; but when it suited her as fearsome as the devil himself. She decided to cheer the boy up, and in spite of the situation it was no great effort. In a short while, both of them were laughing; she told him stories, and asked him to tell her others, which he did with great aplomb. One of these, a silly story accompanied by comic gestures, made one of Sinhá Rita's girls laugh; she'd forgotten her work to look at the lad, and listen to him. Sinhá Rita picked up a cane at the side of the settee, and threatened her:

'Lucretia, mind the cane!'

The young girl lowered her head to avoid the blow, but the blow didn't come. It was a warning; if when night fell the task wasn't done, Lucretia would get the usual punishment. Damião looked at the orphan: she was a black girl, skinny, a little waif with a scar on her forehead and a burn on her left hand. She was eleven years of age. Damião noticed she was coughing, but inwardly and muffled, so as not to interrupt the conversation. He felt sorry for her and decided to take her

under his wing if she didn't finish her task. Sinhá Rita
wouldn't refuse her forgiveness . . . What was more, she'd
laughed because she thought him comical; it was his fault, if
you call being funny a fault.

At this point, João Carneiro arrived. He went pale when he
saw his godson there, and looked at Sinhá Rita, who wasted
no time on preambles. She said it was necessary to take the
boy out of the seminary, since he had no vocation for the
ecclesiastical life, and one priest less was better than a bad
priest. We can love and serve the Lord in the wider world.
João Carneiro, dismayed, couldn't find words to reply for the
first few minutes; finally, he opened his mouth and admon-
ished his godson for coming to bother 'strangers'; then he
asserted he would punish him.

'Punish him – certainly not!' Sinhá Rita interrupted. 'What
for? Go on, go and talk to his father.'

'I can't guarantee a thing, I don't think it can be done . . .'

'It is possible, I'll warrant for that. If you will it,' she went
on in an insinuating tone of voice, 'everything can be worked
out. Go and insist, he'll give way. Go on, Senhor Carneiro,
your godson's not going back to the seminary; I'm telling you
he's not going . . .'

'But, madam . . .'

'Go on, go.'

João Carneiro couldn't work up the courage to go, nor
could he stay. He was being pulled in opposite directions. He
didn't care if the boy ended up a priest, a lawyer or a doctor,
whatever – a layabout would do; the worst thing was that they
were entrusting to him a tremendous struggle with the boy's
father's deepest feelings, with no certainty as to the outcome;

as well as, if the answer was no, another struggle with Sinhá Rita, whose final word had been a threat: 'I'm telling you he's not going back . . .' One way or another there was going to be trouble. There was panic in João Carneiro's eyes, his lids trembled, his chest heaved. He looked at Sinhá Rita in supplication, and with the slightest tinge of reproof. Why couldn't she ask something else of him? Why didn't she ask him to walk, in the rain, all the way to Tijuca or Jacarepaguá? But to ask him to persuade his dear friend to change his son's career . . . He knew the old man; he was quite capable of smashing a jug in his face. Oh! If only the lad could drop down dead, on the spot, in an apoplexy! That was one solution – cruel, it's true, but definitive.

'Well?' Sinhá Rita insisted.

With a gesture of his hand, he told her to wait. He rubbed his chin, looking for a way out. God in heaven! A decree from the Pope dissolving the church, or at least abolishing seminaries, would bring everything to a satisfactory conclusion. João Carneiro would go back home and play gin rummy. Imagine Napoleon's barber being put in command of the army at the battle of Austerlitz . . . But the church was still there, seminaries were still there, his godson was still there, his back to the wall, eyes downcast, waiting, and giving no sign of apoplexy.

'Go on, go,' said Sinhá Rita, handing him his hat and stick.

There was nothing for it. The barber put his razor in its sheath, gripped his sword and went off to the wars. Damião breathed easier; on the outside, however, he remained the same, his eyes fixed on the ground, dejected. This time Sinhá Rita held his chin up.

'Come on, get some supper, don't be so miserable.'

'Do you really think he'll get anywhere?'

'He'll sort it all out,' Sinhá Rita replied, with confidence. 'Come on, the soup's getting cold.'

In spite of Sinhá Rita's jovial nature, and his own easy-going ways, Damião wasn't as happy at supper as earlier that day. He didn't trust his godfather's pliable nature. However, he ate well; and towards the end of the meal returned to the funny stories they'd been telling in the morning. When he was eating his dessert, he heard the noise of people in the next room, and asked if they were coming to take him away.

'It must be the girls.'

They got up and went to the sitting room. The 'girls' were five neighbours who came every afternoon to have coffee with Sinhá Rita, and stayed until it was dark.

The pupils, when their supper was over, went back to their work cushions. Sinhá Rita presided over all these womenfolk, those who lived there and those from outside. The gentle clicking of the bobbins and the neighbours' chatter were such homely noises, so far away from theology and Latin, that the lad let himself be drawn in by them and forgot everything else. For the first few minutes, the women were a little shy; but that soon wore off. One of them sang a *modinha*, accompanied by Sinhá Rita on the guitar, and the afternoon passed quickly by. Before the end, Sinhá Rita asked Damião to tell a certain story she'd been amused by. It was the same one that had made Lucretia laugh.

'Come on, Senhor Damião, don't play hard to get, the girls want to be off. You'll like this story.'

Damião had no option but to obey. Even though the expectations had been built up, which reduced the surprise and the effect, the story ended in laughter from the girls. Damião, pleased with himself, didn't forget Lucretia and looked at her, to see if she'd laughed too. He saw she had her face close to her cushion to finish her task. She wasn't laughing; or maybe she'd laughed inwardly, just as she coughed.

The neighbours left, and twilight came. Damião's soul blackened as night fell. What could be happening? Over and over he went to look through the shutters, and came back more and more disheartened. Not a sign of his godfather. It was plain that his father had told him to shut up, called a couple of slaves and gone to the police to ask for the loan of a constable, and was on his way to take him back to the seminary by force. Damião asked Sinhá Rita if you could get out of the house by the back; he ran into the backyard and thought he could jump over the wall. He asked if there was some way of escaping to the Rua da Vala, or if it was better to ask some neighbour to do him the favour of taking him in. The worst thing was his cassock; if Sinhá Rita could get him a jacket, or an old frock-coat . . . Sinhá Rita had just the thing, a coat, a memento from João Carneiro, or perhaps an over-sight.

'I've one of my late husband's coats,' she said, laughing, 'but what's all this fuss for? It'll all work out, don't worry.'

Finally, just as night came, one of his godfather's slaves appeared with a letter for Sinhá Rita. The business wasn't settled yet; the father was furious and on the point of smashing the furniture; he'd shouted that no, sir, the young dandy would go to the seminary, or he'd put him in jail, or the army. João Carneiro had had a terrific struggle to persuade his friend not to take things in hand now, but sleep on it for the night, and think whether it was right to destine such a rebellious and vicious young man to the religious life. He explained in the letter that he spoke in those terms the better to argue the case. He'd not won it yet, he said; but on the next day he'd go and see him and insist again. He concluded by saying the boy should come to his house.

Damião finished reading the letter and looked at Sinhá Rita. 'She's my last refuge,' he thought. Sinhá Rita had a horn inkwell brought over, and at the bottom of the letter itself, on the same sheet, wrote this reply: 'Joãozinho, either you save the boy, or I'll never see you again.' She sealed the letter with a wafer, and gave it to the slave, telling him to take it quickly. Again she tried to cheer the seminarian, who had once more donned the habit of humility and dismay. She told him to calm down, for this was now her affair.

'They'll see what I'm worth! I'm no pushover, wait and see!'

It was time to gather in the work. Sinhá Rita examined it: all the pupils had finished. Only Lucretia was still at her cushion, weaving her bobbins in and out, unable to see; Sinhá Rita went over to her, saw that her task wasn't finished, flew into a rage, and grabbed her by the ear.

'Ah, you little good-for-nothing!'

'Missy, missy! For the love of God! For Our Lady in heaven!'

'Good-for-nothing! Our Lady doesn't protect idle girls!'

Lucretia struggled, pulled herself away from her mistress's grip, and ran inside; Sinhá Rita went after her and grabbed her.

'Get here!'

'Please, mistress, forgive me!' The little girl coughed.

'Certainly not. Where's the cane?'

And they both came back into the room, one held by her ear, struggling, weeping and begging; the other saying over and over that no, she was going to punish her.

'Where's the cane?'

The cane was at the head of the settee, on the other side of the room. Sinhá Rita, so as not to let go of the girl, shouted to the seminarian:

'Senhor Damião, pass me that cane, if you please.'

Damião went cold . . . Cruel moment! A cloud passed before his eyes. Yes, he had sworn to give the girl his protection – she had got behind in her work because of him . . .

'Give me the cane, Senhor Damião!'

Damião got as far as going towards the settee. Then the girl begged him for the sake of everything he held most sacred, his mother, his father, Our Lord himself . . .

'Help me, young master!'

Sinhá Rita, her face on fire and her eyes starting out of her head, demanded the cane without letting go of the girl, who was now paralysed by a fit of coughing. Damião felt a pang of guilt; but he needed to get out of the seminary so badly! He went over to the settee, picked up the cane and handed it to Sinhá Rita.

Midnight Mass

I'VE NEVER BEEN ABLE to understand the conversation I had with a lady, many years ago, when I was seventeen, and she was thirty. It was Christmas Eve. I had arranged to go to Midnight Mass with a neighbour, and decided not to go to bed; it was fixed that I'd wake him at midnight.

The house where I lodged belonged to the notary Meneses, whose first marriage had been with one of my cousins. His second wife, Conceição, and her mother had made me feel welcome when I came from Mangaratiba, some months before, to study for my entrance exams. I lived a quiet life, in that two-storey house on the Rua do Senado, with my books, a few acquaintances, outings from time to time. It was a small family, consisting of the notary, his wife and mother-in-law and two female slaves. They had old-fashioned habits. At ten at night everyone was in their rooms; by half past ten the whole house was asleep. I'd never been to the theatre, and more than once, hearing Meneses say he was going, I asked him to take me with him. When this happened, the mother-in-law made a face, and the slaves stifled their giggles; he didn't answer, got dressed, went out and only came back the next morning. Later on I found out that the theatre was a living, breathing euphemism. Meneses had an ongoing affair with a lady who was separated from her husband, and slept away one night a week. Conceição had suffered at the outset from the existence of this rival; but finally she'd resigned herself to the arrangement, got used to it, and ended up thinking it was just fine.

Dear, good Conceição! They called her 'the saint' and she merited the title, so easily did she put up with her husband's neglect. In truth, she was of a middling temperament, given neither to floods of tears nor to bursts of laughter. In the department we're talking of she was like a Muslim; she'd accept a harem, so long as appearances were kept up. God forgive me, if I misjudge her. Everything about her was passive and attenuated. Even her face was average, neither pretty nor ugly. She was what we call a nice person. She spoke ill of no one, and pardoned everything. She didn't know how to hate; maybe even she didn't know how to love.

On that Christmas Eve, the notary went to the theatre. It was in 1861 or 1862. I should have been back in Mangaratiba, on my holidays; but I stayed till Christmas to see 'Midnight Mass in the big city'. The family went to bed at the usual time; I went into the front room, dressed and ready. From there I could go into the vestibule and leave without waking anyone. There were three keys to the door; the notary had one, I'd take another and the third was kept in the house.

'But, Senhor Nogueira, what will you do all this time?' Conceição's mother asked me.

'I'll read, Dona Ignacia.'

I had a novel with me, *The Three Musketeers*, in an old translation published by the *Jornal do Commercio*, I think. I sat

down at the table in the middle of the room, and by the light
of a kerosene lamp, while the house was asleep, I leaped once
more on to d'Artagnan's scrawny horse and embarked on my
adventures. In a short while I was completely drunk on
Dumas. The minutes flew by, instead of dragging as they
usually do when we're waiting; I heard the clock strike
eleven, but only by chance – I hardly noticed a thing.
However, a little noise I heard from inside the house awoke
me from my reading. Someone was walking along the
corridor leading from the parlour to the dining room; I lifted
my head; soon I saw the figure of Conceição appear at the
door.

'Haven't you gone yet?' she asked.

'No, I don't think it's midnight yet.'

'How patient you are!'

Conceição came into the front room, trailing along in her
bedroom slippers. She was wearing a white dressing gown
loosely tied at her waist. Thin as she was, she looked like a
romantic vision, not out of keeping with my novel. I shut the
book; she went to sit on the chair in front of me, near the
settee. I asked her if I'd made a noise and unintentionally
woken her; quickly she replied:

'No! Of course not! I just woke, that's all.'

I looked at her a little and doubted what she said. Her eyes
didn't look as if she'd just been asleep; she looked as if she'd
been awake. Someone else would have made something of
this observation; I hurriedly rejected it, without realising that
maybe she'd not been sleeping because of me, and was lying
so as not to worry or annoy me. I've already said she was a
good woman, very good.

'But it must be nearly time,' I said.

'What patience you have to wait up, while our neighbour's asleep! And alone! Aren't you afraid of ghosts? I thought I gave you a fright when you saw me.'

'I was surprised when I heard the steps; but you soon came in.'

'What were you reading? Don't tell me, I know, it's the *Musketeers*.'

'That's right; it's very good.'

'Do you like novels?'

'Yes.'

'Have you read *A moreninha*?'[1]

'By Dr Macedo? I've got it in Mangaratiba.'

'I'm very fond of novels, but I don't read much, for lack of time. What novels have you read?'

I began to tell her the names of some. Conceição listened to me with her head leaning on the back of the chair, her eyes peeping between half-shut lids, fixed on me. From time to time she passed her tongue over her lips, to wet them. When I stopped talking she said nothing to me; we stayed that way for a few seconds. Then I saw her lift her head, entwine her fingers and rest her chin on them, with her elbows on the arms of the chair, all this without taking her big sharp eyes off me.

'Maybe she's bored,' I thought.

Then, out loud:

'Dona Conceição, I think it's about time, and I . . .'

'No, no, it's still early. I saw the clock this minute, and it's half past eleven. You've got time. If you can't sleep at night can you get through the day without sleeping?'

'I have done in the past.'

'Not me; if I lose a night's sleep I'm useless the next day unless I nod off, even for half an hour. But I'm getting old too.'

'You, old, Dona Conceição?'

Perhaps my saying this so warmly made her smile. Usually, her gestures were slow and her attitudes calm; now, however, she suddenly got up, went over to the other side of the room and paced back and forth between the street window and her husband's study door. Like this, in this respectable state of disarray, she made a singular impression on me. Though she was thin she had a kind of sway to her walk, as if she found it hard to carry her own weight; this had never seemed as marked as on that night. She stopped from time to time, examining a piece of curtain, or putting some object into its right place on the sideboard; finally she stopped in front of me, with the table between us. The circle of her ideas was narrow; she went back to her surprise at finding me waiting up alone; I repeated what she already knew, that is, that I had never seen Midnight Mass in the capital, and didn't want to miss it.

'It's the same as in the country; all Masses are alike.'

'I believe you; but here there's bound to be more show, and more people. Holy Week in Rio is more colourful than in the country. Not to mention St John's Night, and St Anthony's . . .'

Little by little, she'd leaned forward; she'd put her elbows on the marble top of the table and her face between her outspread hands. Her sleeves weren't buttoned, and fell naturally; I saw half her arms, very pale, and not as thin as you might have thought. I had seen her arms before, though not often; at that moment, however, they made a great impression on me. Her veins were so blue that in spite of the dim light I could count them from where I was. More than the book, it was Conceição's presence that kept me awake. I went on saying what I thought about festivals in the country and the town, and other things that came into my head. As I went on I changed the subject without knowing why, going from one to another and then back to the first, and laughing to make her smile and see her white, gleaming teeth, all neat and even. Her eyes weren't exactly black, but they were dark; her nose, long, narrow and slightly curved, gave her face an interrogative look. When I raised my voice a little, she restrained me:

'Not so loud! You might wake Mama.'

She never abandoned that position: with our faces so close, it filled me with delight. It was true, there was no need to raise our voices to be heard; the two of us whispered, I more than she, because I talked more; at times, she looked earnest, very earnest, with her forehead a little furrowed. In the end, she tired of this; her manner changed and she moved. She came round to my side of the table and sat on the settee. I turned round, and secretly caught sight of the tips of her slippers; but this was only while she was sitting down, for her dressing gown was long and instantly covered them. I remember they were black. Conceição said in a low voice:

'Mama's room is way off, but she sleeps very lightly; if she woke now, poor thing, she'd take a while to get back to sleep.'

'I'm like that too.'

'What?' she asked, leaning towards me to catch my words better.

I went to sit on the chair next to the settee and repeated what I'd said. She laughed at the coincidence; she was a light sleeper too – that made three of us.

'There are times when I'm like Mama; when I wake up, I can't get back to sleep. I roll around in the bed, get up, light a candle, walk round, go back to bed, but it's no good.'

'That's what happened to you tonight.'

'No, no,' she interrupted.

I didn't understand her denial; maybe she didn't either. She picked up the ends of the cord of her gown and tapped them on her knees – her right knee, rather, for she'd just crossed her legs. Then she told me a story from a dream, and told me she'd only ever had one nightmare, when she was a child. She asked me if I had them. The conversation began again, slowly, lengthily, without my thinking about the time or the Mass. When I ended one story or an explanation, she invented another question or another subject, and I began talking again. From time to time, she restrained me:

'Not so loud, not so loud . . .'

There were pauses too. Twice I thought I saw her going to sleep; but her eyes, shut for an instant, opened soon after, with no sign of sleepiness or fatigue, as if she'd shut them to see better. At one of these moments, I think she saw me absorbed by her presence, and I remember she closed them again – whether slowly or hurriedly, I don't know. There are impressions from that night which seem truncated or confused. I contradict myself, and get mixed up. One that I still have fresh in my mind is that, on one occasion, this woman who was merely nice looked beautiful, truly beautiful. She was standing with her arms crossed; out of respect for her, I tried to get up;

she didn't let me, put one of her hands on my shoulder, and made me sit down. I think she was going to say something; but she shivered, as if she had felt the cold, turned her back on me and went to sit on the chair where she'd found me reading. From there she gave a glance at the mirror, which was above the settee, and talked about two pictures hanging on the wall.

'These pictures are getting old. I've already asked Chiquinho to buy some others.'

Chiquinho was the husband. The pictures spoke of the man's principal interest. One represented Cleopatra; I can't remember what the subject of the other was, but it was women. Both were vulgar; at that time I didn't think they were ugly.

'They're pretty,' I said.

'They are, I agree; but they're stained. And anyway, to be honest, I'd prefer two images, two saints. These are more suitable to a young man's room, or a barber's shop.'

'A barber's? You've never been to a barber's.'

'But I imagine the customers while they're waiting, talking about girls and love affairs, and naturally the owner likes to cheer their surroundings up with nice pictures. In a family house, though, I don't think it's suitable. That's what I think; but I think lots of funny things like that. Anyhow, I don't like the pictures. I've got an Our Lady of the Conception, my patron saint, very pretty; but it's a statue, and you can't put it on the wall – I don't want to anyway. It's in my oratory.'

The idea of the oratory reminded me of Mass; I remembered it was getting late and thought of saying so. I think I got as far as opening my mouth, but I soon shut it to listen to what she was saying, sweetly, charmingly, so softly that a laziness spread over my spirit and made me forget the Mass and the church. She was talking about her devotions when she was a child and a young girl. Then she told some stories about dances, things that had happened on outings, memories of boat trips to Paquetá, all jumbled up, one thing following on from another. When she tired of the past she spoke about the present, what she did in the house, the burden of family duties. They'd told her before she was married it would be bad, but her duties were no bother. She didn't tell me, but I knew she'd married when she was twenty-seven.

She wasn't moving around now, as she had done before, and stayed almost in the same position. Her eyes no longer had that wide, distant look in them, and she began looking aimlessly round the walls.

'We should change the wallpaper,' she said a little later, as if talking to herself.

I agreed, so as to say something, to get out of the kind of magnetised sleep, or whatever it was, that was paralysing my tongue and my senses. I wanted to end the conversation, but didn't want to at the same time; I made an effort to tear my eyes from her, and did so, out of respect; but the idea that she might think it was boredom when it wasn't brought my eyes back again to Conceição. The conversation was slowly dying. In the street, the silence was complete.

We stayed completely quiet for a while, even – I can't say for how long. The only tiny noise was the gnawing of a mouse in the study, which awoke me from my state of somnolence; I went to speak of it, but I couldn't find a way. Conceição seemed to be daydreaming. Suddenly I heard a knock on the window, from outside, and a voice shouting: 'Midnight Mass! Midnight Mass!'

'There's your friend,' she said, getting up. 'That's funny; you were going to wake him, and it's he who's come to awaken you. Off you go, it must be time; goodnight.'

'Is it time already?' I asked.

'Of course.'

'Midnight Mass!' the person repeated from outside, knocking.

'Go on, off you go, don't make them wait for you. It was my fault. Goodnight; till tomorrow.'

And with the same sway to her body, Conceição went down the corridor into the house, treading softly. I went out into the street to find the neighbour waiting. We went off to the church. During Mass, the figure of Conceição came once or twice between me and the priest; put it down to my seventeen years. The following morning, at breakfast, I talked about the Midnight Mass and the people in the church without arousing Conceição's curiosity. During the day, I found her as she always was, natural, kind, with nothing about her that reminded me of the previous night's conversation. At New Year I went to Mangaratiba. When I came back to Rio de Janeiro, in March, the notary had died of apoplexy. Conceição was living in Engenho Novo, but I didn't go to visit, nor did I happen to see her. Later, I heard she'd married her late husband's apprenticed clerk.

Pylades and Orestes

QUINTANILHA BEGAT GONÇALVES. That was the impression they gave together, not that they were alike. On the contrary, Quintanilha's face was round, Gonçalves's long, the former was small and dark, the latter tall and fair, and overall they were quite different in their appearance. We can add that they were about the same age. The idea of paternity sprang from the way the former treated the latter; a father wouldn't have lavished as much affection, care and thought as he did.

They had been students together, lived together, and graduated in the same year. Quintanilha didn't go into law or become a magistrate, he went into politics; but after he was elected a provincial member of the Chamber of Deputies in 187—, he finished his mandate and abandoned the career. He'd got an inheritance from an uncle, which earned him about thirty *contos de réis* a year. He came to see his friend Gonçalves, who was a solicitor in Rio de Janeiro.

Though he was well off, young, and a friend to his only friend, you can't say Quintanilha was completely happy, as we'll see. Let's put on one side the distress caused by the hatred of the other relatives; it was so bad he almost gave up the inheritance, and the only reason he didn't was that his friend Gonçalves, who used to give him ideas and advice, convinced him it would be the height of madness to do it.

'Is it your fault you deserved more of your uncle than the other relations? It wasn't you that made the will or sweet-talked the old man, as they did. If he left you everything, it's because he thought better of you than of them; keep the fortune, according to the will of the deceased, and don't be a fool.'

Quintanilha ended up agreeing. Some of the relatives tried to make it up with him, but his friend showed him what their hidden intentions were, and Quintanilha shut the door on them. One of them, seeing him so close to his ex-student friend, told anyone who cared to listen:

'There you are; he abandons his relatives and goes around with strangers; we'll see where that leads.'

When he heard about this, Quintanilha hurried indignantly to tell Gonçalves about it. Gonçalves smiled, called him a fool and calmed his worries; there was no sense in getting con-cerned about tittle-tattle.

'There's only one thing I want,' Gonçalves went on, 'and that's that we separate, so it can't be said that . . .'

'So what can't be said? That's a good one! That'd be a fine thing, if I started choosing my friendships according to the whim of a lot of barefaced layabouts!'

'Don't talk like that, Quintanilha. You're very rude about your relatives.'

'The devil take my relatives! So I'm to live with people recommended by half a dozen scoundrels who want to come and live off my money? No, Gonçalves; anything you want

but that. It's me, and my own heart, that chooses my friends.
Or are you . . . are you tired of me?'

'Me? You're joking.'

'Well then?'

'But . . .'

'No buts about it.'

Their lives were as united as it was possible for them to be.
When Quintanilha awoke, he thought about his friend, had
breakfast and went to see him. They dined together, visited
friends, went for a stroll or ended the evening at the theatre. If
Gonçalves had some work to do in the evening, Quintanilha
dutifully went to assist him; he looked for legal texts, marked
them, copied them or carried the books. Gonçalves often
forgot things, a message, a letter, shoes, cigars, papers. Quintanilha acted as his memory. At times, in the Rua do Ouvidor
watching the girls go by, Gonçalves would remember some
documents he'd left at the office. Quintanilha flew off to fetch
them and came back so happy you wouldn't have known if
they were legal papers or a winning lottery ticket. He sought
him anxiously with his eyes as he ran in, all smiles, and dead of
fatigue.

'Are these the ones?'

'Yes . . . let me see . . . the very ones. Give me them.'

'It's all right, I'll carry them.'

At first, Gonçalves would sigh: 'What trouble I've put you
to!'

Quintanilha laughed at the sigh so good-naturedly that his
friend, so as not to upset him, would no longer accuse himself;
he agreed to accept these favours. With time, they turned into
a job. Gonçalves said to his friend: 'Remind me later today of

this or that,' and Quintanilha committed these things to memory, or wrote them down if there were a lot of them. Some had to be remembered at a given moment, and it was quite something watching the good Quintanilha sigh, waiting for a given moment to arrive, to have the pleasure of reminding his friend of his affairs. And he carried his letters and papers, went to get the replies, to look for people, to wait for them at the railway station, or went on trips into the interior. On his own initiative, he discovered good cigars, good restaurants or good shows. Gonçalves could no longer mention a new book – or just an expensive one – without finding he had a copy at home.

'You're a spendthrift,' he'd say in a tone of reprimand.

'That's a good one! Is money spent on literature and science wasted, then?' Quintanilha would conclude.

At the end of the year he thought Gonçalves should spend the summer holidays out of the city. The latter ended up agreeing, and the pleasure this gave Quintanilha was enormous. They went up to Petrópolis. On the way back, as they were coming down the mountain, they were talking about painting, and Quintanilha noted they didn't yet have a portrait of them both and had one painted. When he took it to his friend, Gonçalves had to tell him it was no good. Quintanilha was speechless.

'It's rubbish,' Gonçalves insisted.

'But the painter told me . . .'

'You don't understand painting, Quintanilha, and the painter took advantage and put one over on you. Is this a decent face? Is my arm twisted like this?'

'What a robber!'

'No, he's not to blame, he did his job; it's you that's got no feeling for art, or any experience of it, and you've bungled it. With the best of intentions, no doubt . . .'

'Yes, I had good intentions.'

'And I bet you've already paid?'

'Yes.'

Gonçalves shook his head, called him an ignoramus and ended up laughing. Quintanilha, embarrassed and annoyed, looked over and over at the picture, till he took out a knife and ripped it from top to bottom. As if this gesture of vengeance wasn't enough, he gave the picture back to the artist with a note in which he informed him of some of the things that had been said, and added that he was an ass. These things happen in life. Moreover, a promissory note of Gonçalves's that fell due some days later, and that he couldn't pay, gave Quintanilha something else to think about. They almost had a fight; Gonçalves's intention was to renew the loan; Quintanilha, who had endorsed it, thought it not worth the bother asking for this favour when the amount was so small (a *conto* and a half); he would lend the sum, and his friend could pay him when he was able. Gonçalves wouldn't consent to this, and the loan was renewed. This was repeated when the second due-date came, and all Gonçalves would do was give Quintanilha a promissory note, at the same rate of interest as the first.

'Can't you see you put me to shame, Gonçalves? How can I take interest off you?'

'Either you accept it, or nothing doing.'

'But, my dear friend . . .'

He had to agree. The two were so united that a lady called them newly-weds, and an intellectual, Pylades and Orestes.

They laughed, of course, but Quintanilha's laughter had something like tears in it; there was a soft tenderness about his eyes. Another difference is that Quintanilha's feelings had an enthusiasm about them completely lacking in Gonçalves; but then enthusiasm can't be invented. Of course, the second of the two men was better able to inspire it in the first than vice versa. In fact, Quintanilha was most sensitive to any kind of favour; a word or a look could light up his brain. A tap on the shoulder or the stomach, just to signal approval or merely underline their intimacy, could melt him with pleasure. He would recount the gesture and its circumstances for two or three days.

It wasn't uncommon to see him get irritated and stubborn, and lambast others. Frequently, too, he could be seen laughing; sometimes the laughter invaded him completely, bursting out of his mouth, his eyes, his forehead, arms and legs – he exuded laughter from every pore. Though not strongly passionate, he was far from being unemotional.

Gonçalves's promissory note came due in six months. On the day itself, not only had Quintanilha no thought of asking for the money, he'd decided to have dinner in some distant part of the city so as not to see his friend if he was to be asked to renew it. Gonçalves spoiled the whole plan: early in the morning he brought him the money. Quintanilha at first made a gesture of refusal, telling him to keep it – he might need it; the debtor insisted on paying, and paid.

Quintanilha watched all Gonçalves did; he saw how hard he worked, and the energy he put into his cases. He was full of admiration. In truth, Gonçalves wasn't a great lawyer, but within the limits of his abilities he acquitted himself well.

'Why don't you get married?' Quintanilha said to him one day. 'Lawyers should get married.'

Gonçalves answered with a laugh. He had an aunt, his only relative, whom he loved dearly, and who died when they were just reaching thirty. Days later, he said to his friend: 'You're the only one I've got left now.'

Quintanilha felt tears in his eyes, and didn't know what to say. When he thought of saying that he 'would die for him' it was too late. He redoubled his endearments, and one day awoke with the notion of making a will. Saying nothing to his friend, he named him executor and only heir.

'Keep this document for me, Gonçalves,' he said, giving him the will. 'I feel fine, but death can easily overtake us, and I don't want to trust my final wishes to just anyone.'

It was around this time that something happened, which I'll now recount.

Quintanilha had a second cousin, Camila, twenty-two, modest, well brought up and pretty. She wasn't rich; her father, João Bastos, was a bookkeeper for a coffee firm. They had quarrelled over the inheritance; but Quintanilha went to João Bastos's wife's funeral, and this act of respect brought them together again. João Bastos easily forgot some rude things he'd said of his cousin, said some nice ones, and invited him to dinner. Quintanilha went, and went back. He listened to his cousin's eulogies for his dead wife; on one occasion when Camila left them alone, João Bastos praised his daughter's rare qualities, and said she was, in moral terms, her mother's absolute heir.

'I'd never say this to the girl, and I ask you to say nothing either. She's modest, and if we begin to praise her it could be her undoing. So, for example, I'll never tell her she's as pretty as her mother was when she was her age; it might make her vain. But she's even prettier, don't you think? She can play the piano too, which her mother couldn't.'

When Camila came back to the dining room, Quintanilha felt the urge to tell her all, but held back and winked at his cousin. He asked to hear her play the piano; she answered, in melancholy tones:

'Not yet, it's only a month since Mama died; leave it for a time yet. Anyway, I play badly.'

'Badly?'

'Very badly.'

Quintanilha winked at his cousin again, and remarked to the girl that only if she played could he judge whether she did it well or ill. As for the time, it was true that only a month had gone by; but it was also true that music was a natural pastime, and a very respectable one. Besides, all she had to do was play something sad. João Bastos approved this view of the matter, and suggested an elegiac piece. Camila shook her head.

'No, no, it's still playing the piano; the neighbours are quite capable of saying I played a polka.'

Quintanilha thought that was funny and laughed. Later he agreed and waited till three months were up. In the interim he saw his cousin a few times, the three last visits being the longest and the closest together. Finally, he was able to hear her play the piano, and liked what he heard. Her father confessed that at first he'd not liked these German pieces; with time he got used to them and enjoyed them. He called his daughter 'my little German girl', a nickname Quintanilha adopted, only in the plural: 'our little German girl'. Possessive pronouns give a certain intimacy; in a little time, it was shared between the three of them – or four, if we count Gonçalves, who was introduced there by his friend; but let's stick to the three of them.

You've already sniffed it out for yourself, sagacious reader. Quintanilha ended up falling for the girl. How could he not, when Camila had such languid, bewitching eyes? Not that she rested them on him often, and if she did it was with a certain embarrassment at first, like children obeying the voice of a master or a father; but she did rest them on him, and they were such that they gave a fatal wound, though unintentionally. She also smiled frequently and was amusing to listen to. At the piano, however reluctantly she might play, she played well. In short, Camila might not have been acting on her own initiative, but she was no less bewitching for that. Quintanilha discovered one morning that he'd dreamed of her all night, and at night that he'd thought of her all day, and concluded from this discovery that he loved her and was loved in return. He felt so giddy that he was ready to announce it in the newspapers. At the least, he wanted to tell his friend Gonçalves, and ran to his office. Quintanilha's affection for him was complicated by respect and fear. When he was about to open his mouth he swallowed the secret before it was out. He didn't dare tell him that day or the next.

He should have; there might still have been time to win the battle. He put the revelation off for a week. One day he went to dine with his friend, and after much hesitation told him everything; he loved his cousin and was loved by her.

'Do you approve, Gonçalves?'

Gonçalves went pale – or, at least, he looked grave; pallor and gravity took on the same aspect with him. But no; really, he went pale.

'Do you approve?' Quintanilha repeated.

After some seconds, Gonçalves was going to open his mouth to answer, but he shut it again, and fixed his eyes 'on yesterday', to use the words he used of himself when he stared at some point in the distance. In vain Quintanilha insisted on knowing what was the matter, what he was thinking, was this love another piece of 'foolishness'? He was so used to hearing this word from him that it no longer hurt or affronted him, even in such delicate and personal matters. Gonçalves surfaced from his meditative state, shrugged his shoulders with a disillusioned air, and murmured these words in such a low voice that his friend could hardly hear him:

'Don't ask me anything; do what you want.'

'Gonçalves, what is this?' Quintanilha asked, shocked and grasping him by the hands.

Gonçalves let out a big sigh, which, if it had wings, is still flying around somewhere. That, though he didn't put it in these paradoxical words, was Quintanilha's impression. The clock in the dining room struck eight. Gonçalves claimed he had to go and see a judge, and his friend made his farewells.

In the street Quintanilha came to a halt, stunned. He couldn't understand those gestures, that sigh, the pallor, the whole mysterious effect of the news of his love. He'd gone in and said his piece, expecting to hear from his friend one or more of the usual, familiar epithets, 'idiot', 'blockhead', 'simpleton', and heard none of them. On the contrary, there

was something akin to respect in Gonçalves's gestures. He
couldn't remember anything at dinner that could have offended him; it was only after he confided his new feelings for
his cousin that his friend had been so upset.

'But it can't be,' he thought, 'what is it about Camila that
prevents her being a good wife?'

He spent more than half an hour standing in front of the
house in this quandary. Then he noticed that Gonçalves
hadn't gone out. He waited another half-hour; nothing.
He was tempted to go back in, hug him, question him
. . . He hadn't the strength; he went off down the street
in despair. He arrived at João Bastos's house and was unable to
see Camila; she'd gone to bed with a cold. He wanted to tell
her everything – and here we must explain that he hadn't yet
declared his love to his cousin. Her eyes didn't avoid his; that
was all, and it might have been no more than flirtation. But
there could be no better occasion to make the situation clear.
If he told her what had happened with his friend, he had the
opening to let her know he loved her and was going to ask her
father for her hand. It would have been some consolation in
the midst of this agony; chance had robbed him of it, and
Quintanilha left the house in a worse state than he'd gone in.
He retired to his own home.

He didn't get to sleep until two in the morning, and then
sleep gave him no respite – only made him more perturbed, in
new, unfamiliar ways. He dreamed that he was going to cross
a long, old bridge, between two mountains, and halfway
across a figure rose up and stood firmly in front of him. It was
Gonçalves. 'Villain,' he said with burning eyes, 'why have you
come to take away the love of my life, the woman I adore,

and who is mine? Take my heart, take it, and finish the job.'
And in a trice he opened his chest, tore his heart out and put it
in Quintanilha's mouth. The latter tried to grasp his friend's
vital organ and put it back in Gonçalves's breast; it was
impossible. In the end, his jaws closed round it. He tried
to spit it out, but that was worse; his teeth bit into the heart.
He tried to speak, but there wasn't much hope with his mouth
full like that. Finally his friend lifted his arms and stretched his
hands out to curse him, as he'd seen in melodramas as a boy;
immediately after, two immense tears welled up from his eyes,
which filled the valley with water; he plunged in and disappeared. Quintanilha awoke hardly able to breathe.

The illusion caused by the nightmare was such that he put
his hands to his mouth, to pull his friend's heart out. He found
only his tongue, rubbed his eyes and sat up. Where was he?
What was going on? What was the bridge? And Gonçalves?
He came fully to his senses, realised what was happening and
lay down again, unable to sleep, though this time he lay awake
for less time; he fell asleep at four.

When dawn came, remembering the previous day, both
the reality and the dream, he came to the conclusion that his
friend Gonçalves was his rival, loved his cousin, and maybe
was loved by her . . . Yes, yes, it might be so. Quintanilha
spent two agonising hours. Finally he pulled himself together
and went to Gonçalves's office, to know his fate; and if it was
true, yes, if it was true . . .

Gonçalves was drawing up a legal document. He paused to
look at him for a moment, got up, opened the steel cabinet
where he kept important papers, took out Quintanilha's will,
and gave it to the testator.

'What's this?'

'You're going to change your legal status,' Gonçalves replied, sitting down at the table.

Quintanilha heard tears in his voice; at least, it seemed so to him. He asked him to keep the will; he was its natural guardian. He pressed him; the only reply was the harsh sound of the pen on the paper. The pen wasn't running smoothly, the writing was shaky, and there were more corrections than usual – probably he was getting the dates wrong. He consulted the books with such a melancholy air that it saddened his friend. Sometimes he stopped everything, the pen and the consulting, to fix his gaze 'on yesterday'.

'I understand,' said Quintanilha, 'she's yours.'

'Who d'you mean, she?' Gonçalves went to ask, but his friend was already shooting down the stairs like an arrow; he went on drawing up his document.

The sequel needn't be guessed at; all we need to know is the end. It can't be guessed at or even believed; but the human soul is capable of great feats, good and evil. Quintanilha made another will, leaving everything to his cousin, on condition she married his friend. Camila wouldn't accept the will, but she was so happy when her cousin told her about Gonçalves's tears that she accepted both, Gonçalves and the tears. Then Quintanilha could find no better solution than to make a third will leaving everything to his friend.

The end of the story was told in Latin. Quintanilha was a witness at the wedding, and godfather to the first two children. One day, when he was taking sweets to his god-children, as he was crossing Fifteenth of November Square, he was hit by a rebellious bullet (this was in 1893, during the naval revolt), which killed him almost instantaneously. He's buried in the cemetery of St John the Baptist; it's a simple grave, and the stone has an epitaph which ends with these pious words: 'Pray for him!' And that's the end of my story. Orestes is still alive, with none of the remorse of his Greek prototype. Pylades is now a silent character, just as in Sophocles' play.[1] Pray for him!

Father against Mother

WHEN SLAVERY ENDED, it took with it certain trades and tools; the same must have happened with other social institutions. I'll only mention some of the tools because of their link with certain trades. One of them was the neck iron, another was leg irons; there was also the tin-plate mask. The mask cured the slaves of the vice of drunkenness by shutting their mouths. It had only three holes in it, two to see, one to breathe, and it was fastened behind the head with a padlock. Not only did this curb the vice of drinking: the slaves also lost the temptation to steal because they generally used their master's small change to slake their thirst, and so two sins were eliminated, and honesty and sobriety were assured. The mask was grotesque, but order in the human and social realm is not always achieved without grotesquery – cruelty, even, sometimes. Tinsmiths used to hang them up, for sale, in the doorways of their shops. But let's not think about masks.

The neck iron was applied to slaves with the habit of running away. Imagine a thick collar, with an equally thick shaft on one side, left or right, which went up to the top of the head, and which was locked behind with a key. It weighed a lot, naturally, but it was less a punishment than a sign. A slave who fled with one of these showed that he was a repeated offender, and wherever he went was easily caught.

Half a century ago, slaves frequently ran away. There were lots of them, and not all of them liked being slaves. From time to time they would be beaten, and not all of them liked being beaten. Many were simply reprimanded; there was someone in the household who acted as their godfather, and the owner himself wasn't a bad man; besides, the sensation of ownership acted as a softener, for money hurts, too. Escapes happened repeatedly, however. There were even cases, exceptional though they were, when a contraband slave, no sooner had he been bought in the Valongo, took to his heels, even though he was unfamiliar with the city streets.[1] Some of those who went into private houses, as soon as they were used to their surroundings, asked their masters to fix a rent, and went to earn it outside, selling items in the street.

When someone's slave escaped, they offered a sum of money to whoever returned them. They put advertisements in the newspapers, with the distinguishing marks of the escapee, his name, clothes, physical defects if he had any, the neighbourhood where he might be and the amount of the reward. When the amount wasn't mentioned, there was a promise: 'There will be a generous reward', or: 'You will be well rewarded'. Often the advertisement carried above it, or at the side, a little vignette of a black man, barefoot, with a stick over his shoulder and a bundle on the end. Anyone who gave the slave shelter was threatened with the full rigour of the law.

Well then, catching runaway slaves was one of the trades of the time. Maybe it wasn't a noble one, but since it was the forcible instrument whereby law and property were safeguarded, it had that other implicit kind of nobility we owe to the law and its demands. No one entered the trade out of a desire for entertainment, nor did it require much study; poverty, a sudden need for money, unsuitability for other jobs, chance, and sometimes a pleasure in serving too, though in another walk of life, provided the incentive to anyone who felt strong enough to impose order on disorder.

Candido Neves – Candinho to his family – is the person linked to the story of an escape; he gave in to poverty when he took up the trade of catching runaways. This man had a grave defect – he never lasted in any job or trade, and lacked the necessary stability; that's what he called a run of bad luck. He began by wanting to learn typesetting, but soon saw it would take some time to learn the job well, and even then perhaps he might not earn enough; that was what he said to himself. The retail trade attracted him – a fine career was to be had there. However, the obligation of attending to everyone and serving them touched a raw nerve of pride in him, and after five or six weeks he was back in the street of his own free will. An assistant in a notary's office, office boy in a government department attached to the ministry of the interior, postman and other jobs were abandoned soon after they were obtained.

When he fell for young Clara, all he owned was debts, though not that many since he lived with a cousin, a wood carver by trade. After several attempts to get a job, he decided to opt for his cousin's profession, and in fact had already taken some lessons. It was no bother to take some more, but since he tried to learn in a hurry, he learned badly. He couldn't do delicate or complicated work, only claw-feet for sofas and common decoration for chair backs. He wanted to have something to work at when he married, and marriage wasn't long in coming.

He was thirty years of age, and Clara twenty-two. She was an orphan who lived with an aunt, Monica, and did sewing jobs with her. Her sewing didn't stop her flirting a bit, but her suitors only wanted to pass the time of day; that was as far as it went. They came by of an afternoon, looked her up and down, and she them, until night fell and she went back to her sewing. What she noticed is that she regretted none of them, nor did she feel any desire for them. In many cases, she may not even have known their names. She wanted to get married, of course. As her aunt said to her, it was like fishing with a rod to see if the fish would bite – but they kept their distance; all they did was swim round the bait, looking at it, sniffing it, then leaving it for others.

Love has ways of making itself known. When the girl saw Candido Neves, she felt that he was the husband-to-be, the real, the only one. They met at a dance; such was – in keeping with her suitor's first trade – the first page of this book, which would be published badly typeset and with its stitching in a worse state. The marriage happened eleven months later, and it was the biggest party they'd had all the time they'd known one another. Some of Clara's friends, less out of friendship than envy, tried to prevent her taking this step. They didn't deny he was a nice lad, nor that he loved her – some virtues couldn't be denied; what they said was that he was too fond of a good time.

'Well, thank goodness for that,' replied the bride, 'at least I'm not marrying a corpse.'

'No, not a corpse; it's just that . . .'

But they didn't finish the sentence. Aunt Monica, after the marriage, in the impoverished house where they lodged, spoke to them about possible children. They wanted one, just one, even if it made their poverty worse.

'If you have a child, you'll die of hunger,' said the aunt to her niece.

'Our Lady will feed us,' replied Clara.

Aunt Monica should have warned or threatened them this way when Candido came to ask for the girl's hand; but she liked a good time as well, and there'd be a great party at the wedding, as in fact there was.

All three of them were happy. The happy couple laughed at everything. Even their names, Clara, Neves, Candido, were the subject of jokes;[2] they didn't provide food, but they made you laugh, and the laughter was easily digested. She did more sewing now, and he went out on odd jobs; he had no fixed employment.

But none of this made them give up on the child. This creature, however, ignorant as it was of this procreative urge, lay waiting in the eternal realms. One day, however, it announced its presence; male or female, it was the blessed fruit that would bring them the happiness they longed for. Aunt Monica was dismayed, but Candido and Clara made fun of her fears.

'God will come to our aid, Auntie,' insisted the mother-to-be.

The news went round the neighbourhood. All they had to do was wait for the great day. The wife was working with a greater will, which was the way it had to be, since, as well as the sewing she was paid for, she had to make the baby's clothes with offcuts. She was looking forward to it so much, measuring nappies, sewing shirts. There wasn't much material, and she could only do it from time to time. Aunt Monica helped, it's true, though she complained.

'Yours is a sad lot,' she sighed.

'Other children come into the world, don't they?' asked Clara.

'Yes, and they always find something certain to eat, even if it's not much . . .'

'What d'you mean, certain?'

'Certain – a job, a profession, something to do, but how does the father of this unfortunate creature spend his time?'

As soon as he heard about this warning, Candido Neves went to talk to the aunt, not harshly, but much less mildly than usual, and asked if she'd ever gone without food.

'You've only ever fasted in Holy Week, and that's when you don't want to eat your supper with us. We've always had our salt cod on Good Friday . . .'

'I know that, but there are three of us.'

'So now there'll be four.'

'It's not the same.'

'What do you want me to do, more than I do already?'

'Something more fixed. Look at the joiner on the corner, the man who keeps the store, that typesetter who married last Saturday, all of them have got a fixed job . . . Don't get angry; I'm not saying you're a layabout, but your job's too uncertain. You go for weeks without a penny to your name.'

'Yes, but then one night I'll make up for it all, and more. God doesn't abandon me, and runaway slaves know I'm not to be trifled with; hardly any of them put up any fight, many give themselves up on the spot.'

He was proud of this, and talked of this hope as if it was secure capital. Soon he was laughing and making the aunt laugh; she was naturally jolly, and looked forward to a great party at the christening.

Candido Neves had lost his job as a wood carver, just as he'd given up on many others better or worse than that one. Catching slaves had novel charms for him. He didn't have to sit down for hours at a stretch. All it needed was strength, a sharp eye, patience, courage and a bit of rope. Candido Neves read the advertisements, copied them out, put them in his pocket and went out to do his research. He had a good memory. When he'd memorised the distinguishing marks and the habits of a runaway, in no time he found him, caught, bound and returned him. A lot of strength was needed, and agility. More than once, on the street corner, talking of something else altogether, he saw a slave pass by like any other, realised he'd escaped, who he was, his name, who his owner was, where he lived and what the reward was; he interrupted the conversation and went after the criminal. He didn't catch him straight away, but waited to find a suitable spot, then one leap, and the reward was his. He didn't always get away without losing some blood, as the victim's nails and teeth did their work, but usually he subdued them without the least scratch.

One day these profits began to dwindle. Runaway slaves no longer gave themselves up to Candido Neves as they had been doing. There were other, skilled hands at work. As the business was growing, more than one unemployed man got his act together, grabbed a rope, looked at the papers, copied advertisements and set out on the hunt. Even in the neighbourhood there was more than one rival. This meant that Candido Neves's debts started to mount, with less of those timely or near-timely payments than in the early days. Life became a hard grind. They ate badly, and on borrowed money; they ate late. The landlord insisted on the rent.

Clara didn't even have time to mend her husband's clothes, so great was the necessity to sew for money. Aunt Monica helped her niece, of course. When he came in every evening, you could see on his face that there was nothing in his pocket. He had his supper and went out again, looking for some runaway or other. Sometimes, though not often, he even got the wrong person, and grabbed a faithful slave going about his master's business. Once, he caught a freedman; he was full of apologies, but he got a healthy drubbing from the man's family.

'That's all we needed!' Aunt Monica exclaimed when he'd come in and told the story of the mistake and its consequences. 'Give it up, Candinho; look for another way of earning your living.'

Candido truly did want to do something else, not because of this advice, but because he felt like a change of job; it would be a way of changing skin or identity. The trouble is that he couldn't find any job to hand that he could learn in a hurry.

Nature did its work; the foetus was growing, until it was heavy in the mother, and the birth was not far off. The eighth month came, a month of worries and necessities, though still less so than the ninth, which I'll skip too. It's best to come to the effects of all this. They couldn't have been much nastier.

'No, Aunt Monica!' shouted Candinho, rejecting some advice which I find difficult to write down, though less difficult than it was for the father to hear it. He'd never do that!

It was in the last week of the final month that Aunt Monica advised the couple to take the child when it was born to the Orphans' Wheel for abandoned babies, set in the wall of a convent.[3] Nothing could be harder to bear for two young parents awaiting their child, to kiss it, care for it, watch it laugh, grow, fatten, jump up and down . . . Put it where? What did she mean? Candinho stared wide-eyed at the aunt, and ended up thumping the dining table. The table, which was old and falling to pieces, nearly collapsed completely. Clara intervened:

'Auntie doesn't mean any harm, Candinho.'

'Harm?' Aunt Monica answered. 'Harm or no harm, whatever, I'm telling you that's the best thing you can do. You're up to your eyes in debt; there's hardly any meat or beans in the house. If some money doesn't turn up, how can your family grow? There'll be time later; later, when you've got a surer way of earning your living, the children that come will be received with the same affection as this one, or more. This one will be well brought up; it'll lack for nothing. Is the Wheel some beach, or a rubbish dump? They don't kill people there, no one dies unnecessarily; here, it's certain to die if it doesn't get fed enough. Oh well . . .'

Aunt Monica ended the sentence with a shrug of her shoulders, turned her back and went to her bedroom. She had already hinted at this solution, but it was the first time she'd done it so openly and passionately – cruelly, if you prefer. Clara held her hand out to her husband, as if looking to him to buck her up; Candido Neves grimaced, and, under his breath, said the aunt was crazy. The couple's show of affection was interrupted by someone knocking at the door.

'Who is it?' asked the husband.

'It's me.'

It was the landlord, who was owed three months' rent, and was coming in person to threaten his tenant with eviction. Candido begged him to come in.

'There's no need . . .'

'Please do.'

Their creditor came in and refused to sit down; he glanced at the furniture to see if any could be pawned; not much, he thought. He'd come to get the rent they owed, and could wait no longer; if he wasn't paid in five days, he'd put them in the street. He'd not worked for the benefit of others. When you saw him you wouldn't think he was a proprietor; but words made up for appearances, and poor Candinho shut up rather than answering back. Instead he gave a bow, promising and begging at the same time. The owner gave no ground.

'Five days or out you go!' he repeated as he went out, his hand on the latch.

Candinho went off in another direction. When he was in a fix like this he never despaired; he always counted on some loan or other, how or where from he had no idea, but from somewhere. Then he cast his eye over the advertisements. He found several, some already old, but he'd been looking in vain for a long time. He spent some hours to no effect, and went back home. Four days later, he'd still found no way out; he tried to find backing, and went to see people friendly with the owner, but was only told to pack his bags.

It was a tight situation. They couldn't find a house, or anyone to give them temporary lodging; it was the street or nothing. They couldn't count on the aunt. Aunt Monica managed to find a room for the three of them in the house of an old rich woman, who promised to lend her basement at the back of the stables, on one side of the courtyard. Moreover, she deliberately said nothing to the two of them, so that Candido Neves, in despair at this state of affairs, would start by putting the child on the Wheel and finding some secure and regular way of getting money; putting his life in order, in short. She listened to Clara's complaints, without echoing them, it's true – but she brought no comfort. The day they were forced to leave the house, she'd surprise them with news of the favour and they'd go and sleep better than they'd expected.

That was what happened. Thrown out of the house, they went to the rooms they had been lent, and two days later the child was born. The father was very happy, and unhappy at the same time. Aunt Monica insisted on giving the child to the Wheel. 'If you don't want to take it, leave it to me; I'll go to the Rua dos Barbonos.' Candido Neves asked her not to, wait, and he'd take it himself. We might note that it was a boy, and that this was the sex both parents had wanted. They'd only given him a bit of milk; but, as it was raining that evening, the father agreed to take him to the Wheel the next night.

That evening, he went through all his notes of runaway slaves. The rewards for the most part were just promises; some mentioned a sum, though nothing much. One, however, was for a hundred *mil-reis*. It was for a mulatta; there was information about her looks and her clothes. Candido Neves had searched for her without success, and had given up on it; he imagined some lover had taken her in. Now, however, looking again at the amount and the need he had for it gave Candido Neves the energy to make one last big effort. He went out in the morning to look for signs and ask questions round the Rua da Carioca and the nearby square, the Rua do Parto and the Rua da Ajuda, which was where she might be, according to the advertisement. He didn't find her; only a chemist in the Rua da Ajuda remembered selling an ounce of some drug, three days before, to someone with those marks. Candido Neves talked as if he were the slave's owner, and politely thanked him for the information. He had no better luck with other runaways whose reward was meagre, or less certain.

He went back to the miserable lodgings they'd been lent. Aunt Monica had put some food together for the young mother, and had the child ready to be taken to the Wheel. The father, in spite of the agreement they'd reached, could hardly hide his pain at what he saw. He refused to eat what Aunt Monica had kept for him; he wasn't hungry, he said, and it was true. He thought of a thousand ways whereby he could keep his son; but none was any good. He couldn't even forget the shelter where he was living. He consulted his wife, who seemed resigned. Aunt Monica had described the child's future upbringing: more and greater poverty – perhaps he would die in utter destitution. Candido Neves was forced to fulfil his promise; he asked his wife to give their son the last milk he would drink from his mother. This done, the child went to sleep;

his father picked him up, and went off in the direction of the Rua dos Barbonos.

We can be sure he thought more than once of going back home with him; and that he wrapped him up warm, kissed him, and covered his face to keep the damp night air off. When he entered the Rua da Guarda Velha, Candido Neves began to slacken his pace.

'I'll give him up as late as I can,' he murmured.

But since the street was not infinite, or even long, eventually he'd come to its end; it was then that it occurred to him to go into one of the alleyways that linked it to the Rua da Ajuda, and he saw the figure of a woman on the other side of the street: it was the mulatta who had escaped. I won't depict Candido Neves's commotion here, because I can't convey it with enough intensity. One adjective is enough; let's say it was enormous. As the woman went down the street, he went too; a few steps away was the pharmacy where he'd got the information, as I've already recounted. He went in, found the pharmacist, asked him if he'd be so kind as to look after the child for a moment; he'd be back to get it, without fail.

'But . . .'

Candido Neves gave him no time to say anything; he hurried out, crossed the street, up to the point where he could catch the woman without creating a disturbance. At the end of the street, when she was turning to go down the Rua de São José, Candido Neves came close to her. It was her, it was the runaway mulatta.

'Arminda!' he shouted, using the name in the advertisement.

Arminda turned round without suspecting ill intent. It was only when he'd pulled the piece of rope from his pocket and grabbed her arms that she realised and tried to flee. It was too late. Candido Neves, with his strong hands, tied her wrists and told her to get moving. The slave made as if to shout; it seems she even let out a louder cry than usual, but she soon realised that no one would come to free her – quite the contrary. She then asked him to free her, for the love of God.

'I'm pregnant, master!' she exclaimed. 'If your worship has a child, I beg you for the love of him to let me go; I'll be your slave, I'll serve you for as long as you want. Please, please let me go, young master!'

'Get moving!' Candido Neves repeated.

'Let me go!'

'Don't keep me waiting; get moving!'

There was a struggle at this point, for the slave, groaning, was dragging herself and her unborn child along. Passers-by, or people in shop doorways understood what was going on, and naturally didn't get involved. Arminda alleged that her master was a very bad man, and would probably punish her with a whipping – which, in the state she was in, would hurt much more. No doubt of it, he'd have her whipped.

'It's your own fault. Who asked you to have a child and then flee?' asked Candido Neves.

He wasn't in the best frame of mind, because of the child he'd left behind in the pharmacy, waiting for him. It's also true that he wasn't one for saying anything very profound. He dragged the slave along the Rua dos Ourives, towards the Rua da Alfândega, where her master lived. On the corner of this last street, the struggle got worse; the slave planted her feet against the wall, and pulled back with great effort, to no avail. All she did was make it take more time to get to the house than it would have done, and it was nearby. Finally, she arrived, dragged along, desperate, gasping for breath. She even got down on her knees, but in vain. The master was at home, and responded to the call and the commotion.

'Here's the runaway,' said Candido Neves.

'That's her all right.'

'Master!'

'Come on, get in . . .'

Arminda fell in the corridor. Then and there the master opened his wallet and took out the hundred *mil-reis* of the reward. Candido Neves put the two fifty *mil-reis* notes away, while the master was still telling the slave to get inside. On the floor, where she was lying, carried away by fear and pain, and after a short struggle, the slave had a miscarriage.

The product of a few months' growth came lifeless into the world, amid the groans of the mother, and the owner's gestures of despair. Candido Neves saw the whole spectacle. He didn't know what time it was. In any case, he had to run quickly to the Rua da Ajuda, and that was what he did, with no wish to know what the consequences of the disaster were.

When he got there, he saw that the chemist was alone, without the child he'd handed over. He felt like strangling him. Fortunately, the chemist explained everything in time; the child was inside with his family, and both went inside. The father grabbed his son with the same degree of ferocity he'd used to grab the slave-woman a short while back, a different ferocity, of course – the ferocity of love. He thanked them hurriedly and awkwardly, and left in a tearing hurry, not to the Orphans' Wheel, but to the borrowed room, with his son and the hundred *mil-reis* of the reward. Aunt Monica, when she heard the explanation, forgave the return of the child, since he brought the *mil-reis* with it. She did, it's true, say some harsh things about the slave, because of the miscarriage, as well as the escape. Candido Neves, kissing his son amid genuine tears, blessed the escape and was unconcerned about the miscarriage.

'Not all children make it,' said his beating heart.

Translator's Notes

Translator's Introduction

1 *Dead Souls* is discussed at length in one of Machado's newspaper columns, and it is almost certain that the 'Diary of a Madman' provided vital elements for the plot of *Philosopher or Dog?* This is less surprising than one might think – Mérimée admired Gogol, and wrote about him in terms which would have attracted Machado, in the *Revue des Deux Mondes*, which was widely read in Brazil as elsewhere.

2 In my comments on this story, I am indebted to José Miguel Wisnik's wonderful article, '*Machado maxixe*', in *Sem receita* (São Paulo: Publifolha, 2004), pp. 15–105.

The Mirror: A Sketch for a New Theory of the Human Soul

1 Luís de Camões (*c*. 1524–80), the great Portuguese poet and author of the national epic, *The Lusiads*, is said to have uttered these words on his deathbed. In 1580, the Spanish king, Philip II, ascended the Portuguese throne, and Portugal ceased to be independent until 1640.

2 This institution, originally founded in 1831 as an instrument of social control by the landed oligarchy, had by 1880 become a largely decorative affair.

3 King João of Portugal fled to Brazil, escorted by the British fleet, in 1808, and Rio de Janeiro became the temporary capital of the Portu-

guese Empire. The transformation involved eventually led to the colony's becoming an independent empire, with King João's son Pedro as the first emperor.

4 From 'The Old Clock on the Stairs' (1845).

5 A phrase from 'Bluebeard', one of the stories collected by Charles Perrault in *Mother Goose Stories* (1697). Imprisoned by Bluebeard, the heroine anxiously asks her sister if her brothers are coming to save her.

6 Tomás Antônio Gonzaga (1744–1810), the most famous lyric poet to have written in Brazil in the colonial period.

An Alexandrian Tale

1 Herophilus (*c.* 335 BC–*c.* 280 BC) is a historical figure, reputed to have been the first to carry out autopsies. The activities attributed to him here have a basis in historical accounts.

A Singular Occurrence

1 A now forgotten one-act play, *Je dîne chez ma mère* (1855), by Lambert Thiboust and Adrien Lacourcelle.

2 A phrase ('*la nostalgie de la boue*') from a play by Émile Augier, *Le mariage d'Olympe* (1855), written to counter the view of the reformed prostitute in *The Lady of the Camellias*.

A Chapter of Hats

1 Literally, *The Dark-Skinned Girl*, by Joaquim Manuel de Macedo (1844). A slight, sentimental romance, it remained popular well into the twentieth century.

2 A Catholic novelist, born Pauline de La Ferronays, and married to an English diplomat, the Hon. Augustus Craven. *Le mot de l'énigme* (1874) describes a virtuous woman who, though given every justification and incentive to commit adultery, refuses to do so. Madame Craven's novels

were popular at this time, and were among Queen Victoria's favourite reading.

3 *The Formation of Vegetable Mould, through the Action of Worms* (1881).

4 By Giacomo Meyerbeer (1836). It was one of the most spectacular operas of the nineteenth century, and one of the most popular.

5 The Cassino was an upper-class ballroom.

Evolution

1 'One misfortune leads to another.'

2 An annually published guide of commercial establishments, official institutions, etc., in Rio de Janeiro.

A Schoolboy's Story

1 The Regency began with the abdication of Emperor Pedro I in 1831. It was a period of political unrest, which the premature majority of Pedro II (he was only fifteen) in 1840 largely succeeded in putting an end to.

2 After the Portuguese court's flight to Rio in 1808, King João stayed in Brazil until 1821.

3 An unidentified popular tune: the literal translation is 'A rat in a frock-coat'.

Dona Paula

1 Then a semi-rural retreat in the steep hills surrounding the city of Rio.

2 The 1850s, a boom period in Rio. Stoltz was the most famous opera singer of the time; the Marquis of Paraná was the leader of the so-called 'Conciliation' ministry, which included members of both political parties.

The Diplomat

1 Emperor Pedro II's birthday.

2 A public garden on Guanabara bay, near the centre of the city.

3 In 1865.

The Hidden Cause

1 *Capoeira* is a kind of fighting without weapons, originally developed by the slaves as a means of defence and attack, in which all depends on skilful use of arms and legs. In the nineteenth century gangs of practitioners, but these ones often armed, roamed the streets of Rio and constituted a serious public nuisance. They were finally stamped out at the beginning of the 1890s as part of the drive to 'civilise' the city and make it attractive to foreign immigrants. In more recent times, *capoeira* has become a popular form of martial art, in Brazil and abroad.

The Cynosure of All Eyes

1 Vincenzo Bellini's last opera (1835).

A Famous Man

1 Sinhazinha was a familiar appellation used by slaves to refer to the young women in their owner's family.

2 Emperor from 1822 to 1831.

3 The date, in 1871, of the Law of the Free Womb, which declared that all slaves born after the law was passed would be free at the age of twenty-one.

4 The Duke of Caxias was the leader of the outgoing conservative government.

Midnight Mass

1 See note 1 to p. 66, 'A Chapter of Hats'.

Pylades and Orestes

1 In Sophocles' *Orestes*, Pylades is present on stage, but never says anything.

Father against Mother

1 The Valongo was the main slave market in Rio, where new slaves from Africa were sold. They were 'contraband' after 1831, when the transatlantic trade had been officially abolished, under pressure from Great Britain. It really ended in 1850.

2 All the names refer to whiteness in one way or another – *neves* means snow.

3 This partitioned wooden turntable was set in the convent wall, so that neither the giver nor the receiver could see each other. The baby would then be taken to a foundling hospital.

A NOTE ON THE AUTHOR

Joaquim Maria Machado de Assis (1839–1908) was born and lived his whole life in Rio de Janeiro. The son of poor parents, and mulatto, he worked his way up to a successful career as a civil servant and writer. He was revered (though not understood) in his lifetime, and was unanimously elected President of the Brazilian Academy of Letters when it was founded in 1896. He is still universally regarded as the greatest Brazilian writer.

A NOTE ON THE TRANSLATOR

John Gledson is Professor Emeritus of Brazilian Studies at the University of Liverpool. He is the author of books in English and Portuguese on the nineteenth-century novelist and short-story writer Machado de Assis and the twentieth-century poet Carlos Drummond de Andrade. He has translated several works by Brazilian authors, including *Don Casmurro* by Machado de Assis, *The Brothers* and *Ashes of the Amazon* by Milton Hatoum, and Roberto Schwarz's critical work on Machado de Assis, *A Master on the Periphery of Capitalism.*

A NOTE ON THE TYPE

The text of this book is set in Bembo. This type was first used in 1495 by the Venetian printer Aldus Manutius for Cardinal Bembo's *De Aetna*, and was cut for Manutius by Francesco Griffo. It was one of the types used by Claude Garamond (1480–1561) as a model for his Romain de l'Université, and so it was the forerunner of what became standard European type for the following two centuries. Its modern form follows the original types and was designed for Monotype in 1929.